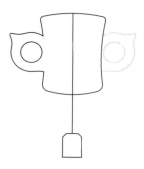

Plats

John Trefry

a text from Inside the Castle

Completed in 2008 by John Trefry
THIRD PRINTING MARCH 2015

First printing in limited edition of five letterhalf zines
released as From the Ground volume 08 in 2008.

If I Choose to Stare the World Happens to My Eyes
A Conversation with John Trefry
by Joe Milazzo
Originally appeared on Entropy Magazine in October 2014

The text is set in 9pt Minion Pro.
For more to read and look at:
www.insidethecastle.org

The cover is designed by Ashley of Post Baroque.
For more to look at:
www.postbaroque.com

ISBN-13: 978-0615981666 (Inside the Castle)
ISBN-10: 0615981666

Plats
:1

If I Choose to Stare the World Happens to My Eyes
A Conversation with John Trefry, by Joe Milazzo
:159

LOS ANGELES

The apartment blocks cycle past. The sun, diffused stucco dust in taupe haze, descends in a continuous track from the moment that dawn raced over this whole city, revealing unpainted crevices, reflected faces, evaporating damp reserves, sinking quickly, satisfied. She rotates north slightly, east on to Idaho, to tread back toward the dawn, but first toward the entopic dusk while the sun slides between her shoulderblades and she :1 dives beneath the asphalt to meet day where the city sleeps, to illuminate the space between her sleeping body and her disintegrating character. Her hands cradle her eyes, apartment blocks cycle past and rise away from the road when she bows her head and rests her elbows on her knees to stare at nude stockings through chinks in her fingers, and she sinks.

The seas settle to the west, buffered by hints of earth in glimmering eddies, chrome sunlight, coasting inland, shimmering. A sense of the looming marine void weighs on her neck, distant, hidden, present in light playing across continuous clouds, in the incompleteness that is desire, the automatic distance from tangible objects and forms through the machinations of the senses. The sea is not there because she had seen it, or was offered it, but because she wanted it to be, an empty directionlessness, where, afloat on her back, active tidal currents draw her ever outward from lines, walls, roads, lines converging to waterless eastern deserts. Behind her back is the apophenia of morning. She walked eastward, away from the sea, with high heat on her shoulders.

I need to take hold of something. The sun is limp in the window, between the blinds. It has been floating around my room for so long that my teeth can feel it swirling around them, liquidly, milky, sending me back into sleep and rising me back through itself every so often to think about rolling over, readjusting the pillows, or wondering how orange it could ever get. I will lie here and the light wont change. It will get dark then later again will get light. It wont change color. When it is barely light and the brick wall outside my window is silver, I can almost see through it. It would continue the color of the sky, and my room is silver. It is damp for a moment at sunrise and then becomes desert dry. In those silver seconds I have my eyes open.

To the bedimm'd hall beneath the hulking midcity hotel, the Minnetonka Ballroom, woven furtively beneath stacked and arranged furniture, chairs in columns, circular tables with legs folded into flat pinwheels, and accoutrements, linens folded and stacked, mugs on wrought iron trees, napkins fanfolded in glasses on carts, fields of legs rising up from the vast expanse of empty carpet to whose center the condensate sprawl of the room in day is focused, when the bits of the day drew to a close, objects huddled close to await the dusk, to conceal shadows cast in the artificial blonde light, the folded hands and feet beneath tables, everything swirls under, subjugated, beneath the heap, peering out across the carpet, it was there that we will pass through the night.

Against a bare plaster wall a questionable tracery of milky green light undulates. Pressed against the opposite wall, your buttocks forced outward to the water stained plaster, your arms splayed outward with fists loosely curled, your feet stacked in gray canvas shoes, on your side, you are. In an alcove, low, above the high water line, far enough to only see dry between the outdoor walls and off to the low horizon of your alley eyes on concrete, you gaze awake into the palazzo courtyard from the alcove floor. The invaginated contortions of the Lido's Arms pour strange sourceless light around corners, through chinks, off of reflections into a mess on your open eyes, dryly specular. There are twists and turns you do not see, from the edge of the ruin, it is there that you pass through the night.

When substances themselves recede so far from light, through time or drowning depth, themselves they become darkness and not things. Even in the anodyne duration of darkness the spots that have felt the sun and will again are blind lithified corpses. Movement, consequences, the pulse of life, the furtive eyelashed looks of disbelief, of forethought, the absence of breath and loss of resistance, the smoothness, the collection of mistaken objects born of each second who would swirl in blinding pandemonium, the physical pretence, the blood, the spittle, the end, the distinction that anything is separate, a beginning never will begin in the ink that renders all in the body of itself, of the geologic darkness where you had passed through the night.

The setting sun, somewhere over her left shoulder races westward across the flat southern sky. Now she glances upward. Her eyes diverge. Her hair frays, backlit, leaden. The louring day reflects upon the disease of apartment blocks, Saltair, Minnetonka, that she passes slowly and comes to a full stop before. The deceleration causes the sedimentary hair resting on her left shoulder to slide limply to her chest. The faltering halted light reflected from an array of stucco faces upon her skin bears a bouquet of jaundice, a floral, yet plastic and pock-marked hue that in other approaching nights might calculate out to warmth. The nights of others. Her received pallor is of the idleness practiced by arms, and arms, and arms preparing for sleep behind stucco walls.

Freedom is release from will. Parallel to the hills roads run ever distant in furrowed ruts converging into later afternoons in a segmented band of colors refracted from the sun into the asphalt. It is a stumbling spectrum converging to a point while she gains ground, and, while it creeps further away from her, claims her future with the pointless exploration of its compressed impressions and mysteries. She follows the horizon through serpentine high walled corridors that claim space not through distance and division but by coverage, claiming every spot in a surface by wrapping into a continuous mess of fluid turns where the uncertainty of direction and extent rivals the ubiquitous straight line. She pauses intermittently, between the stations of the sky.

My eyes may have been open for hours, but when the light trickles across them I know for certain. In that sketch I wonder whether I am waking up somewhere else, someone else, in a room filled with things made of dark wood, with oval mirrors and mirrored trays with glass phials and atomizers, picture frames with faces and a sky above the window that is waiting for the sun to change in the days changes, showing unfamiliar colors. I wonder whether it is all canceled out in the silver. The special things and idiosyncrasies that make me someone are canceled out against each other in reflections, or that just waking up, or just seeing the light waking up the city it will take a moment for me to snap into myself and into a day that moves with the natural cadence with the revolving earth.

The body is alone. Pass the tip of a limb between two adjacent perpendicular limbs, bend around one, then over and under the other. Rows of contortions are punctuated by crossing limbs making smaller increments. More frequent punctuations sacrifice coherence to impenetrability. The composition cedes to disorder where limbs, unable to weave completely, fray in varying degrees of contraction and rotation: completely extended and taut, entirely folded back upon themselves, patterned with frozen wrinkles of exertion. The renitence of the rind which unifies the array is segmented by long gasps absent of pattern. Stretches of the body that would be solid open dark chasms between parallel limbs, shadowy mechanisms are here revealed then quickly sealed.

The ruined surfaces of ruinous things swim in various shades and hues of night light bouncing pale green to deep opaque sea and dried grass to gaseous orange and back on breezes. Fingerprints, strands of hair, dried fluid stains remain when the lights disappear. Out of the dim emerge the edges of objects and imperfections drawn in streetlamp shadow, darkening your cheek in the sand, flowing in from tidal canals to submerge you where you settle, until the buoyant objects you clutch wrestle you through the depths. Where you had struggled not to sink by holding them, you now cast away rising bits of the world allowing you to sit for a moment more in the dark, beyond yourself, yet you rise faster on the tide until you sink deposited on a bed of silt.

What you feel in the darkness isnt consistent with any physical possibilities, if you knew the shape of your body or where it lay. It is diffused and adrift. Your senses burn where they shouldnt, amidst you, all of it is you and you are filled with so much vague geography. In the rolling black shiver that fans through you the touch is consistent, liquid ice, or oil asymptotically kissing freezing. You dont reach final states. You remain on the verge. It is so still and so uniform that it touches you completely at once, with the same anesthetic pace across your unfolded perception, a perfect unreflective blackness from which your own extents, in the way that you want them, are not visible or present. You feel the coldness describing them, but they are gone.

The day sun lays bare the fragmented shells of pale stucco standing immobile in tightly spaced and regular increments along every eastbound street. Behind the walls that close the city into square patterns, the breath of a character promotes a more meandering order upon its current. Faced with the rigid city, she cannot move or take action, quiescent even to her continual debasement. The city grid does not yield; it lines up breezes that skirt her and dance charitably from the sea to lay their golden kiss upon the recumbent dingbat facades. She and the city remain inert, silhouettes idly welcoming dusk with that treasonous false zeal that eventually accepts a preference for awakening its own shadowy inhabitants over the waning stasis of the diving sun.

In a shifting stand of weak beige grass between a fence and the street, a sheet of red paper leans limply. Stride on stride, her gray canvas slip-on shoe reaches the paper which she shuffles out of the reeds, taps it lightly with the ball of her foot onto the sidewalk where it lies face up. The paper is softened in spots, worn gently, eroded, folded into a pocket, sat on, furrowed, showed greater signs of wear. Three Bedroom Apartment for rent, Venice, freshly painted. Most of the paper, through wear, is feathery mauve with blooms of pure red. She curls her toe inside her shoe whose sole, at its tip, falls open, her stocking toe transfers the paper to her hand, where she refolds it and places it in the breast pocket of her smock, on the chest side of a thick stack of worn cards and scraps.

I wait through silver moments. In the space of time that light laps against the opposite wall and returns to me, it carries my hopes, faith in regenerative avoidance, in an array of pictures of tidy arranged views across appointed tables and out windows through swaying leaves, rooms filled with light, a breeze playing through the open window, through my hair, dries my lips and the walls. I can only conjure so much. If anything assembled in the flash of magic at dawn, an unveiled life that I had forgotten about, I didnt want to open my eyes on to it. Watching something happen is less believable than happening upon it. I need to set this day apart to be something. I close my eyes before it becomes another, with the last, without the fullness that I picture from deep behind my eyes.

The perpetual readjustings, contortions, rasping, and decay of a cloudy mechanism cycling pose and gesture throughout an interior night and into early morning necessarily inhabit many variations of its initial program. This machine is the vast series of instantaneous states of its own history, all existing internally and concurrently. In isolated moments

there is clarity to the actions when compared with one another. Moved out into the frays of focus, in the frosty blue and pale of fluorescently lit dew, the limbs, patterned after a specious wholeness, do not support the corporeality of a machine, but of many bodies and perspectives. A limb from the heap flexes forth from its cavern to deflect the dewy integument in part of an imperceptible geometric chain of events.

Moments make other moments. Moments and moments and moments make things. In the courtyard, around the corner, your breath falls and unfurls a sequence from your face around walls, stairs, arcades, still water, overlooks, wrought iron railings, and salt caked windows to a chink in horizontal blinds the size of the thickness of her pointer finger. From the dark she watches you in the dark lying, low, looking through the streets and canals, the footprints in sandy banks and estuaries lead back to things that you have touched and arranged. The cups, towels, bedclothes, scraps of paper, shining tools, black oily pools, tea bags, gun blue filings, and chips of enamel are loosely picked up on the tide far behind you, roll away, sink, wash ashore, gather, and she puts them in an apartment.

In the undifferentiated dark you devolve into a feeling, a geometrically consistent question on the slow current. You are a question of time and setting and vessel, and then you are a question of character and action, and then you are a question of motivation, or lack, and effect, and then you are a womans body, and then you are the dark itself where the very substance is effect, the substance is in question, and then you are all of the questions and all of the things. Nothing can begin without a change, without seeing your hands out before your eyes, without something beyond them, or this is the end, the beginning is lost somewhere at this precise moment but just out of plane, in an adjacent plat, a tangent in the murk, and it has all happened and will all happen without anything at all.

Roused to motion when the car rocks forward she leans back to her left shoulder, still facing north. The apartment blocks cycle past, Bruneau, Palm Plains. Skirting beneath the graying horizon, captured along streets bound to the logic of the city she recedes back, too low a thing to exist in them all at once. Being only here, in the immediacy of forgetting, facing the road ahead dumbly, she fails to come to an understanding with the grid, her places in it. She lets her eyes ride the rolling scape of the gently sloping roofs about whose crests the streets mesh in a panoramic network. She gestures with projected envy at the yellowed roofs by lacing her fingers together to block them out. Diffused light falls upon her face, drawing an icteric pallor from the hazy dusk horizon.

Venice, wade, into the intersection of afternoon, awaken from napping sunshine, out from the shadowy grog cast by apartment buildings, Ca d'Oro, Canaletto Breeze, onto the sidewalk. Pale sunshine falls across white asphalt in small, hesitant, changing reflective paces, each connected in potential with the entire stretch of road in either direction, to horizons of sorts, where the road slopes ever upward out of the sea, to dense highwalled islands, within whose chambers and passages the horizon and the sea fall away, left only inscribed across eyes that have just left them and see them in every window ledge, kitchen table, and expanse of blue carpet, dappled with floes of yellowed green. Awaken from a nap of hours inland to sunlit grog, inland, any place without the sea.

If I can make myself see through the brick wall, or look all the way through the mirage of time, through this lump that will be a day, when I sit still in it, seeing myself crepuscular in the next morning, in the same place but a different person, who maybe isnt running, or collapsing, it makes me have no need for hope, only acute vision. With my eyes closed I feel these things. I dont need to compare them. I need only to feel the water wick'd from the air and from my sheets, to know that I should stack pillows and covers into the corner where the bed nests into the corner, and entomb my head within it. I need to set aside a day that makes a nick in my life that others will fall into. How do I do that. When I open my eyes, the day will have passed. The segments overlap.

In isolation the limb may be scrutinized. First station, first body. Each limb registers each knot in the textile pattern on which it lies through a contract with gravity and sleep. Although existing in its surroundings, the perpetually shifting relationships within the body are nothing more than the calculated repetitions of the machine. The thigh normal to the floor on which the knee, bearing, draws it to the calf, which extends 20° above level touching at its tapered tip the cleavage of two thighs drawn tight by the groin at floor level. Involuntary movement does not begin, it is borne. An eddy, registering in the dewbank, is borne by the movements that precede it and the breath in which it occurs. The knee rasps across the rug. Full close.

You lie in the dim but not concealed. All traces lead to you and they will be traced. The only hiding is moving or drowning. In the night the city empties. The traces drape back over the horizon leaving the stolen moments of the day bobbing or sinking into the sea to come at you again from the opposite horizon at dawn. This is a windowless room, the door ajar and nothing but a disembodied light floating beyond view. There is nothing in the dark night but what this little hollow has captured. You lie wedged in place on the floor. In the empty night the space you fill is endless. You cannot move because in the emptiness there is nowhere you are not. The world is snuffed out. You are only where you are because she sees you there, and you have been there so long.

This is the only dark place. It is awaking lost and misshapen and not even awake. It is in between. All of the moments that freeze you in disintegrated poses are waystations between some forgotten fall, the failure of live birth, every morning, and the torrent of light, casting enough shadows through the chasms that divide you to make you look whole, but spectral. The breathless scribblings that ink your sleep, that pause time for your body to tremble automatically, write the dawn and day just the same. They are never silent. They fold opaque paper around you and seal you from the city, stealing the immaculate communications between what you want and what will happen. There is either nothing or a solid cloud of light. The roads partition either chaos or timid tombs.

The drape'd firmament, closing down, uncoloring itself, slowly seeps begrayened wintry night out of the early spring heavens toward the horizon. The faint outlines of the roofscape remain lightly hovering beneath the dusk. Those enclosures and the characters they retain are descending into a medium being in which they are surfaces trimmed and filled with leaden night, but sit just before the dark, almost crowned in dimness by the shadows they cast upon the sky. She could hook her fingertips around their drawn extents, peel them away to the secret deviations therein, and find only continuous dusk. Held in patterns through the day they step out from the darkening background across hoary lawns and at the curb; they all crumble in unison with the sun.

Napping, gone, whilst sunlight falls in parallel lines, brown and blue upon surfaces, a yellow kitchen table atop which sits a plain bone colored mug with thick walls and a pronounced rim; the handle is thick and flat with a small hole and an outsweeping thumbrest. It is untouched in a chamber of absence inexorable. In the vessel is a dry scaly pale lavender skin. The napping body lies still in the sunlight. Objects left fixed, untouched, alone for so long, become their settings, their original forms willed to implode into the spot where they have rested and they, within the voids they cradle by their shapes, change those settings they have become part of; when implored, the tiny vessel floats in a kitchen sea of sun golden solitude.

At this moment the lights flutter slowly into cycle across the empty ceiling, their shivering captured in the frail glass cylinder is tangible enough to rattle the dust on my painted metal table, settled into waxy oils, and my empty chair casts a dark shadow under the table on the worn terrazzo. I was in bed. I didnt see people, only their names. I had given up on neighbors, populations. Sorting through all of the names, fearing the numbers in the addresses, the fixity of their existence in the world, made me want my room to be empty enough to run away from. I didnt want it to fit me. It couldnt anyway, so I wouldnt let it try. At this moment my station was empty, I was absent from the whole world. I couldnt even see myself, my legs, my chest, my room, my day. I saw nothing.

In the machine, although repeating, the harbingers of each station differ. Second station, first body. Although systematized, the translatory movement of the rasping knee, drawing the calf to penetrate the two press'd thighs until they are separated by its diameter, is unfamiliar in the conditional cloud of this instant; it is a native accident. Condensate of the refrigerant night air in tenuous patterns of beadlet and woven rivulet, lubricates the continuous movement of the calf. The widest diameter of the calf passes through the thighs, full splay, then the thighs draw back together. The space of the skin against the skin is sealed by the damp and by pressure from the groin which squeezes the thighs to resist the company of the calf, without anticipation or intent.

She is behind the chink in the blinds. She pulls it shut and withdraws the spear of light, the probing scrutiny condemning your face flat in a black puddle, your socks thorny with dried sweat and salt, your dress filled with memos from other days, your hesitant sleep in the thin dirty sand. The heavy copper salts return to the sea through your burning nose. The spears of light, the eye, the fiery haze, roll back across your empty body. They wear slowly, an intangible erosion at the edges of you, where you stop and the air starts, until even that distinction is filled with the contact of her scrutiny and the window light, insinuating themselves across your neck and beneath your bound collar. It is not their inevitability, but their inconsistency that keeps you alert. You wait, you are smothered.

If you are awake then this has begun. The world doesnt form for dreams. If you are awake, time is not passing. Beginnings are limbos that wander through the unscuttled twilight moments, stretching themselves into bright hours when you still hide, dull paralyzed breeze asides and naps, the long afternoon burning your nose and souring your body, perpetually in a series of beginnings each stopping short of fruition, each tiding to each, until it is dark again or still dark. The darkness is immeasurable; you are endless in it, an ineffectual, limp forever. You need the sun to cast a shadow, to put things behind you, to change, to divorce, to co-opt, to happen, accidentally, and then forget, and lose yourself when you are real, lost again.

In the flagrance of day, sunset is never an expectation. Desperation accompanies the final moments when the sun is seen racing away loathe to receive supplications, leaving the homes scattered with ash from its flaming last caress whose dinge is visible briefly in the afterlight of dusk; the train of light is drawn over the rooftops. She entreats it to step back out of the sea enough to throw senescent lines of wavering steel across her grog for a moment more. Bent in expectation of full night it makes no gestures to stand out of its half mourning pose, where beneath the hulking fold of the distant sea she desires to sink and repent to the sun, a lukewarm and low collection of limbs spat out of dusk with stock movements; she is made to look away.

Your senses are lukewarm. The afternoon apartment is still. Lowering sunlight hits west windows at forever angles buffeting them with deepening hues impossible to shut out. Blinds are pulled completely to. Plastic slats soften the edges of the brown rays which still penetrate and fall on the carpet in stripes of blended light and shadow. Dust is frozen breathless haunting the room and deeply drifts in the crooks of moldingless walls. The carpet is covered with spots gummy and dried; the walls are cold glossy, running with condensate drips that ran and were painted over. In the far back room above the tussled pallet through the window blinds chink, east, across the intersection a fence holds back tall unkempt beige grass. Your hands are chapped.

I felt the sheets whose cold open window dew declared a life apart, nobody would let me live this way, awake in the cold, when the fabric dried for a twinkling, and turned warm and pasty with my sweat. My old breath filled the cavern of pillows. I see the morning in bits. I didnt try to live straight through them. They belonged in different places, at the same time all around the city. I see bits while they happen. I wouldnt notice, but I see the voids in the dust, the crescents of emptiness around cups and jars, fingerprints in the sand. I need to drop each bit into the sequence. If it happened yesterday, it was a separate compartment. If it happens this afternoon I want to happen with it. I need to be sure before I fall out of bed. Some one morning I will run through it all in order.

At ease. Third station, first body. Involuntary movement is a thing, not an action. The movements of the machine, conspicuous, incongruous, isolate it into a thing to be observed and registered. Action is when there was or is to be anticipation and intent, a contextual course of events. Movement, is a thing, is blind, fidgety. The thighs are cleared by the fullness of the calf and waver upright, at ease. Glossy moisture, coruscating in beadlets about the calf, wavers in the pregnancy when there is no fore and is no aft momentum. Symmetrical about the knee, the thigh and the calf, themselves in full splay, waver at 30° above level. The faded end of the thigh describes an housing with its arc within which the thing is taking place. The returning knee sinks, and drags across the rug.

Your consciousness flutters in a fine period. The symmetries of the city appear to you in the confluence of objects, atmosphere, and light to play back through your lost walking hours in a carnival of assumed memories. Reminiscent rebuses of morning moments cobbled together in piecemeal mosaics begin to shake out of the failing darkness, pulses of fluorescent light, sunlit cigarette butts in the sand, stained tissues folded into quarters on a window sill in milky light, the slick surfaces that shine cold against your warm wet hair. You are weighed by the repetition. Again the freshly bathed dusk grog begins the night without the day ending and you swim into the detritus of the day in reverse, floating to the surface in the dark alcove on the moisture borne lights from the courtyard.

You will try to see things where there is nothing and things will float past you, before your shrugging eyes, undetected. The blocks that hem this void are paper thin. They dont shut things out, they hold them in to keep them from connecting to the greater composition. Your tendency is to see occurrences only for what they prefigure, leading you in sequence to the next. You look for things to be whole and continuous. This cant happen that way. This is not for you. But this is the end already, or the fork to it, the last attempt, with so much already gone by you already know things you shouldnt know, you look for things you shouldnt see but that you know are there, you remember things that have yet to happen. In this mess it wont help you.

She opens her eyes to coordinate the descent of dark with her own. Transitional moments give shape to her floating life. The half lit roadway rolls out with the limp sorrow of dawn transported here to join with dusk. In these halfway atmospheres are drawn the profiles of time, held through long stretches of day and night in hesitations of dreaming, thresholds, cave mouths. The slim figures of tree trunks, mailbox posts, powerline uprights stretch into canescent sheets, rotating with the earth, caught in her parted glimpse they insinuate themselves outside the movement of her body, of the sky, the eyes. The seconds between the full stops of light and dark or dark and light, smear into one with she and her retinue of apartment windows submerged in their aged, crumbling lot.

Wade into the slowly moving rio, pressed tight between walls, from the street surfaces where collections of distant expanses are all occluded, all suspended grains of a relationship are drawn in fragments. She cannot clutch the city whilst getting caught drifting into reeds around corners. Yet, lost down within, a relationship impossible through racing straightness is cultivated, she is subject to the invisible eddies, the deep currents, the stagnant dead ends, the life cast into the reeds, she sees why, for self preservation, the streets redirect themselves, why they hide through covered sotoportego the sun cannot touch, standing water connects continuously with the great network she believes she is refused from but which she cannot leave without drifting throughout.

The days are unbelievable messes. They never start. They are starting all the time, staggered for my troubles. I wont know which place I am waking up in out of them all, at the metal desk, under the table, wrapped in a cocoon on the bathroom floor. I slowly run my eyes across my surroundings. Things are unclear behind a milky haze. It doesnt matter what arises out of it. My eyes dont burn but they feel smothered. The material on the wall where the stripes of my falling fingerprints in some substance trace wont indicate anything about the circumstances that put me there. Clear vision would only confuse me. By the time I have asserted a context I am always at my desk with cold hands. It will never be perfect, but I want to be present when it happens.

Fourth station, first body. The array of limbs finds poses when its sequence becomes identifiable. The history of the thing is not the thing; history is an external proof that action is taking place. Causes for each birth, or present state, other than those that were once exterior effects, are contained within the thing. The thighs stand, full splay, separated by the maximum diameter of the calf, the knee rasps back, setting the nap of the carpet aright, toward the drawing back together of the thighs somewhere beneath the rind. Perhaps the extent of the system is observed in cross section, or perhaps it is being extrapolated from the periodic rise and submersion of that single thigh from the integument, or from the traces and cowlicks in the nap and dew of the rug. Full close.

In the fluctuation you transcribe secrets. You hope they will color bits of memories. You close them into your eyes, but they never do. The light moves in the rippled patterns of blown liquid refracting. Sinuous, electric nets oscillate across the wall, spread out from particular spots and shiver in decreasing frenzy out toward the alley. Soft filtered color traces through some of the lines, transforming whilst they twist 'on themselves, idle yellow to lukewarm gray spueth across the wall, disappearing, impoverished, arising charitably and truthfully clear again, the green hopes of the regenerated creature precede its old rose anguish, and truthfully clear again before the void, where the strand of light wastes its gift and recedes further. In its absence the black seal of death, the orange end.

You see a white shapeless luminance beginning in a sparse fog and flooding through the gaps it initiated to fill your eyes. It is bright through solid matter, through your eyelids open or closed. Keep them open. Put on the semblance of wanting to surface. The water is shallow enough to kneel in. You lie chest down with your dress rising and falling against the sand it sways filling with water and billowing then blown tight across you. The light and salt burn your eyes. Salt flumes in your eyes shimmer across finer and finer shapes etching out of the surface a horizon with indistinguishable attitude, and you sink again, your arms wilting ahead of you. Wet or dry you sag. You could be pulled anywhere in the world in a long long instant and be still a breath away from disappearing.

Full descent. The streetscape renounces the caresses of the sun. There is no trace of it now. It is her lot, for these moments of atmospheric pause, to shudder herself into void. There is no light on the street now. The sun leaves night. Full night. In an asynchronous dappling up across the high plains, the posts and peaks of the street lamps rise out of the dim slowly toward the east end of the avenue while shades of darkness assume their pose on darkened surfaces. The night blooms with dark dapples enfolding the gray walls of the apartment blocks. Hidden wells of night creep forth in lacework inscriptions, translucent black drapes, drawn out from rediscovered edges that had been obliterated by the sun. Her eyes follow with rote gestures; she rides further forward.

On all sides are walls. Afternoon sun flows through southfacing gaps and falls upon her neck and shoulders. Long spells and days spent watching the shadows drift across the opposite wall, and shadows of clouds drift through those pale frames of light at conflicting speeds, bring her the protection of familiarity, willing everchanging skies. She is claimed by this space, identified by its coordinates, its stillness, its address, its name, all of which she adopts. Sheltered, though the road extends far out to the horizon, she stares. The city falls away, the repeated blocks, the names, and the mysteries. She stalls here and there not from personal interest, or any sense of fit or acquiescence to the rigor of gridded walls, but by vacantly occupying it with the tides allowance.

To be in that one place, days from now, I place myself in my toes, the sheets are still cold through my nails, the dew is cold through the spots bared through to my flesh and the sheets are stiffly rough on the scraps of skin that are not horned over, each toe is warm where it connects back to my feet even in the stillness of the livid blood, I find a moment sealed away and stopped, I am in my fingertips and feel the singular evacuating pain through my fingernails from stored cold underneath the pillows. The cold confluence of my blood, each bit of me, pools in my chest, all beneath my skin. I lie and visualize myself walking in the white sun. Out there could be anywhere. Outside my skin is an omnipresent texture of fabric. I feel its incremental identity slide over my skin when I adjust my body.

The effect of involuntary movement is further involuntary, but not unaccepted or unforeseen, movement. However, insentient animate things, having no ability to perform informed actions related to their locations or translatory movements, have come to be found where they are only through sequences of involuntary effects. Movement suites can be

apparently synchronous yet over time cause adjacent bodies, atmospheric conditions, and landscape patterns to migrate drawing new systems into the sequence. Isolated, the second through the fourth station of the first body and some fragment of the duration between the first station approaching the second and the fourth station approaching the first, bear a kinetic effect on an adjacent body.

The tendrils of light that swirl around you do not harbor memory. You do not remember. The places still are and the objects still where your hands aligned them. Things touch places forever. The end in long orange dusty fingers is pressed into your eyes in sleep, the tiny daily suicide. In it is the empty afternoon apartment, yellow with self scrutiny, leave the city, leave the long rays through blinds that ignite the gray dust of your breath, leave the musty palazzo, wake up to a green sky through the alley window in your empty bedroom at dusk across the hollow sky dome. On the street is black prenight emptiness, black puddles, black churches, solid places not carved open by memories, leaving you sealed, moony, with your sleepless accusations.

You are always near the end, floating just before the tide, the rain washing through the desert, until it is dry and the edgeless wind blows you, or the clean hand of night reaches beneath your collar and replaces you with cold condensation. You have a long way to go. You know the increments meted out before you and those past, not what happened in them anymore, but their duration. A piece is taken out from before you and moved to behind you. The construction is forgotten. Those tired vessels laid out toward the horizon are unorganized and mute. It makes you want to stop and survey if you could. You dont need to. You dont even know who you could be. You would do anything, only if it was nothing to you.

The walls are papered in seals of death. In this tiny night between sunset and the streetlamp light, buildings can sleep. The freedom from unfetter'd emissaries of the city and its diurnal machinations leaves her startled and aware of her minimal extents. In darkness, without visual continuity into the car, the road, the lawns, she feels the surfaces at which she ends and from which she is isolated. She reclaims those distant parts of her drifting away; they lay their slumbering facades bare to her scrutiny. When the night has plaited its voiding capes across her, she feels a contained self-consciousness. They conceal her secret wholeness within their chambers. She rides forward, almost fully erased from the continuity of the city, and she meanders from its slumbering grid.

Stiff reeds weigh against a rusty diamondshaped chainlink fence in conditions which would only have been possible had the fence been placed long after the grass had stopped growing, involuntarily following the sun, living, to prop it out of the sidewalk and preserve it in the plat of this particular apartment building. In the reeds halfway into the lot lay arid flotsam, a tea bag, steeped, then pressed out with a thumb and dried in the form of a pillow recently vacated, a gray plastic spoon with a white oval in its shallow vessel around which a turbid lavender corona skirts, fragments of paper, circulars, napkin, the frothy filter of a cigarette amongst the short reeds that would blow in the breeze, a folded sheet of red paper, softened at its creases and stained with liquid tannic blooms.

My room is empty in the sunlight. Empty rooms claim whole bodies to balance against the vacuum, waiting to receive a character and prescribing each scrap to its place. I went to the room an afternoon, long sunlight clouding the air, and I was torn to pieces. I come in late, after the streetlamps set and leave before I wake up. Today I am awake in the room; the morning draws on. Something will happen. I want to sit at the kitchen table, watch the sidewalk through the tall window, or force sleep, avoid controlling my consciousness. I want to make one choice and let it flow out. I want to make myself fall into the sand and let the wind blown dunes transport me where they might. If I choose to stare the world happens to my eyes. At my desk I look into a fluorescent light and it is days later.

First station, second body. The abdomen, propped on a mess of limbs and pinned by another mess, slopes downward at 30° above level to the buttocks, wherefrom the hips rise back symmetrically at 30° above level to rest atop the thighs of the first body, press'd tight together. Stations, although diverging infinitesimally over time from these minute characterizations, are identified by the positions of the two thighs in relation to one another, full close, and the inclination of the hips above level, 30°. These actions occur completely embedded beneath the integument. Fragments of bodies cannot move without a plan, a fragmented suite of intermediate stations to suitably identify a possible range of motion and a cast of key functionaries.

Everything floats and sinks in unison, a tidal city riding the tides. Tepid water seeps in beneath the legs of kitchen tables, beneath mugs on kitchen tables, beneath your kneeling knees, the soles of your feet, lifting you and they all away from the surface of home together and some time setting it all back down, the entire city sinking back into the wet sand gently but deeply and slightly rearranged. Where you were in relation to the things around you is the same. Things do not just move. Some thing disappeared. An empty print remains in the dust. You are implicated. Beyond the doorways, outside and inside, around gated corners, all may change. The effects you fear that you have caused are played out all together, all around, and always, but not by you. You are part of them.

You dont need to be brought along or situated. You dont need a back story. It would be the same, reduced or obscured, flooded with salt water or wasted by blown sand, just floating. You must be the only one but you arent. You wait to be seen. Real things need corroboration. Real things have shadows and aspirations. Nothing has happened. Each start surfaces with everything ahead of it, each blink an endless coastline from the sea. You dont need to put anything together. You couldnt. You dont know if you are even visible. You see your hands loosely clawed into the sand. Shapes with edges happen outside of you. Where they meet your skin they part and flow around you then coalesce while they disappear. You are left with nothing.

Lawns and road retain a silvery cloak, the sky is swollen with livid haze, the lawns and road draw accents of purple into their grain. In a night with its own emerging luminance, the body of the city inverts to be darkened and absent. The evacuated chambers empty and overlooked in day are solid black against a purple sky, a void with the silhouette of an apartment block. It displays wasted gifts of erasure with an iconic pronunciation that would seem proud, if it were an object that existed. Back there in the false night, shadows hang deceptively 'fore conspirators in warm lit apartments. Wavering capes chain'd at the horizon splay'd and torn, behind which exists immemorial infant darkness. In the impoverished unbeing of shapeless form, the buildings are erased into existence.

Tender, parasitic yellow flowers bloom without greenery, living off of the decay, dried sap within the brown husks of grass. She stood fenced from the cast away tea party, drawn to the apartment windows beyond fence and thicket by the absence of a cup, and fingers around its thick handle, another hand flat on the grass with a stiff arm on which she leans back into the grass, finishes the mint tea which has slowly turned purple in the bottom of the cup, and rests down onto her side and elbow beneath the sunflowers. She removes a scrap of paper from her blouse, looks down her legs and feet in the sun. The smell of salt low in the still air wavers with the motions of the brackish water, nearby, to the west, just through the reeds, where it laps gently into footprints worn into a sandy stone step.

It isnt the empty room that pulls me to pieces. It is the mocking potential that any room has to strip back down to its paint and forget you. Every freshly painted hollowed out spot could appear in any memory, any desire. It has to. Each shade away from my skin fits even less than the last, from my underclothes sharing indescribable curves, out to each layer of fabric more and more victims of the desert breeze, out from the rooms where shadows degrade me and hard corners push back my fingertips from ever falling completely into their vertices, I can only shape the dust. At least in the room I have extents. In the cone of light that describes my desk at night after the fluorescent grid has set I know where I am and where I am not, where I end.

When the thighs flutter into a state of cleavage, full splay, the hips descend about the axis of the buttocks, sliding down the inside surfaces of the thighs, 5°, toward the intruding calf. Second station, second body, a body affected purely by its received lot. Any performative consistency it purports to have is passed on to it, inherited nominally through action, but is a reaction. The system of names, numeral designations, through which actions take precedence over the actions of other things is rote, external, and insecure. There is no secure way to categorize the existence of the machine. The bequest of an ur-station to the machine is foreign, strange. All actions and capabilities, all states in which actions have and will occur are concurrent with the aseitic history of the machine.

The flowing world fritters back and forth, in and out of rented doors and ceaselessly up and down endless streets. You lie still bracing your eyes to reassemble the junked moments of the day, to place the trinkets and potions dragging behind and jostling in the great moonlit pool together in sequence, you held the mug and let it cool on the table, you crawled beneath the table, on steps that had led down to a mooring, or in the reedy banks in unkempt corners, floating away leaving you with no token object to remember through, to be through. You are left without reprieve, distraction, acquittal, or escape. Every still moment is aggravated by a lost opposing moment filled with perlustration, distant shaking, betrayal, empty investment, and by its inevitable return.

You are a blot without origin. You are contingent. Let each block, each plat, packed to the frame with shivering shapes, go away when you pass into it, let it be merely a moment in supersessive series, one after another until you have forgotten enough to be someone. Who will you be. Nothing inside you will be changed. How will you be seen. Will you be seen in the sun first hesitantly touching your skin. Will you be that same woman from another day. Which humor will comprise your debut. Dont expect more than the rootless dust, the unidentifiable vapor, the overflowing arroyo, or any vantage that will give them form. What will you see first. It nods suspended in your eyes casting pins of shadow out of the white sky, from the white shape of a face and of hands.

The silhouettes of withdrawn spaces willed to hold the horizon are full of mountain haze flowing beneath the apparitional night they are masked from. Arcs of orange sky ignited beyond the horizon vibrate with the chapped faced anxiety of birth in distant parallel streets where lamps seem to bloom. She is moving parallel to the streetscape and stops before a gable broad in profile, left side coming almost to the ground, hirsute with antennae, and electrical wires seen over her right shoulder clearly within the luminous night sky. She approaches the threshold of emptiness, where she looks into herself looking upon a captured mouth of darkness in the shape of an apartment home. She steps into a placeless sleep from which she would rise enclosed in one of those chambers, behind the sky.

Her shoes are filthy. Those spots of white rubbed through the dirt, those shoes are caked with walked-in dust, asphalt lagoon silt, laid in the dirt dust asleep with legs together and feet stacked, rubbed in sleep those coats of dust branded into white fabric, gilt gray into the white fabric, the tiny particulates of rubbed rocks rubbed into something old, an old shoe and old worn stiff socks, ignored extremities, she does not know she is rubbing them together, can you not feel tall grassland seeds that creep through holes in your sole, migrate through arches and into heel holes where they imbed in your fractured skin, those dirty skins, hardened, unfeeling callouses, these feet are in a different realm, below her horizon, forgotten, submerged. Standing water makes the dirt on your feet real.

Outside is the opposite of the empty room. The city is at once. It is a torrent that I cant separate myself from. I clench my head to crush it all out into a safe orbit cloud and the sand flood slides back over to bury me, a point in an endless landscape made of the same stuff from which all else is wrought. When I shift in it I dont know it. I am an effect. When I happen upon a street it is every street running all the way back to the ocean and all the way through the desert. When I see the lights of the windows at dusk they are every other window. It is all the same in each glimpse but I know it is always changing. I can never see the end of it because I dont know if I have moved. Then I am in a room. The bedsheets and pillows are my rind. They are a terrain of whom I am the earth.

The body is never causally isolated because there is no fixed point from which causality is gauged, even the rug roils beneath. Third station, second body. The hips and the buttocks do not move toward the thighs when they raise back slightly to 15°. The breadth of the asplay thighs, at ease, corresponding to the diameter of the calf which is never wider than the buttocks, causes a rise and fall of the hips with no lateral motion. The spaces between stations, in which action is assumed, where cause bears effect, are insignificant, a breath. They are the wispy spaces between the lines of the instructional set, the conflicts loosed from the machines increments. The body, although inseparable from its internal causality, is forever gated from its desire to move differently, more correctly.

Your memories are repetitions, not moments. There is not time to file your heap of things, they come again, the same but different, each a corruption of your recollection. You meet them all again in the way you met them last, finding that place they occupied before you slept. You find the black censer chandelier over front steps, the green painting, the red plastic telephone, in some order, awakening in you nothing beyond the shapes your head recognizes. They arise in different places carrying their stains of disuse and dusty nests to deceive you and your days fall apart and quickly forward. You leave behind your fingerprints and hairs, reflections, shadows, and you take with you flecks of paint or glaze, dust, stains, incriminations in your wake where only she can see them.

Your fingers inch softly into the warm sand. The thin black water pulls away from your hands, slowly undressing itself from you across your arms and your hair washed forward and your burning eyes filled with the softened haze of white morning. It is not awakening. Things are not other things. Events are not other things. It is the water pulling back, leaving you. You are heavy and there is nothing to you. It is an arrival. The heaviness is inside somewhere absent. Youve taken on water. The sand is damp underneath your body. You let your eyes wash with the blankness of the new morning. Faces and eyes and fingers and reflections rise and settle into the layers of white painted on your vision. You put your cheek in it and sink enough to leave a mark in the shoreline.

She risks losing her course disappearing through shut eyes. The shape of the void, the apartment block, is masked on her retina. In the white haze of her head lies an apparitional apartment home appointed to clutter the red throb of her eyelid. The shape approaches chastity, a wholeness ignorant of the bits that fill it, lost in burning fractious night. In this solidity lies the goodness to which all characters are integrated, a vessel of truth that does not threaten to envelop the sky or road. It floats before the sky, an optical bastion against the end of an Idahoan plain. Also, within the white, are things and places: teakettles, toile armchairs, silk floral arrangements, braids, low-lit dens, closets under stairs, hiding spots under kitchen tables, candlelit tables, windows standing up to the sky.

The holes, grimy blooms, washing over your shoes are from somewhere hidden. You have not seen the sun reflected and be annihilated, the worn spots in the sea where land rose and washed away, down to wooden piles, dirt caked splinters, feet sink, down through silt where currents fill them with dark green water rocking gently ever forward, the trudging life, your shoes are grimy, socks sagging around blue ankles, clotted gray, stretched elastic, frayed, wavering in ripples where she steps, shake them out, peel them off and let them float atop a fresh puddle, let them breathe free from your skin, leave them to dry in the sun, afternoon evaporates water from flat stones, your socks left by recessional tides, let them be free of you, go in peace, her shoes are old and worn out, ruined, walk them to shambles.

This day is mine. If it were the last it could be the last and nothing would come of it outside of my skin. I have become a point. For a long time I have been a shadow in unconscious dreams. Parts of me have disappeared. Things that I have left behind have usurped me and denigrate and incriminate me. If I could buff away the fingerprints I made on shop windows I would scour the city for them. My fingerprints no longer lead to me. This day will become between me and my skin. If it is the last I wont leave anything to reflect on. If I go on I will be painted over, because I am not moving. This is the way to open myself wide into something that I have never been. I am too material. I will disappear, or change, or I will want to walk on the sand at the beach.

The upright thighs, cleaved by the calf, full splay again, prop the hips at 5° above level sloping downward to the buttocks, wherefrom the abdomen rises back at 30° above level, propped on a mess of other bodies and pinned in place by another mess of bodies. Fourth station, second body. The body retreats toward implied states of familiarity in respiration, nictitation, and circulation. Each phase in the perpetual recycling of movement moves the instruction set closer to reconciling itself with the body. There is a point in the cycle of the machine at which the catalogue of movements becomes a memory, and the memory becomes an identity, and the machine can recognize its history, and it can operate with intention, although it can not react, nor can it deviate.

You shake. The night is moon warmed and orange skied. You are pulled and pulled slightly from all around, from hidden places and your immediate surroundings, from far before and from this moment. The pull of the morning ocean rolling back from the shore and the chaos of light and breath tug limply from hundreds of glimmering points and you hang in the balance. The devious symmetries of sleep hold you almost just where you are, but do not keep you from shivering. What your eyes saw and your hands touched and the still air you breathed from all of the days apartments, grows outward from you in both directions, act and consequence, the crushing symmetries of guilt paralyze your body on display in the open center of the lit universe.

The sky meets the ground all around you. You look up the beach to the dry sand warming, full of light and bare white feet laced with succulent veins, green in a barren morning. Even with all of the false starts at day it moves on naturally, it creeps. It moves on more quickly than you can follow and white clouds shape disguise omens in the white sky. You only inch through the twirl of the sun and unlacing of the clouds. When day is all moving over you and you lie or stand, rotating on all axes in liquid air, packed in smooth sand, and forgetting to breathe it moves quickly and you know that when it passes you by you are being held in time by a gaze but you cannot appraise it. An eyeless white head shines over you. The sand in your shadow is still damp. You feel the looks. You enter my day.

Inside her the distance of the sky, against the inside of her eyelid, glimmers and fingers fray through blinds a terminal afternoon orange, intruding in clouds of breath, in hands raised to hold out the first signs of dusk, held at a virginal distance from the liberated airs of mind without body. The wise nothingness of that white home remains a receptacle for her, held out inside her closed eyes to receive her days longing for sleep projected behind it, from further in her head where shimmering gray desires are domesticated. Sleep becomes a makeshift pallet and settles about the eye. In that white shape she strains to project a body that might take shape through ajar doors and stretch its limbs into a clean corner where rugs lie upon dry floors meeting board and batten walls.

Look away into a yard, an alcove, you briefly stall but not stop, the tide has set you down on a stone stair reaching into the canal, the tide again rises, never high enough to deposit you across the dead lawn, without tracks, spare your tattered treads, your closed eyes awake there, gently laid on the bristly yet yielding reeds, rising up around you, washes of dust fall across your clothes, silt around your flesh dries in the sun mummifying you into stillness, a place to lie down, where the stalks are laid flat, pale brown, pale blue flowers dappled amongst the grass on an empty dress, a place to lie flat, the afternoon sun bestows upon the grass and upon your still body a regenerative rot that leaves the body but sweeps away the impulses, the person, release from networks of quarantined canals.

I lay my cheek into the thick brown sand. It doesnt cascade but crumbles in miniature. The sun is gray and low for midmorning, over a pink block of apartments. A band of shapely black clouds strikes a fine faint line of sky between its belly and the sea horizon. I never made that first choice from which all others would flow. In old recollections I see a similar sky. I couldnt work out what day would have put me under it; these skies are so infrequent here, real skies. They are unending because they end, and I can capture them, from end to end. I can see their ends and that makes them something. It is not everyones white sky with everyone under it. The tails of the black clouds taper north and south up the beach and curl further inland while they diminish, enfolding the coast.

The body, and bodies, find an internal coherence that retroactively gives form and purpose to the mechanism they are found in. The thighs stand fully erect, full close, propping the hips which slope down 30° below level, at whose highest point, the bicep and the forearm lean, drawn convergent upon the elbow. The underside of the inverted V of the arm is mirrored in the tops of the press'd together hips on which it leans, forming a pillowy diamond-shaped void. First station, third body. The reconciliation of the mechanism with its form and purpose through misapplied external associations is only pertinent within the body, where it is needed; external to the body, explanations about diamonds swirl away and disintegrate in vapor.

You cast a long shadow that reaches down byways and twists around corners, carrying silent charges about your character, your facelessness, and when it settles, in a vast empty parking lot surrounded by the back bedroom windows of all the night apartments, its shivering perimeter rattles in exaggerated panic. She closes one eye and unfocuses the other through the tiny hole where the cord of her window blinds passes through a slat, sees your shadow, steps back from the blinds, her silhouette diffuses into lightness. You ran your hands through your hair and touched her cold window glass. From her window she can see it all, into every pore, across tiny craters of sand far above the tide line, through time and consequences, reaching back, unsuspecting, beleaguered, alert, and unprotected.

The days are reflections. You cant place yourself in any of them. Each is more populated than the last with the things you have forgotten. Each reflects each until you no longer appear in them at all. Looking into the oncoming days you face the consistent loss of you. Still lives from a world of sunlight and sunlight filled clouds fill in your shape. You dont see things anymore. They are within or behind you. You have had them make you. If the sky is there, you are there. If the sand is there, you are there. The streets are too long for one day. The heat rising off of the horizon reflects the sunset or the days old sunrise far down the road. These effects focus into a single body, enormous, yet immaterial, happening all at once in an equilibrium that renders itself and its contents insignificant.

Wrinkles fan out geometrically from her clenched eyelids. She pressures objects, thighs, vases, folded napkins to assume her place, instead of following her; her form looks foreign. She fills her absent body with stock domesticity: aprons bound by cords, large metal handled spoons, a large round stone holds open a garden gate. She turns her hands over to face her palms upward and presses the tips of both thumbs between the knuckles of her pointing fingers. She presses the knuckle of each pointing finger into her closed corresponding eyes. Her eyeballs cave against the pressure. The inverted silhouette of the black apartment block remains, empty, white, awaiting the hopes of the regenerated creature. Citrine spots wash the white apartments of her eyes.

Her shoes are caked with dried layers of fine mud, you cannot walk it off, it comes from walking, when the soles erode the rind of filth thickens, kick your foot against the splintered wood pole, she kicks her foot out, kick beside the pole, scrape your shoe, each shoe, mud binds the shoe to her worn sock, all you have collected, all that coats you is dried by sea breezes into viscous powder. She is kicking and shuffling her shoe against the wood pole in a fine cloud of dust, carrying away the roads, slept-in puddles, sun off of the facets of the sea carried in a mosaic of sand grains, the dead thicket, the grass threads through the entire length of fence wavering with the lapping current of her foot shuffles. Her steps in endless repetition walk the days into the ocean, sinking, behind her back.

I dont dream. When I realize that I am dreaming I am awake, my hands flutter over the metal desk. They disappear in their movements and detach themselves bloodlessly from my body. They continue to sort and file but they are gone. I see the tips of my sleeves limply still and a foggy blue stain in the air that doesnt float away. That is there. When I dream in my bed I am sitting up, my back against the wall under the window. I clutch my wrist because I think it is someone elses. I hold it to be sure it doesnt leave. I watch the shadow of the palm in a rectangle of light on the blank wall. I focus on whether I am feeling the contact in my hand, which is touching, or my wrist, which is being touched. My skin is always prickled by the onset of fever or by the warmth of someone watching me.

Held between, or within movements, delineation of the diamond capturing the void of the inchoate third body, enters the second station, and the void sags into a flat downward pointing chevron. The two arm muscle groups between the thighs parted by the calf, and, more integral to the character of the movement, the hips, loosely forming the vertices of the void, incomplete only by the thickness of the damp night air. The forearm and bicep span, only momentarily, before the chevron is rushed by all manners of fingers, heels, apples, and blades. It is not possible for a body to stand, be defined, assured, and differentiated when clad with the company of so many scrambling bodies; yet, a body, even lost now, can always be scrutinized.

You know the judging eyes, they shred you. You need not see them precisely quivering to maintain focus on you or your shadows or your wake of errors and failures and misperceptions. You see the eyes blankly cast into the dark rooms of afternoon, and still into dusk and when the city lights awaken all about they are glazed in fluorescent glimmers, dry and unblinking, fully white. In all the days all the open eyes can scour your footsteps and peripatetic dreams. In the dark you need not see the eyes to know that they loom. They address all facets of your descent and departure, your progress, your productivity, your worth and contribution, your shape, the questions and the motivations, your growth, your erasure, your punctuality, your collections, your deposits and throwaways.

If all of the light, and all of the events, and all of the hopes of the days and days return to you, and to everything else, you are relieved of the burden of causing anything. They will come again and again. If they changed you would change with them to be just what you are in them now, on their breeze you drift. You have no more future responsibility than all that has played out behind you, and that is all gone. It only exists in the glimmers of a damp eye where the receding tide flashes in reflection. You see the bits of the day stippling into your eyes in a luminous sandstorm, your hands form claws in the sand and you let your hair fall across your face across the white sun. You are a full vessel, sinking, you cant receive anything else but a coat of paint. You are waiting. I watch you wait.

She begins at the pressure point of her knuckle sending concentric waves of fresh green sands sparkling in depthless space until the shimmering hue sprawls out across the eyescape. The verdant mist laps against the boundaries of her inner vision and reflects back in softer currents, the foamy crests of wavelets catching golden glimmers, and slowly the haze encroaches on the zone where her knuckle presses, where the apartment is cloaked in the perennial sap of translucency, of humility. Pressing deeper. The visible concavity expands with a slightly deeper hue; radiating explosions of golden flecks degrade the profiles of home further. In this central depression, in the grown over remains of inverted domesticity, she wanders the ways of final repose.

All things in the city must collapse upon themselves, roads become hillside cul-de-sacs, sidewalks pool into parking lots, water from drains meets the sea. Her feet streak across the concrete and the concrete travels upward to fill her stockings with hard unfeeling stone. She kicks her shoes when she walks on each vertical element rising out of the concrete, some tall enough to strike into the white sky, others just barely high and stiff enough to resist her limp motion, metal street sign posts, black iron security fence struts which she merely drags her leading left foot across, the legs of mailboxes, wire uprights of disposable for-rent signs, high striped mooring posts, marking out a linear pen that stretches up to the horizon and diminishes.

I layer my clothes to brace my skin from the air. It is too sensitive. I feel eyes that can see around corners, whose pupils are shadows, piercing through the breeze and sun. The sun is over the end of a street now where it is blocked off from the sand and ocean. I dont think Sepulveda hits the ocean. It goes on forever. I should make a day to find the end of Sepulveda. I want it to start and end distinctly. I want to see it in the dark so the beige hills that crush the valleys and trump the horizon are lightless and black. They make me shake. The tail of the ridge jutting out to the north is an heavier shade of white from the sky with a thin silver corona. I see the sun behind it, snatched from the southern sky, able to rifle dusty afternoon into the bathroom windows were I home.

In so much buzzing and dripping, and clawing and stepping over the limp and the mechanized who move in machines in the dark, all that a body can do is to sleep, and to vibrate. All that a body can do is to not be there. Dark streaks between parallel pale limbs on the rind, where it is clear that the body is one thing, loose it from a night of continuous capes to be naked. The voids feign corporeality on a body turning to mist at fluorescent dawn. The third body is defined by where it is not and where its actions are not. The third station, the thighs are slightly parted, at ease, the hips ascending, waver slightly before dropping, and the arm muscle groups tense minimally, arching back to define an upward pointing chevron-shaped void, framing a refrigerant cloudbank.

Her gaze bears down and drives you harder to the earth each night, grinding you into nothing against the asphalt and dropping you into corners crushed from the burden. You are broken into pieces and her eyes see them when they float away. You remain kneeling before her glassy eyes and you remain hurriedly stepping away from them and lying in the dark and sitting behind a counter forgetting. She sees the past admissions falling away from you in clouds of dust, in sweat that falls on the table. In all the days of all the eyes in every moment you never cease to be broken apart, yet you never outrun the big clumsy body that has wasted so many dreams and footsteps. In every moment, even those in which you know yourself not to be, they record, taunt ceaselessly, and place you there.

You cant know how this situation will redirect me. You are responsible. Whatever the outcome your guilt is sealed in the vapor that perpetuates my life. You have nothing to do. Let this moment free into the reflective moisture of my breath, the fine clear crystals of the sand endlessly flickering between cause and effect. Let yourself be lost in the sun. It will all happen whatever you do. The sky is half white atmosphere and half luminous white cloud from end to end of the beach. You squint across the sand. I get up to leave. You have not changed position. The scrutiny presses down on you. You have jettisoned yourself over and over into the sand to keep your body from sinking into it because you dont know what is there. I know what is there, I was buried from the beginning.

In the obscure distance she can discern the impersonal forms left in the apartment. To recall these cast aside items is to destroy their importance, to cross a threshold into an intangible home on the night, on the street, to blow away with the breath of a wink the cloud that binds them here and her to them. At the cusp between the pleasure of permanent damage and entrance to this memorial home the sparkles shimmer behind your eyes with roseate benevolence. With continued descent lights consume the eye and smother out the remaining wisps of recognition. She is seeing within her eye an entire space of senses free from the population of her mind and the street. The natal sight, the ancient directive to gaze behind figures of the material world, is awakened.

She is bound by external impulse to tap her foot until her shoes have disintegrated, are clean, by impulses from beyond the horizon, beneath green dusks, march her forward away from the sea until she crumbles into dust under the rattle of endless footfalls. Each step into a new reflection, a lengthening shadow, is a new doom, a new empty urge to satisfy. In her reflection are endless lists of scorned surfaces to erase and incompletions to amend. She presses her palm against the breast pocket of her smock. The stack of paper relieves a soft rectangle out of the fabric. Each card and folded sheet explains a failure, a boundary. Papers drift into the canals from vaster seas upon weak tides drawing only the most base of concerns, the elementary shortcomings for her to find, second-hand.

I stayed all night at my desk. That morning the sky was green. During the night the hills had fallen away and loosed the smog and sun from the morning sky. I stood absently in it for a moment before going back to my desk. During the day, in there, the sun didnt move, there were not shadows. My actions didnt progress. When my hands started moving over the desk, they didnt stop, the paper didnt stop, the fluorescent lights in the ceiling, the metal lamp over the desk, all of the other empty desks light the room into a shadowless gas. It was momentary. I had only to move one envelope and I had moved and placed all of them for a lifetime. It wasnt a matter of how long it happened, only that it had happened. I believe that one moment is different from the next. I wasnt there. I was at the beach.

Fourth station, third body. The vertex of the void, formed by the hips ascending the insides of the thighs, forced outward to press the arm muscle groups out of the sagging chevron, now taut, approaches the shape of a diamond. The arm muscle groups forced into a peak, through whose frame, which breaches the rind of the machine, a gray stria of light bisects the scene, directly through the soft vertex which would lie opposite of an elbow. The body curtain parts upon a luminance, a vermilion guardstrip draws the edge of the rug at the bottom of the stria. Light clings to the night, light clings to sweat on skin. The curtain is drawn back, the taut blacks are pulled before the light casting shadow back onto the body through a diamond shaped orifice, slightly before it goes limp.

Things become solid in the dark. The past becomes tangible. Guilt, suspicion, and scrutiny are forces that you are cast adrift upon to meander through the night. You yearn to sink down into opaque silt. Her eyes pass you from one moment to the next, floating empty beneath you, never filling a place or failing with you. The lost spots where you have fallen, spilled, given up, cheated, intruded, hidden, decayed and languished, leave inlets for scrutiny to fill, her eyes flooding your past and eroding it into wandering islets and spits that you never find again in the backed up stagnation of the trapped tides. The moments that fall away, into the soup, swim suspended beneath you always, always rubbing amongst one another, borrowing and infecting, and losing you with their foreignness.

The day is a long morning, waiting to start, for the sky flats to wheel into place and the buildings mocked up. Then things are hidden around the city, notes to yourself, bits of food, beds, clothes, tragedies. They are attractors. Not each on its own but the mess of them. You couldnt be drawn to a specific thing. You have no needs. The sky is swollen with a single cloud. It contains the sun. The cloud is viscous benign smoke. A breeze emerges from down the beach and pulls the hair from your face across your chest and is still. Where the sea horizon meets the beach at the edge of the city a black soft edge of sky blends into the water. It grows. You dont see it rising filling half of the sky. A cold wind filled with sand and bits of soft paper fills the beach.

Sense without stimulus passes time slowly. It does not occur. The pressure on her eyes sculpts a flourishing chamber of lights with depth and shade. Glowing discs rise out and grow to fill the entire space, detailed arrays rise from the disc and undulate with arithmetical ease matching the pure logic of the sleeping absent city. It is all a memory. A visceral vibration that leaves the flesh unaffected, cycles with the sparkling pink of the crushed vitria. She finds the distancing relationships of geometric alienation in the orbs of her own eyes. She presses deeper with her knuckles and the light peters out in a single circular wave leaving a cavern of darkness and senselessness. She feels the cool conditioned air against her forearms wrestling her from vast oblivion.

On a landmass that is always sinking into that sea she climbs continually. When she finds sleep in dry secureness she awakens drowning in rising shadowy dampness. She watches through the pickets that line her canal the doors of apartments hanging open, shade, carpet, and mirrors, and the dropping sun in reflections, stopped and still burning white. She kicks her foot across gray battens and silver weathered boards that bound the sidewalk. She stands on the sidewalk side of this wall just a few paces along its length. All shadows make their way toward the horizon, marching in unison and slowly turning pale, before being all washed into dim beneath the great shadow of the sea. She drowns there, fluid, drifting into some alcove or beneath an open shelter, draped in marine umbra.

The sun is behind the tail of the cloudband, far to the south. The clouds have encroached on the beach to the extent that their steely underbellies are visible. The sea to the south shimmers with white dashes. The rest of the ocean is black. The sky between the clouds and the ocean is white, then pale blue, then gray. Every bit is on its own course. The sun is on my face and neck then it is gone. It is too easy to watch the day become finite. I know that it is all changing. It is moving forward. The things around me dont move or change. In the sunlight I feel every moment slip away while it happens. The day is a series of recollections. My life spirals away in the sun and dry breeze but I let it fall into those immediate recollections that I neednt experience. I know that the day ends and then is another day.

With each petite sweep of the limbs a breath retains light; with each
cycle the body draws a breath; with each breath the reflection from the
cave walls transform, dripping surfaces, hollows with becalmed limbs
dreaming of action, crevasses masticate shadowy crotches, crooks, groins,
pits, arches, cages, smalls, napes, deliberately touching each body in the
hall with irritating dampness. The fourth body. The mechanism replays,
involuntary, draws a breath, the body splayed limply from station to
station, each being merely a twitching sign on a knot of fabric riding a
pleat through a pulmonary void, exhale. Whatever lines had been traced
into the dew on skin, either naturally or by intent, have been buffed gently
since dusk by the action of fluttering limbs.

All of those solid lost moments, all of the wide open eyes lying
beneath bury you from below. The tension on your lungs and your heart
from inside constricts their chambers and sacs with the nagging weight
of trifling thoughts and complexes until they are crushed from within or
pulled to pieces floating alongside the unforgettable slipstreams of guilt.
You breathe laboriously. But the slight fragments of you are not guilty,
nor are you, now. When you drown you will be nothing. The fragments of
objects and scenarios from a desperately recent past align in the thickness
of the lagoon to create a perfect window out to the unlit and starless sky.
All day you drown and every night you spit out the humors and misdeeds
that clog your chest, run down your shirt, and fill your shoes.

Where crests of sand were scribed by wavelets, fine sand is let loose
into the air. It drifts high against your arms and chest and crackles in your
teeth. Salt breaks on your neck and sticks against your upturned collar.
The beach is smooth and the sky is bright and black. Material distinctions
are apparent and definite. Things dont cause other things. Are they in
order. When you happen again and again is there anything left from the
others. When have you wronged. Is the guilt from a post-dated wrong.
Objects and terrains have edges that at different times pretends different
things. They can open up with a diaphanous imitation of inclusiveness,
but the things that float into the tentative midst are themselves closed and
tired, unaware. You are conscious only that you end.

She lets wash away upon the breathing lights throbbing through the chamber, the residual profiles of her presence in the world through which her eyes float, through where there were things and stimuli. There is no respite in touching wood, vinyl, or chrome surfaces. They too struggle to continually outline her body with incongruent lines and edges that draw rooms through which she has no capability of passing. The stasis of all those canceled things, objects, abandon their impetus for being here in her company. Histories, conceptions, correlations, the desires from which she was wrought and the reconfigurations that nest her body into the world of things, sparkle only in the brilliant, rosy median between grief and joy.

Wood drifting out of the old seas of preoccupied days upon still sandbars, or kept, after waters recede, in the obstructed arcades and embedded routes that burrow through rooms and chambers in order to open at some point along the water, grows silver and desiccated. You should simply sink. Drowning is a death that preserves your form. A slow saline impregnation just below the seaside city sidewalks, the sun plays down through suspended silt to heat the salt from the water, to replace your matter slowly with silt and salt upon water vapor in the shape of the cavity you have evacuated. The water about your calves flows. Thready ripples fan out in a wake trailing in the direction from which you came yet you are still.

At my desk the still flood of time, with me in it, begins from whence it ended. I dont know that the earth or sun are moving, that the tides are ebbing or clouds churning, that someone is walking in the sun or lying in the dim, that the late afternoon glare shines through dust floating in my apartment, that my body decays, that my heart is beating and blood is pooling in my feet. I dont need to. So much of living is sleep that I dont need my body at all. When there is nothing I only need faith that time is moving forward. Out under the wide open sky that faith isnt possible. If I had the control in there to abandon my body, abandon the world and let myself expire, out here I am alive and heavy. I cast a pale shadow on the sand; if I lie here long enough it will stretch into the dunes and desert.

Bodies form coats 'round other bodies, nest'd layers of the character, which must be taken by the fingertips and pulled aside to gain egress from the body, into the night. Beyond the coat flaps, upon the carpet, stands a hall seen through a deep recess. The coat opens within the crevasse of two tumbledown towers of stacked linen. Upon a breath the coat pulls shut. The coat opens within a hall of metal chair legs nested and stacked in columns. Were this a cavern, these inverted scapes would be uncharacteristically straight and staccato. Were the body, the character, to calve with the folds of the coat, into subsequent bodies, it would be left, peel'd, satiny refrigerant dewcovered and wavering beneath stacked chairs, between linen columns, pleated immaterially into a lavender night.

Out on the sidewalk or in the weeds and dust you arrange, quantify, and recall the clots of mess that have flowed back toward you against the falling tide, where they collect strange notions that discourage recollection or closure, or absolution. All night you drown in those confusing or stolen memories. The humid electric air is thick; your body disappears within it. The solidity and stability of every edge of you tingles with grog. Sleep in the warm bath of night. Let the emptiness of your body, between all of its lost nodes, swell with warm wet steam and evaporating blood. You fill with water and sink in pieces. The solid things in a vaporous night fall through the refracted moon and distant green kitchen light and rise to condense on windows and mirrors with dusky steam for a body.

You wonder about rolling over onto your back. The sea has receded. There are no in between positions, no engagements. You are a series of pairs. You and the sea, the sand, you and me, the darkness, the dimness, you and you, dreamy afterbirth, you are passed from station to station, each one you and an action, you walking, you prostrated, you dozing, you appearing, disappearing, and reappearing from plat to plat, you stealing, you longing, you forgetting, you beginning. The sun shines hot in the white bulb of morning. You walk across the sand. Your feet are hard and borrowed. You dont feel them. Who does. You feel the heat from the sand rising beneath your dress. Your stockings sweat and sweat between the stockings slowly seeps and rolls back to the sand.

Her memories of shapes, profiles, and volumes of these things are folded into the inert hollows of her closed eyes. The lights bursting across her eyelids do not invoke the catalogue she distances herself from; the eyes float free of their communicative tethers. Why dream of chairs and bureaux in a night filled with fluid light and cool clear blood swirling through careening vitria. What rattles forth is an anguished collection of the senses of a body blind and numb from the start. The senses merely close a zone around her body that engulfs stucco walls, asphalt glimmers, particleboard telephone alcoves, and doorknobs her gaze passes translucently through. She and those purely evocative parentheses are left afloat in a boundless storehouse of memory shivering to find its forms.

The water drops, leaving a darkened wash from the high water mark on your stocking. The water falls beneath a second pair of stockings rolled to just below your ankles and recedes down to the sidewalk in front of a recessed porch beneath an apartment facing the street. Silver smooth webs of driftwood branches lean against the wall beneath an overhang in a drift. Precarious in lunar gravity they cast lengthening liquid shadows on the whitewashed board and batten. Pinned and draped behind the wood a collection of gray frayed fishing nets is discarded. A single door hangs open on darkness beyond the debris. A carving of an osprey with wings flatly outstretched on a shield marked with the faces of lions, head and beak turned east, stoic, hangs east of the door, above the driftwood.

I have been here for days. I see the sunshine passing by on the wood floor in the front room. This isnt the place where night happened. It is too porous and indefensible. In the morning the white sunlight shows the dust in the corners, hanging at the top of the walls, and beneath the table, the arm chair, and the bed. It casts shadows. Someone looking over the horizon is right in my window, shadowless. I feel a pressure in my head. It pulls inward. The steam or the wetness is trying to press through the side of my eye. I sleep indiscriminately and I wake up in different phases of the sun. I think about sleeping at my desk, without the sun. When I am there the sun falls into the apartment in the same way it is now. I have thought the stillness is old.

Even the most vigilant components of the sleeping body are, adrift in the curtainscape of night, consumed in blond obscurity. The stria of blond light refracts through the cloudy coat, shed from the body, and projects a hand reaching out to dip fingers into the mist, pinching the hurtling beadlets to hold them to the body. Brassy chairlegs, clutched between pale blue fingers that hold the body firmly in the hall, drawn out on the rug, when the character, drifting out from it upon the cloud, is built and torn to gauzy fineness by refrigerated air and by fluorescent moonlight. These recreated tropes of night coat scrutiny and incongruity over the character, which, covered in a highly suggestive surface, quietly refracts the surroundings without context or scale in an artificial pose.

Beneath the kitchen table she has laid out a large, thin overcoat, rumpled arms casually but deliberately folded across its chest. Dampness on the slick painted walls catches her pacing shadowfalls high on the wooden ceiling. You remember the room, the ceiling. You pull your dress around yourself. Your eyes open onto rooms. The shadows and glimmers of apartments, long cool nights and damp bedclothes rustle together around you. Why do you claim to yourself to recall the walls, how the ceiling sloped and the moonlight fell on the brick wall across the alley. Why would you have been there. Who would have seen you, but her, lying beneath the kitchen table, watching your shadow shiver across the asphalt, then slink off the street and appear high on her ceiling.

The entire sky is black and simple for a moment. A thin rain falls. Your feet kick the sand away from the asphalt and low steam rocks from side to side while the streets are slaked. You walk and stop. The rain falls on your hair. Oily water traces down your neck and between your shoulderblades. It should irritate you. It stops there on your back and you feel it with all of your skin. The rain falls across the stacks and scraps up across the sand to fill the day. It fills in and smooths away footprints. The apartment blocks look soft and pliable and the rain eases the stucco into richer shades and washes the dust from the gray fronds and needles that flutter in front of fences that disappear into the curtain of the front advancing into the horizon. The rain is singular.

The limbo of these ephemeral constructs is hesitantly penetrated by an emerging physical pressure. She is withdrawn from the pressure of all surfaces and atmospheres; she is not supported or touched. The sensation arises from the void manifesting itself in the disruption of the particulate patterns within the globes of her eyes. Her eyes being slowly immersed in a burgeoning tingle, her bare presence lofted upon incarnadine webs of light that prick forth memories of the body. The flesh wraps and folds across the hollow surface of the eye to form a wickerwork vortex of light. The vortex is not a passage. It is terminal, a vessel. At the center of the vessel is a darker rose of light in the process of being snuffed out by her knuckle. The world of reaction and constraint bears upon her.

:39

Flattened by afternoon shade of the dead end apartment your face alone is captured immaterially reflected in a small mirror through the shade swelling within the open door. Your face, brass eyebrows and spun dim lashes, peeled away from the sunlight sidewalk, you cannot touch your blank features. Your absent face has taken with it the late warmth of the sun whose radiance, from the end of each hair, begins to glow outward across the wall on which the mirror hangs in a lethargic single wave, swelling from the center of the mirror yet not expanding beyond its frame. When the simple molding in the reflection at the floor and ceiling wash into view the molding in the emerging passageway wavers into view, growing more defined toward the mirror.

The walls are decaying into powder and blowing into creeping sands. The thick paint stays. It is built up in change and neglect, the bark of a desert tree, sickness of the brain. In the afternoon I sweat in the bed, the dust burns. The sky, the ocean and heavy things fill the days I am away. This empty apartment slips into soft dusk, the shadows fan into shade and into darkness. Why not stay away. Why not seal the windows with heavy curtains filled with weights, turn on all the lamps and wait. I think it could end that way. The sun will keep rising and falling and slipping twixt clouds and sand will drift high against walls and the door will rust shut in the sea breeze and I wont go back there. The numbers will fall off of the wall and they wont come here. No one comes. The palms scratch at the windows.

Bodies rising from the stupor of repetition bring a continuity of sense through the nested character. Out before it, alert digits, pale blue skin, veins translucent in fingers where veins are atypical, trace out windows to bare metal through dew condensing on the abutting layers of chairlegs. Brown crust, flaky drifts collects around the elliptical feet of the chairlegs. Touch flakes, crush between fingertips, shavings of sallowed shellac. Fragments of the hall, bits contained in each breath toward a hall that is also a body: a pale linear luminance, vertical parallel soft edge'd shadows, a sea of droplets, each refracting milk-colored flowers. Among tableaux of information, none is more recognizable than that hand, several fingers looped, to grip the chairleg, yet loosely lying upon the rug.

In a cool night with storms hovering offshore, beyond the sandbars and canals, the walls glisten with damp. Long lamps throw deep yellow light across water rippling broadly. The leading edge of the wavelets carry the light to you in diminishing stacks. The city is all reflective, covered in damp skins, open windows and dim mirrors in barely dark corners. You are reproduced in tiny reflections of dewy coats and prismatic waves of brackish dark water. You see nothing, buried in time and dust. The apartment lights snuff out. She sees you from beneath the kitchen table. Early in the day, stepping out of the sea, your face, green with sea lights, filled the bathroom mirror, now in the darkness, refracts across the glossy walls of her apartment, or from a distance, or from the past.

At the end of the road the rain hangs in a pale curtain where the edge of the sky opens onto the desert. When you stop under a tree you feel its bark. Nothing. It is damp. Your fingers are damp. The road doesnt end in this direction. That doesnt mean anything, then there is the desert where days are nurtured in the emptiness. You should want to lie down in the cradle of hot rocks and sandy fire. You have nothing to turn yourself into. The notes on the papers are yours, you hide them in your pockets. Your nests are washed away at night. Things are ruined. Then at morning more and more things back up against the storm sewers. The refuse is yours. Each step leaves a step left behind. The road keeps going. All left to be yours is the walking and the desert rain stopped up in the washes.

The force of the knuckles reaches a terminal pressure. The vitria crushed concave, her eye throbs and sparkles full with an almost uniform drift of pink pearls. She straightens her fingers and extracts her knuckles from her eyes. She presses the backs of her hands against her cheek bones and rubs her wrists against her eyelids. Her eyelids remain shut reflexively shielding the cavity to which bruised eyeballs wander forth. She sees a plain white circle inside each enclosed eye where the knuckles have evacuated. The circles are broad and stretch almost to the edges of her vision. Her eyelids remain closed. The white chamber expands to draw together her body and the voided eyes she floats within under the same cloud. The whole world of streets is buffed out in this benevolent pall.

The walls glisten coolly. The crest of the light drifts away from me standing on the sidewalk, carrying vapor from my sweat, and lint from my hair, washing toward my reflection, deep within the apartment. Light washing over a door on the left wall, moist plaster run through with long running beadlets, motionless. The carpet is spectral, the light proceeds, across a white shoe, and another white shoe, stacked ankle to ankle, toe'ing out from the ajar door where bathroom tile in small murky mint squares is visible, she spreads out with limbs curled toward her body, you cannot sprawl out here, it is too compact, you cannot stand, your knees hit the water closet lid and hands fall limp smacking the vanity. Her fingers trace the baseboard and tile, trace over the dimpled sole of the shoe.

I look into the white sheet over the earth. It settles limply across my face when I crane my neck off of the sand. Long droops and drapes of dimmer value billow easily within the unending whiteness. It is luminous. When I blink I bring it with me but it is tissue pink. The discolorations remain. I cant figure if I am looking directly into the sun or into a continuous thin cloud with the sun behind it. When I scan the beach the distinction between materials is faint. All I spend my time doing is checking back on things. I look to see if they have moved or turned. I watch round things carefully. I use the same cup for everything. With jars and bottles I hesitate to touch them 'else I encounter them later rotated out of their resting position and lock myself in the bathroom to sleep.

All of the clouds and leaves represented in the patterned landscape take in the beads of sweaty dew that run down the chairlegs in periodic rivulets. Liquid rolls away from the body and saturates the groundcover, seeping into the network of knots before floating back into the night in a small atmospheric cycle. A cloudband in the textile refracts into an immaterial slick of floating liquid orbs. Now a real cloud, it filters and recomposes light just above the horizon. The orbs glimmer in anticipation of the distant silver morning, rising away from the rug in twisted interlocking festoons. Mauve light from beneath the double doors gives depth to the negligible surface of the cloud, hovering somewhere before and after the hand grasps the bronze chairleg.

She sees what your hands have touched, moved, placed, and discarded. You never touch your skin. You touch your clothes, running pointer finger and thumb together along your cuffs, the seams at the tops of your breast pockets, the hem of your dress or your coat. You smooth rumples in the fabric to eliminate traces. Your hands fight the inexorable building up of wrinkles, silt, salt, frays, stains, flakes, rubbing them out, clawing at the gravel, smoothing incessantly. You run your hands along door frames, pressing apartments away from you, sliding them into the sea, into the shadows, or out from the throw of streetlamps. You smooth the beach sand, bury cigarette butts, and scoop sand into footprints. Wear can be divested of cause. You run your fingertips along the frame of a mirror.

The city decays. In days of dry breezes the landscape dies peacefully. Your straightline mouth withers into a grin. At a distance the buildings around you are monstrous. The dry mold on their skin subdues a pinkness that the morning sun let clear through the air must have made into another living thing on the sidewalk with you. They are beige. Great windowless prisms that absorb light line the street, far back from it, miles, down other roads, or right before your eyes. You could pick them up. Reach out your hand and wave it through the air missing anything solid and slapping greasy raindrops. The powdered things, the unused and retired cobbles of the city, wash back downhill to the ocean in the running rain. Things take their places. You dont get near anything.

Clarity accompanies pain, but clarity of the pain. She senses that the body, returning to capture her eyes, has emerged from a burning cloud, then moved away from the street in her absence, taking her with it. It had returned to her or she had shrouded it continuously in a velvet pileus, each leaving each surrendered to the strains and shortcomings that insist upon the interdependence of her memory to her flesh. She is lost back within the extents of her body, the streets taper out into the night. She has returned to the sensate register of her experiences where she remains still, contained, a passenger. She sees the terminal concavity of virginity within the eyes, the road blocked abruptly by darkness, the door at the end of the bare hallway, shut and in moonless shade.

Apartments are for collapse, for contorted sleep, you cannot fit in the spaces, you would not fit in the spaces, your empty body would not alone fit in the spaces. Move in. Light from the street fills the frame of the mirror. Her back lit face is obliterated in shadow. The coiled warmth of a filament in a lightbulb washes outward from the ceiling creating a rust-colored circle on the floor. The soft shadows of lamps in the daytime cannot kiss your skin. The empty light of a lamp in the afternoon is swept away by the long rays of the sun. Even your reflection, not even a transmigration of your matter, only an empty illusion, is transitory in the dim apartment. The lamp reflects in the corner of the mirror, the rest of the frame filled with pale plaster, glistening.

The horizon is soft and rolling with black swells against the white sky. They are so consistent that they arent changing. The same with the walls and floor. Things happen across them or within their emptiness, but the edges are exact. There are places I can believe in that can recalibrate my senses, the shadowless wall of my bedroom, the desert tree outside my kitchen window growing out of the sidewalk with ancient black bark. The ocean doesnt check the tumult. It is a dark room I am locked out of, dark on the outside. Maybe I let it come to me. The spittle brown foam is blowing in chunks across the sand toward me. I feel how insides disintegrate. I couldnt walk into it. I would let it come over me and if I couldnt see in it then I wouldnt need to find a way out or find that I was gone.

Pale fingernails languidly penetrate the pile of the rug up to the bluish cuticles, and flex, bending the distal knuckle flat, the metacarpal knuckles creep forward in space. Hand and wrist emerging into moonlight, thighs and shoulders burst forth from the integument yet still huddled beyond the mouth of five chairlegs, three chairlegs dwindling into the periphery, the body cloud emerges toward the background. Seen from within, every orb of dew a witness to the whole other body, struggling to not be seen, the cloud unfolds into view, replacing home with far off destinations. The cloud is framed by a window that is of itself. Cloudbands of textile knots, exhalations punctuated by detached blossoms, threaded about the neck, shoulders, chest, refracting them, showing the body in patterned sleep.

The mirror is fogged over and nothing is visible beyond the fluorescent lamp over the mirror which shines directly down to your hands over the rim of the sink. A pale apparition dissolved into steam pushes away from the mirror, your hands behind your buttocks touch the glossy tile, each tiny square the size of your fingertips. Your fingertips correspond to the spots left on the tile in fine silky silt. Your hands fold across the flat bodice of your smock, smoothing it and the water bloused it outward, crossing them briefly, mummified, afloat, and placing them palm down over your breasts and pressing the stack of papers against your skin. Water and silt cast and disseminate your hands across the city all into the night. Submerging her eyes, they touch her face, and wash over it.

At the end of the road, where it collapses in a point, everything on it, near it, or beyond it, comes to a single function, where the air is a body and body to body the horde of points collects to propose an insurmountable conclusion. If there was an end it would be because you end. You dont know where you are in the assortment, only that there is a single point at either end of the road. You always see it. You will never be a part of it. You are endless because you were there when this began, in some capacity, and when it began again you were there even more, and when it ends you, in fullness, begin. It is a burden. The reins belong to someone else. You could end the same, being anyone or be anywhere, and it seemed important that you were mutable, and the shepherd of all other ends.

Consciousness, with its frayed edges, haunts the ends of night in every direction, draped over the crest of an avenue, pouring into the mouth of a cavern, forcing entry to an empty apartment, her movements draw it no nearer because it is the night that must move and has moved over her; with it she has placed the city of streets within each of her closed eyes. Each vessel cradles silvery white tears filling the basin of the plains, running forth from each damaged befogged eye. The loose memories of lights trailing across chrome coagulate into groups of obstacles, enclosures, distances, stretches, and arms waiting to open. These afterimages of the night from which she continually flees assemble and float fore from the crepuscular glimmers of damp airy crests on these old buried seas.

The walls, which let out to hidden spaces along the passageway in shadowy breaks in continuity, are a fresco of multiple occupations. Where surfaces meet, layers of the back story fall away revealing strata of heavy paint coats, murky, translucent colors gleaned from discarded objects catching sun through filmy water in which they are suspended. Light filtered through drifting clouds of wet fur clotted with household dust, when passed through a soiled teal bath towel, from which the brackish water dissolved plumes of brownish red, casts subdued seagreen and old gold from which a character or pigment can be extracted. In the reflection is another reflection in a vanity mirror, through the ajar door. Pulsing fluorescent light on the edge of a tub. Hands pull downward on a towel.

Gray clouds filled in from the horizon to just beyond the breaking waves out from the sand. I see the rain draped across the water turning it from black to gray. The sky was hot white over the sand and the city. I scanned from north to south and slowly back. Two slender white hands surfaced out of the black water near the shore buoyed in clutches of foam. The tide was receding. I had watched it pull away from my stocking feet. Long salt faded hair swayed out of the blackness forward flowing between the hands. Should I show alarm. I was alone. Faces bring people. Her paper white hands let into bare arms and the billowing sleeves and shoulders of a soaked blue dress. I had started looking at still things to feel myself disappear while those things became real. I gave myself real things.

The bodies exhale vaporous sweat drawn out or condensed to the skin. Pulmonary currents unfurl the body cloud out in pleats that lap and curl over themselves and through the air. These folds carry in their breath the fleeting moments of introspection between the incessant action of the body and the absent listlessness of the awake. There is nothing to see in a pleat but the opposite side. The cloud grows to fill the entire cavern refracting the rug with its floral pattern, the slender stria of blonde light from the mouth of the space, and the body itself, out to which embracing virga reach and fade into transparent chills before making contact. While it decays, the cloud body, from every vantage point in the hall, refracts the clothed body and it draws in a breath, and draws in the cloud.

She watches you step across the damp tile. Your stocking feet leave grainy impressions, buff away bare personal footprints. You step pointedly on old footprints. You hide in your footsteps, thrown across the city. They are hers, or hers, theirs. You cant start guessing tonight. She saw them fall, press in and the sea lap into them, you struggled across the pavement, spiraling around apartments and parking lots. Footsteps to the window, standing tall on toes, to the kitchen table, pausing, stepping backward to the door, straight 'cross the carpet, feet falling at vacuum seams, straight 'cross the carpet and slowly into shadow soft stockings slide. You hide out beyond your footsteps, beside her empty gaze, curling around door frames, table legs, feet stacked side on side your legs drawn upward.

You dont ask for the burdens or projections. You put yourself on display, but only in a blankness that cant take a shape, or a trust. You are a show, a cipher. Against blank pastel walls you lose your edges. What comes, comes. What you become, you become. You notice absently, in the passing of time, a sourness in the way you line up with your surroundings. Will you being in a place make it less of a place. Does it cave in to your diaphaneity. They change your edges. They make you something on the verge of annihilating them. Do they need you. They want to end. You will witness it, to make it certain. You might have fallen with it all before. Every day is a catastrophe that you dont set aside, or every day is a chance, you stumble across them when you wander.

An apartment block, a gable roof falls lower to one side and a voided blank wall is relieved from the night with glossy edges and shades of nothing against a field of pale. The White Plains, The Moondial, The Distant Trace. This figure has conditional transparency. With certain approaches of her attention it ceases to dwell there at all, it becomes the next or prior in the series. It is a spectre of a home. It is home, dreams strewn across clouds, an apparition with eyes shut. With her open eyes it sits mutely across black lawns and squares itself against the city, unpaints itself of light and depth. The moonlight falls blankly upon it. The emptiness is more vast than the night that surrounds it, it cultivates sheen and multiplies the dull burn of the sky.

A mug, tossed into the still water, floats upright for some time. Breezes or wakes begin to toss ribbons of wavelets over the lip into the vessel so finely that the liquid merely runs down the inside wall and begins to pool. The final wavelet corresponds with the precise weight of the pooled water and the vessel is pulled beneath the surface. The sun casts across it a filthy sallowed bone hue. The edges of these colors, the old potential evacuations built up into a whole forgotten shell, a sandbar full of empty shells, peel away around the dim door jamb underneath her fidgeting and tracing fingernails. Her thumbs spread across the outer surface of the door jamb. Your feet, shod in bright white sneakers against pale green and gold outdoor carpet, jut over the dusty wood threshold.

When I had real time I filled it with loss. I had watched things and come back to them over and again to find the bits of myself I had given over to them. All of my knowledge was contained in other things. I had watched the sky without the ocean but knew the ocean was there, behind all of the buildings and reflections. If all that I am balanced between the sky and the stacked and ordered debris in my apartment then there was nothing to catch the day on but a new sky or new things. I didnt want to let her rise up out of the water. Where would it all go. I have stored so much in compartments and stacks that this errant instant which I had prepared for myself wouldnt fit. I wont let myself see her stand up off of her knees in the soft sand and walk up into the sun and the white sky.

Beyond home, clouds occupy repeating frames, each encompassing all that is seen. For the body becoming cloud, all that is visible is that cloud, seen through itself, seen occupying distant extents, curling around the midnight. To see the body is to ignore all that it is seen against, to register without context its poses and gestures. A rug, a filigree of mottled hortulan knots, is seen in each frame the cloud occupies. The roving gaze cannot discern seams which would define the repeat of ordinary textiles. The cloud is the window upon which the entire night composes itself. Mauve, periwinkle, beige, pale rose, taupe, cornflower, and sand tinged characters with diaphanous profiles refracted through each beadlet in the cloud, grade into one another in a barely discernible tessellation.

Your fingers are hooked into a claw, now, and earlier, when she watched you pausing on the sidewalk outside the black steel gate, you held your dress at the hips, your fingers pressing thin floral fabric into palm, and pulled up on your skirts, pushed the fabric back on top of your hips; a tartan seam circumscribed your knees. You looked up at the window, slowly passing and never stopping in a sweep to the horizon. You smooth the skirts over your thighs. Your curled hand fits over the rim of a pale green bathtub, a doorknob covered in paint, a cool dry mug, wrists, the heel of a shoe, a fluorescent light bulb, soft earth, the oceanic horizon. She appeared large from the window, looming absently in the distant outdoors, and stood upright, pausing on the sidewalk.

When something disappears it has no other corroboration than what it left behind. There isnt a story. Passing time around you empties the days ahead to a catalogue of perpetual loss. There are always more things, more loss. Where do things go when you forget them, when they are gone and gone from you. Are they preserved, desiccated in the sun but still the same. Do they linger in shade. Do they become an inscrutable part of you, the skin on your back, your neck. Are you coursing with dross. You dont make things happen, but you are there when they do, they dont happen to you but you are forced to follow their repercussions through the days and wonder what they have done to you. When the sun sets you sit awake through the night. It is safer to see than to have.

Homes bound together in the night stand in a moderately low continuous surface bounding the street. She cannot penetrate the line into the flesh of the city. She cannot penetrate a single empty home into a spartan chamber that awaits nothing, she dares not gouge her eyes further or close them now because bodies form first out of the darkness. Her body is spread out before her eyes. The pressure continues to draw tenderness. Her legs, crossed at the ankles run parallel to the street, continuing to ignore the desired direction of her character, the cross current fighting the streets and careening into the homes, and collapsing at their feet. She allows profane shadows to bloom across the walls empaneling them into her judgment and distinguishing them from the night sky.

Your inverted palms touch the door amidst debris and driftwood, touching the coats of paint in succession, sliding your fingernails beneath each stratum, you invite yourself into the latent abandonments, recuperations, refusals, surrenders, and fatal triumphs of each apartment that, scattered about by the tides, has merely been replicated, found again elsewheres, reinhabited, repainted, and stocked with discarded items that have washed ashore enough times that they cannot be thrown back, and grow familiar. Each coat of paint covers the apartment that has been evacuated at that particular point in time, its color a memorial. Each coat also creates a new apartment at some distant point in space, which you will undoubtedly step into again, somewhere further east.

The sand has dried around me. It happens slowly and nothing else happens. You experience the things that happen in between actual events, not the events. The feeling of each grain of sand cutting the skin on my wrist sends me to each moment, each injury, in separate voyages. I move my palm over the sand to make a smooth area and then I spiral into it with my fingertip unearthing a cigarette filter. I look away from the ocean because I know it is there. I know it is there when I dont see it. When I wake up turned around I know which direction it is from me but it isnt something I ever need to corroborate. The gravity of the geographic traumas exist in blinks or breaths. To know only what hasnt happened or what you can only guess is there is debilitating.

The argosies that ride the dewy night carry refractions of all they inhabit. The hortulan landscape of wispy dendritic cornflower blossoms and curls, stippled out in the knotted textile surface, become real, amplified through the drifting body. Carry these details inside to make the translucent night familiar. The cloud body consumes and contains the leafy mosaic, its vapor replaced by the pattern, knot gazing upon knot. The rug rolls up upon each breath and sputter. The knots unfurl into long diamonds. Cloudbands ascend, knees rasp, knees grind, festooned limbs reach out to gaze back upon shoulders and other body parts more easily definable by their profiles and characteristics than any consistent location within the body, guardstrips and frames dissolve in vermilion parhelia.

In the dampness things get matted into one another in glistening confusion. Hair, collar, pavement, cheek all flatten and slide across one another. You look out across your shoulder with unfocused eyes toward light from darkness, whatever is distant, a failure fixation, and you cannot touch your toes without bending your knees. Your knees are bent and stacked and your feet are stacked ankle on ankle, your hands curled and empty. The night lights play off of unseen waters slowly rolling and are gathered up in the dew and condensation. You glimpse inert kitchen fluorescent sconces, twill browned lampshade over milk glass, plastic globes, candle flames, and a bare light bulb rejected by every mirror across Venice before dying into the dark water, a dim, uncontested death.

When the rain falls you see each drop in place in the emptiness around you. The air between the drops is dry. You inhabit that scattered territory and watch the drops hit your skin and clothes. You turn up your collar beneath your hair to sheet water away from your neck so that you dont seize up. When it rains in the desert the water collects and looms. There is nowhere for it to go against all of the hard old things. It draws things down into flooded concrete caverns below the dusty dry roads. It becomes deadly. A torrent of needling beadlets blown down Sepulveda, through the hills, while you clung to the bark of a dry beige tree, ramps down your chest and sternum and soaks your skirts. You are looking for somewhere the rain isnt, somewhere the sun wont be.

The recent dusk sky, a solid shell laced together from shades of throbbing orange and purple, depthless, is inexorably overtaken with a porous blackness. The voids through which she insinuated herself into comforts and enclosures are swollen with impregnable white solidity. All relationships at the cusp of day are inverted. The pale and wise glow slowly evacuates her mind. The void is not returning. The void has been present continually since the time she was the void, wholly. It lurks beneath the palliative layers of her perceptions branded into her intangible history, trailing her continually. Her breath, exhausting the pressures and incursions of her own body and her city tosses a drape'd seal of death aloft and settles softly, a sheet falling over a corpse.

Flecks of paint gather beneath her nails. Seen through the ribbed thickness and mixed with oily dirt the small chips are less colorful and characteristic of an environment. They could bear no relationship to the series of opened apartments winding back amongst her drifts from the sea. They are stuck in her, foretold to float or sink but not to remain. Each door opens onto the same pale passageway. The things you carry and collect grow quickly irrelevant. You continually attempt to ascribe to them an initial state born concurrent with your acquisition of them. Things do not have pasts, only the pasts they acquire by drifting through your undifferentiated life. Where did that start. You reinvest in them a more appropriate purpose, trajectory.

I put my cheek into the pit I burrowed with my finger and look across the sand. I see a face there. Her eyes were closed. Her hair fell across her mouth. I look across her now that she is there, some little bit to stop me and redirect me, but I see other things in place of her. It was far away. It wasnt today. I was just now seeing it. It was tossed around the crystal grains of sand, reflected, and that if she looked at me she wasnt looking at me but just looking. I looked back but I knew that she had already changed. She would be looking at something else, something closer. I had taken too long to get to this point. I ignored her because she was moving, sitting up to look at the ocean and spreading out her dress across the sand. She could fill up a day, doing things and going places, but she isnt there.

These scrubby flowers pass beneath the cloud, touching and entering, never left behind. Each particle of this fine vapor, spherical orbs of water so immaterial that they retain the refracted content in an attempt to make a body and pass it off in the absence of their own. Leave home, take on the fashion of this context, don a cloak of blue flowers for each beadlet that floats toward the fluorescent moon. Walk the streets. Breathe, part the prow of the cloud into a pair of forked fingers gesturing toward double doors and clearing for a brief vista of the real rug. Tiny knotted squares trace out in all directions weaving together tendrils, swirls, fronts. With each breath, the flat tracery of the rug is lofted up to receive hue from the twilight through the will of the body.

A light appears across the stone. It disappears without having fled, and then reappears. With its presence she is present and all the days before are present and you focus on turning inside out, emptied, only excuses, breath, and distant throbbing. The light disappears. You wait. In its looming absence you shiver, pushing out a slight expansion of your profile in the soft sand. You feel for the light in the fall of your clothes over your body. You watch for dust on the low alcove ceiling to shift, a hair caught in damp to dislodge, a vacant cobweb to quiver beneath her mincing steps above sneaking to the window, the light switch. Your body, your vision, your drive are rigid and instrumental, unwavering, immaterial, and you are smothered when you slow into nothing but anticipation.

Enormous stucco cubes are so far away, so smooth. They are covered with faint flowing blotches of gloss. They are so large that it rains only on portions of them. They have no inside, no door, no window, no shelter or outcropping. The empty asphalt is shadowless in the rain across windworn asphalt. Nothing stands. Nothing for you in these moments until the city cycles further into the day and the buoyant mysteries you have no use for slide beneath the soft sand. That doesnt mean anything. You inch partially beneath a cloth shelter that collects shopping carts. You watch the water still on the asphalt. Drops find different places to flow out of the open surface. Some slick streams swerve softly to sewers and cascade into darkness, together, or languish for a break in the clouds, or heavier rain.

Streets in the city, tapering into gauzy darkness, terminate charitably into buildings or at the last of her footfalls. The vast sags of land that coast over the distant precipices and continue into sheets of manicured grass plains, where beneath, or beyond, slow water sits and gently erodes the base of a wall that rises up out of the lawn, and looms over the street. She did not approach, it came over her. Across the plains, in all directions, homes. The errant lights warm living rooms throw into the cloud stricken night slowly sink. On a blank horizon the last twilights race away from the profanity of the black mountains, the black basalt, and the black buttes; the highlights describing the edges of the landscape bleed away, and the day is etched from the sky until the entire world is renounced.

When you find things amiss, ensnared in new reeds, laid out on gleaming tile, you stutter, falter, you are ineffectual and you must change your trajectory to contain these dead ends. You reexamine the chain of causality. You were indeed there at its root, it has found you in these wanderings. All things stagger out from your footfalls and handprints. You carry the paint chips 'neath your nails, evidence of your periodic return, or of the twisting back of these streets upon you, with slightly different suns and tides and histories. She picks them out with her other fingernails. Passageway upon passageway each painted the same dry bone hue, yet different, in different layers, while the sun falls away from them and their own lights arise.

Enormous things change. The ocean laps back and forth between the coasts and swirls down underneath itself into lightless caverns. The sand drifts along down the beach and the sky where it was filled with clouds turns bright brown and where it had been white a faint rain falls and will go on falling. I try to keep it off of my skin. It is a sudden discovery of old pain, rootless and rattling. It runs down my coat and over my shoes and through the veins on my hands. I lift the hair off of my neck and when I walk a raindrop falls under my collar, runs between my shoulderblades and soaks into my underclothes. It makes my neck hard and I feel that I need to pivot my head to keep my neck from crumbling into flakes. I stop under a street tree.

Each color body drifts through the fabric of the air bearing the profile of a local object: a chair back, a long conical pleat, a stack of table cloths. With a breath, the spectral furniture is drawn in, and exhaled in a cloud. The poses of the hall are exacted in the emptiness among the richly moist air. The darkness between the floating beads conjures the foliate pattern of the rug in waxy negative space and the air between each bead is the pale mauve of swollen breathing. The air space between each bead, each complete refracted room containing a breathing body, is an empty chasm filled with that breath. Each bead floating away from the rug makes visible the entire expanse of its pattern. In the space between breaths, in stillness, reflection is the ideal depiction of a disintegrating reality.

Through twisted covered alleys, at the dead ends of canals, the floors of crevasses, neither you nor your reflection emerges. You watch the stone patio. Still water traces the stone joints with pale green light, deep ocean phosphorescence, on delicate waves that reflect deep in your dry eyes. The reflections compound off of glass, back to water, hidden mirrors, varnished fingernails, slick stone and watery footprints, eyes, your eyes, her eyes, and swells with uniform intensity blotting out all other traces of light. You look at shapes and faces, expressions, her night window, the blinds pried open by a fingertip, the early morning pure blue lighting the apartment until smoky long afternoon rays slide through the blinds to awaken her, a deep orange with no warmth, bright enough only to shame.

There is never silence, but, you can never discern a single source. All that happens, happens at once, everywhere. The rain comes together pattering the water in the parking lot, celestial infinities of individual water droplets in a continuously falling body. Everyone, and all their refuse, is lost in the greatness of the storm. The flush of it all together amounts to a deep internal quiet, an airless security. If each drop is a moment, an instant alone, flashing against the tar, you are quickly at the end of this. You count back through your breaths in each disappearing drop. Days pass in the only rainy days you can recall. This is a day all at once. One chance. The possibilities of the days that conspire to determine your worth would be exhausted by the flicker of rain, all at once, in a morning.

Night, in here and painted across the windscreen. The cool intruding dampness of the city night, filled with captured light and haze coats her skin, hair, and eyes. She raises her finger ahead in a pointing motion until it connects with the dewcoated glass. A bead of moisture is pressed loose and draws a clear trail down to the dash letting in a wash of darkness. Her eyes bob in black bile that is her body floating. Her eyes are recessed so deep in the gaseous head that lolling brown and orange night traces of light passing through the body are snuffed out before reaching them. These wasted gifts she stores close to her mind are the last thing in which she has dominion over in the night. Blindly, she ignores the wavering darkness and she dreams of day.

There was no movement in any of these chambers, it is you that must move, before you are flattened, painted into the compositions, you linger in mirrors and before glass. You allow reflections to move you through the rooms, translating through chance orientations and angles of incidence. You are incapable of claiming a place, setting your shoes in the chamber beyond the late afternoon sun. A third mirror, in the ajar mirrored door of the medicine cabinet is touched by pale afternoon light that plays off of surrounding buildings and drifts into a northern window piece by piece. It tinkles slowly onto the folds of an unmade bed, the pillow is fluffed and its case is smoothed so that the open end is flat and sealed. Soft shadows float over the rumpled sheet and the room is empty save for the bed.

The anxiety of the rain fills my body. The drop and track of rain down my back are still damp and my skin tenses. It is all forward. Something is in the moment and it displaces the last moment. It replaces the last moment. I push out the life that I live for the one that is coming each moment. After some little shock materializes my body out of nothing I am nothing but my body. The rain drips out of the tree in larger drops and I am nothing but my neck and shoulders, wet through my clothes. I cant climb out of the wetness. It is stuck to me. The noon is filled with fine threads of rain that tickle everywhere. Nothing has happened, a blankness before a vision could arise into it out of the shapes that blankness harbors. I need to find my apartment on this street. I need to replace this, and that.

All of the color effects float in fictitious gases of ink, sprayed into the air in such fine beads that they hang languidly, maintaining the effect of perpetual swirling by hanging above the vegetal and nimbic arabesques of the textile landscape with a translucency that draws the appearance of motion out from the lively pattern. The beadlets merely hang twirling in space, but not around one another. The pause within a breath can be so protracted that it is not apparent in the tableau at this moment if the pose of the pattern cedes to the gesture of the breath. Between the reach of potential and the draw of sleep, awareness simply lingers. The blue stems and palmettes stride across neutral taupe to the edges of focus where they stand independently before dissolving into pure respirable tones.

The parallel lines of shadow softly inscribe the blinds across your all pupil eyes, dry beyond blinking, the shadows of soft dust on silt eyes. The clarity of the lines suffers when your eyes strain. The shadow is more than the thing. The lines interweave and bundle together drawing a silhouette of prickles, dry reeds, hairs, and fibers. Her pale blue skin shows a crescent just above the knee and between opal plaits on her neck. She stands at the edge of the window frame, her right hip and shoulder bearing on the cool jamb. She steps away. She reaches up with her left hand and places two fingers between the blinds and pries them open. Your dress is spread out in a sprawling landscape of flowers, turbid blue green. Her right hand smooths the fabric over her thigh and her eyes squint.

There is a long clear stretch. The sky is brilliant beige and tired heat pastes the asphalt with steam. You put your feet out from the shelter and look at yourself extending into the day. You have done something or seen something, you have forgotten something in the mess of all the things you remember. Simple failures are enough to fill the empty hours of loosened days. Their resurfacing is habitual but their origins are obscure. They become confused with catastrophes in the ways that they make your skin feel. The air vibrates. Were you born incorrectly. It is afternoon and rain is dusting the horizon and dissolving the tall lamps in the distance and all of the hard things that are left out in it. The sunlit air is electric around you and in your nose and lungs.

What of the inexorable descent of that sun, of the day objects now in shade, sweating? The roads grow shorter. They evade the protraction of night by standing beneath poles waiting for the streetlamps to bloom, stretching out on lawns before high black walls, banks of darkened windows waiting to be cast in warm light through slightly parted curtains, hanging beneath the dome lamp in the cab of an auto whose coated windows translucency is opaque from within, shielded from the darkness in a perpetual twilight riven with the beads running in greater numbers down the glass. These are many conditions of night, many postures of the dark and lost of which this impoverished dwelling she longs toward is just one.

Inside, your traipsing gaze draws away from draping sacred sunlight, an accidental occurrence, every afternoon forever, and back through the dim and straight passageway. Dim in late afternoon, with eyes under spells of distraction or detached consciousness in descent, still objects awaken momentarily to creep from the apex of the tides. With them you continue to wash and stains rise high onto the walls and out into the open porch, dusty traces from soft dirt and lint drifts that have blown away. Stains and flakes remain preserved nostalgically, or deterrently. The ruinous apartments where these collect await the tide to rise up and cleanse them, or sweep them away entirely, to deposit them on ahead, or back through some nights on a street closer to the sea.

I had thought that I would spend the stretch of the day watching the sun move across the sky, marveling at how the sky changed and how the sky changed time, how it gave me back time by letting me watch it happen. I would see the sun framed through tree branches, low atop the end of a narrow alley. When it wandered the skies I would find my way in a loop back to my apartment, making amends with empty faces of buildings on the sidewalks and the carpark courtyards that swallow the sun. I would stop at every window and buff it with my sleeve, wipe down every doorknob to every apartment, and seal the city off in a clean corner to be buried by time and dust. In bed, in the dim, without my body oddly visible from my own eyes, plans to fill the day with this are plausible.

The fragile body of flesh, which is always returned to, is the critical point between atmosphere and setting. Through the night, the perpetual readjustings, contortions, rasping, and decay of a cloudy body insistently cycling pose and gesture bring a mark'd change in the position of the bodies in relation to the chair legs and textile pattern. This vibrating locomotion caused by the repetitive sequence of internal movements exerts a rote series of effects on the encapsulating rind that plies the damp underbelly of the body slightly away from the carpet and spreads it down a slight distance away from its initial place of rest. An ephemeral stain lingers within the irregular perimeter of the initial place of rest; a watery shadow is cast in the dark.

You close your eyes. Destroyed faces bloom out of spots all clustered together featureless afire. You step onto the rim of the bathtub in the dark to the high window and wipe an arc of condensation with the side of your hooked hand. The sky is flat and brown over the purple brick wall outside. You push yourself up through the window. In each diminishing instant you are captured, arms hanging forward, ankles crossed and hair draped in a stringy cloak seeking the pavement, in every flying drop of water across the sky, from one to the next, upward into the clouds and from each you see to the next. You breathe out the coolness in your lungs and it is you. You breathe out the cool dampness from cloud lungs and it is you. It gathers on her window and she watches the night through it.

Your footsteps are awake. You breathe through them. Their pattering whispers through concussions in your breath. Your eyes squint against bright breeze washing across the canyonettes and rifts off of the main thoroughfare. Bits of paper and fluff and foam totter and swing in the pulses of dry air that cross the street. The light filling the clouds plastered high arching from the west doesnt show onto the faces of buildings or turns of branches. The air itself is light and hot with the coming rain. Your feet are momentarily shadowless and bright in the round. The papers and frothy bits turning over on the air are flat white reflectors. Your hands and feet washing through the street are a coagulation of charged gas, a trapped accident.

Her eyes have gazed in error at a new face reflected each night on the outside of the windscreen, roamed the darkened palmy bowers that separate the roads from the walls, traced iron railings in straight flights of open stairs, hovered outside ground floor windows, cast silhouettes in high windows, fixed upon that door directly at the top of the stairs, ascended, given tentatively in to the dim door frame, communicated the notions of home in a city that had none, a high plain rolling into populous black buttes, back with the trepidations about apartments across the short lawn into her mind. She grasps the door frame and presses her forehead against the glossy door, slowly rolling downward to press her nose, lips, chest, hips, and toes over the threshold.

The lowered sun fills the whitewashed porch with gentle dry warmth, emptiness amidst driftwood and nets, submersion that cascades in front of the open door, also swelling with empty luminance. The sun reflects white in a parked auto windscreen. Over the crest of the sidewalk dim explosions float from doorways where colors and reflections subside and slough away. You will wait long enough and the etiolation washes through you. It moves when you move, although sliding back toward the open water whilst pulling shades down 'cross these upsloping roads. Do not meet it passively. Stride into it. You wash into neutrality and anemia. She penetrates further inland, centerless amongst the crossings and convolutions of the route. She steps from the open door.

I thought about accidents happening. I planned accidents. Maybe I would find myself at that beach. It would begin to rain. Something would begin to surface in me. I didnt plan her. I have known since I came to be here that she would happen and take the idle things that block out time into something I fuss back upon. Faces rising out of the endless sheets of paper and my face onto the desk were always the same face, her featureless face. In the mess of the papers that I fold up and put in my pocket, her face was an intangible curiosity that I could produce to slow down the empty space of that place. It fit in between the cycles of the fluorescent light, it stopped me from seeing my body. But it was long enough, and then there was nothing else. It was an accident that she was real. She still must be.

Low borne clouds slink past. Involuntary eddies gasp through the refrigerant fog bank. When they are chilled, cohering into an increasingly corporeal cloud, the catalytic characters of sheen and glimmer accentuate the familiar features of the visible surfaces in the hall. Such effects hint at continuity. The collusive essences of light, vista, atmosphere, and diligence, insinuate an external force in the movements of the watery curtain. There is the insistence, through atmospheric theatrics, that these phenomena are reflections from beyond the doors. The characters return by rote to their swollen states but left behind is a passing shadow, a change of color. When the cloud parts, the plane of light bisecting the hall snaps into absolute midnight clarity, tinged with rose.

The light from her window runs through the clouds multiplying into a wild flame. It passes through you but fills you all across the sky, omnipresent and inseparable from sea to desert. You feel things. Your stomach sinks, the blood throbs in your feet and fingers until it comes to rest beneath tingling splitting skin spreading across the paving. With pain the most distant fragments of your vast body override what creeps in between and claim the entirety of past, future, solid, breath, thought, and consequence. You are only the fretful stomach. You are the rotted and degraded foot. The physicality of discomfort and the consuming reflection on pain are tethered to the earth, they have mass, and with it they plummet from the nothingness of emotion and memory.

You are washed away by so little. Little holds you together. In a remote thought, dust clotted lipid eyes far away in a mirror, looking directly into themselves and the sensation of water under your heels, between breeze and the sting of the afternoon rain you can go to bits. The moment is neither yours nor yours to be in and it is creeping with malicious assortments of living questions. When nothing is in control there is no predestination, no desire, an insurmountable buffeting of your particulate flesh, you yearn to be given over to deafness or narcotic sleep, folded in distraction, or to be ravaged by the vacuum into enough small pieces that any communicative notions of emotion propping up your body and experiencing the passage of time are severed and tranquilized. You relate to nothing.

She moves through the unlit interior passages and chambers. Her fingers trace moist walls caked with paint drawing a horizontal line birthing rivulets that race in combed streaks to the wood floor. Several colors of glossy paint are splattered on the floor close to the baseboard. A broad and shallow front hall gives in to an open kitchen room with blinded windows on the shorter side, a dim door frame on the facing side ensconces a deeper darkness indicative of depth. Move through into a long narrow hall lined with closed doors. Doorknobs are cloaked in innumerable coats of glossy paint. Drips that dried hanging bear drips that dried on hanging drips. Rental stalactites. Muted light comes through the chinks in the blinds, through the front hall, and through the doorway.

Alleys branch rigidly from the sidewalk. The network of city roads is not complex, it respects the logic of unfocused desire, the want but not the drive. The roads do not end; you will not go completely missing. You may disappear but you are always on the road. The city is for the comprehensive. Escape from its continuity and redundancy is not achieved through knowledge or familiarity. It is not the city that must be known, it cannot, it continues on, into and beneath the sea, beyond the horizon, and through every crossing road, the same city. You must be forgotten. There are no other cities, only different names for the same disillusionment. You must never stop. You may shuffle the names, reassume them, the streets do not change if you touch them all. Touch them all.

I trudged past the apartment blocks, stopping under trees to stop the rain from falling on my shoulders and my neck. My shoes are soaked through and my socks are soaked through and I feel my feet turning to paste. Each tree has a different view of a different apartment block. The sky is white from within the rain. It is still day, although I dont see the sun, the air is filled with light racing through the moisture and I have grown to feel time pass in my body even when it doesnt. I know it is after noon. Things slow and there are so many dry empty rooms. The windows of each apartment dont reflect the white sky. They are black. No one would look out of them. Neighbors are in other rooms in the afternoon, rooms that feel wet but are only cold and glossy.

Float through the grays of moonborne haze toward a light with hue and depth ruled vertically through the slender mouth of the cavern body. Cycles of hue, from rose to azure, drape across mountainous formations, high rounded chairbacks, crenelations, drift in beneath columns of stacked chairs; the fingers and depressions directly before the body pool with an azure pall; the bronze fluting on the astragal of the ajar doors, from which the light is drawn, catches roseate glares. Out from the body, upon its breath, rides the gaze that rolls itself out upon tiny thunderheads rolling over empurpled landscapes and seeing only muted tones through the haze. In the breath and vapor leaving the hollow, the clarity and color increase, unbeknownst to the emissaries of the body.

She cast her eyes from high in the window, across the massive ever brown sky, a physical flame dirge, setting afire the far rooftops all the way across Venice in a brilliant apartment shaped corona over and over the width of the sky and over the curtainless windows of the uppermost apartments where light leans upon thin plastic blinds and wearily halts. Apartments are warm from the sidewalk. She widens her eyes with each sinking sigh tracing you down from hair to stocking foot into the pavement sinking. She does not prop you up. You drop where your feet were made to fail and fell face first then rolled and stopped. First the weight of the pain in your feet falls first and falls still pounding its way into the earth with you and it is you.

You put yourself together from bits and pieces, descriptions in notes, chance reflections reflected by chance back through a life of damp asphalt mirrors, from your hair when it slips into your eyes and the folds of your skirts sometimes lifting over your feet and how your feet step, persuasively, but a mystery to you until they fell, across the concrete, broken at tree roots, and into high brown grasses that your skirts rustle following the breeze and your hands clasp the old bark of a silver tree. You put yourself together from what you are not. You are not me, we both are alone in an afternoon, where I end you begin, I want to end. You could be me. You kneel in the dry grass and eat what was in a foam carton you find there. It is not a show.

The final shades of orange hued gray die in value until her eyes, suspended in dark, apprehend the trace of a single packet of dusk arcing across a doorknob, the first door on the right, which she causes to open. It is the end again of the apartment. These blocks are shallow. There is a window in the far wall with no treatments. The room is empty. The floor is carpeted with a matted pallid pile. Beyond the window is the front or back of another apartment block blazing in the grainy orange light of an alley or street. She begins to move across the room extending her right arm before her. The light falling across her hand seems to weigh upon it. Her outstretched finger arches slightly when the light upon it intensifies. The night in this chamber of the city is tangible.

The soles of your shoes sag with each step. Grind them to nothing. The portions attached to the perimeter of the shoe hang and drag across the pavement. They are ground slowly away. The thickness of the exposed edges is worn to a tapered flap that creeps inward exposing foot and stocking in an expanding ribbon around the perimeter of the shoe. Your foot comes in contact with the pavement. You put it behind you, each step further behind. The attached portions of the sole erode on the rising and falling motions of each step, when the foot seeks the ground or evacuates it. The wear comes where your foot protrudes or presses with more focus. Your balls and heels seek the ground. They tunnel through this protective layer in search of forward momentum. They want distance.

When I found the apartment again it would be where it belonged. Today I believe mine will be there, on the edge of the Sepulvedan Erg, its walls ending in sand. Lido Mirada, East Winds, The Desert Moon, Sylmar Sands, Debby Den, The Mission Hill, Rinaldi Apartments, Incoloro Caja, The Sepulvedan, Coat de Van Nuys, Ventura Arms, Mulholland Capri, Raymond Patio, Cahuenga Tower, The Dryridge, La Casa Cougar, Bel Air Arroyo, Saddle Oaks, Brentwood Imperial, Santa Monica Manor, Angelander, Park West, Five O Five Idaho, The Culver, Jefferson Riviera, Janice Ann, Royal Westchester, Cathy Apartments, Rexford Lincoln, Lord El Segundo, The Manhattan Beachcomber, The Pale Arms, Los Hermosa, Grace's Torrance, Carson Gardens, Rancho Palos Verdes, Ebbtide.

A bodiless panorama, draped with a cold and faltering glow, has neither the gravity nor the orientation to maintain focus. Both the gaze and its subject flutter intermittently. The character in this venue is a staccato transmission transcribed in bits, through many cycles, read by the appearance of moonlight sliding through the astragal of a slightly ajar pair of doors. The postponement of light through the cloud crowds the character with anomalous shadow features which stand at the soft scape of the perimeter of relevance: the slender straightness of the brassy chairlegs, the milky floral pupils of sleep, the finger imprints in the deep blue rug. These grainy phantoms of colored light give fullness and depth to the character in a medium that cannot be coalesced into body.

You can sink on land. Your own weight pulls at you with layers and layers of damp clothes soaking around your steam body spreading in a pool across the stone. What does not sink into the joints and cracks and down through the piles and silt to wash back out to sea pools in shallow depressions worn by her footsteps, standing with her key at the gate and twisting her feet while she looks across the courtyard to her window, and evaporates at dawn from empty clothes mismatched in a pile with no correspondence to your human body. The bottom of the ocean in darkness ends with rock and sand. All of your sinking is on land. You ease into steaming water and your skirts billow. Your hair sways. Your back and calves are flat against the porcelain.

You crouch, your hands beneath the heatherline, you finish. You arent driven by necessity but by what happens, and if necessity passes you linger most of the time barely noticing yourself. Nothing needs you. You dont stop to see yourself against the things that you touch or pass in front of. It is easier if you dont look. You might forget what you thought would be there, it could turn into something else, or just wash away leaving you painfully occupying nothing but your body, in a void, when you look, the emptiness begs to be filled, when you stop looking, the emptiness lingers, a stage for imminent scrutiny and exposure. At this time of day, in this rain from the full beige sky, you are full in yourself, you are visible, I can see you.

She sees her finger reaching out across to the dewy window while she is drawn continually forward. Her fingertip touches the damp glass and sends a drip cutting downward through the fog. She continues to press forward. The window moves forward with the tip of her outstretched finger. The window is sweepingly convex. She draws her face toward the window sending the bleak walls of the chamber and the paleness they enclose into the periphery. The orange light of the alley cascades down across her shoulders. The night air is cool and damp across her bare neck. She rests back to look across the expanse of glass and lets the light fall across her knees. The entire panorama of the windscreen is washed in black dew, dappled across the glass and floating in the night air.

She stood still, halfway through a block and walked in place, heavily, so that her shoes scuffed violently on the pavement. She trudged onward, not through space but through the soles of her shoes. The action of rubbing and eroding became tearing and severing. She swung her arms in the same motions she allowed them to make whilst walking and bend her neck and head forward. The soles, already loose, began to catch and wrap around to the outside of the shoe with some steps. She ground the remaining tethers back to the shoes against the pavement in a back and forth raking movement until both soles were completely detached from her shoes. She picked them up, rolled them into flat wads, and placed them in her hip pocket.

Those rooms with windows dont have lights. Those empty apartments, why do they have windows. Afternoon exists outside of them. When the sunlight gets to a sweaty, swollen sag within the sky, it is all full of brown light. The light reaching into the apartments brings more darkness than after the sun goes down. It is impossible to let the fullness of afternoon in. When the light falls it becomes dust. The only answer is to snuff it out. The real days at my desk dont go by. They start and end together. Where can I be without the world. I become lost. I stop with my jobs and look into the stillness of the fluorescent light. I am whole empty places. I am, without transformation or comparison, the timeless instant of the hard thing that doesnt fit. What other use does it have than to stop and hold me.

The stria of light rides each revolving orb of moisture in a vast cloak of vertical dashes, each seated upon the vermilion guardstrip, and half illuminated by the ajar door to form an ell of color with an alternately azure and rose vertical leg. Pull back, the ells cede to vapor the color of bland parchment that, where it is drawn before the light, is translucent.

The baffled light and its populous reproduction in the cloud timidly illuminate the character of the profiles and figures that wait for the distant perimeter of the hall to awaken. Only a limpid grayness is cast back. A breath, a shadow from the astragal, ghostly beyond the cloud, is then clearly repeated in the incessant refractions of the mist, then physically swirling the cloud in its path.

Coldness reflects in lost moon yawns, condenses in tangible black powder 'neath your fingernails, oily creases from your pressed shut eyes, in cracks on your soaked feet falling open. There is no deeper to go 'til the apartment too sinks, when the tides rise to pull it 'neath the nightly flood, to wash you both into the open sea, to land far apart after moonfall and never see one another again. Warm black silt fills your clothes, wrests open your teeth and entombs your lungs and you continue to breathe. The steam and the night indoors are narcotic. You coalesce into something shutting down. You coalesce before the seas can process you into darkness, into shifting sands and irreducible currents. You must be all before you can be nothing. You must breathe when you drown or you will not drown.

You are leaning against a tree, visible from high windows and storm drains, a day already pooled around your feet in the hydrated dust pooling square in a cut out of the sidewalk. Your feet are just below the surface of the water and the reflection of your ankles shimmers out of the glowing submerged skin. You are stacked up from deep in the purity of the reflection out into the sweat and panting of the air. You are nervous where you have stopped facing the front of an apartment block. Stillness unsettles you. You are on display. The thick light of the rainstorm wraps you in a parted curtain, draped forever into the ocean and the desert with you at the center. You are the only thing forever, filled with empty sky and tired desiccation.

It is the same night from which she folded her skin and flesh into a void that she is now awash in. Now awash in the humility of the hopelessly adrift. The chrome trim around the window pressed into her arm. The sleeve rode up over her bicep. The dome light is dark and the car is empty. Her impressions were necessarily fallible having retreated so often and so far into places that were not places and could not even suffer the death of the sun for no sense of light or even error was embedded in a vacuum. She placed things out of reach in the darkness. She felt the objects surrounding her: fabrics, a potted plant, small photos behind glass, displacing the night out of all the empty vessels that stowed her. She completed a setting out of the emptiness outside the glass and behind her eyes.

She could begin to erode her feet, her hair would drag behind her, she would hobble on her knees until they were gone and she would crawl the rest of the way, until the posterior horizon was no longer the sea. She had compressed days of ginger steps that needed to carry her further, into one spot. Hurriedly you have forced a process that should have consumed more distance. You cannot put behind you the open doors, the interrupted routines, the shoes resting at odd angles on thresholds, the ocean breezes, by physically erasing them, destroying the artifacts, wearing through the papers in your pocket. With distance these things will fall away on their own, you fall away. You cannot accelerate loss, the sun, the arrival of night, sleep, unmade beds and cold open windows. You stop.

When I look up at each window I pass I see a different direction into some other days that those absent people are dissolving out of without feeling it. Maybe these days are mine. Im never going back. I see the reflections from inside. I could go forever. There is no air in apartments. The vacuum still. I see the reflections of hands occupying themselves and stocking feet on tile long absent. I see chairs with slipcovers, stacks of misaddressed mail, expectant dishes, newsprint books of puzzles, a dry sink, whole rooms almost empty, displayed cosmetics, desiccated silk flowers frayed into mauve threads, amnesiac furniture, things that were sentimental to others, bits of the neighbors trash, notes written on mismatched scraps of paper listing days of the week and placenames.

Characters, figures, stars, gauze, stream forth from the chink of the astragal, the only edge inscribed in the entirety of a murky cavern. This could be the edge of anything. The light falls across a distant papered wall and the wavering seam of a curtain. The curtain remains in focus, its selvedged edge, the termination of some chase of shadows, breathes luminance back through waves in the pleats, drawing closer to the total consummation of the received light over the grayness of the hall. Breaths lie within the bellows of the loose puffing fabric. With each breath a dream of stringy dawn, and with each dawn a dream of repetition. The entire frame fills with the pleats of blond lit stock occurrences: awakening, the throwing open of a drape, a fissure where the body has taken leave.

In your closed eyes are the distant places at the bottom of the black ocean that are in every moment pure dark and endless cold. In the silver warmth of morning you will lose your place there. Shadows begin in your eyes. You are apart from them. Your face is flat against concrete. The horizon hangs at arms length with the entire world above it. The terrestrial heavens and arched mosaic skies and stucco winds all stand above you. You are pressed into an airless film upon the concrete. The bits of light flicker and change shape. Arms, feathery succulents, crossed wires, wavering coats, hands reaching to faces and folded hands on hands looming figures on balconies, and high swaying cypresses haunt the light from her window with their bundle of shadows.

The afternoon expands from you, a great unbounded room with spots of inhabitability, a lamplight marking stations of the narrative threaded out for objects that coast down sand dunes in lightning storms, and you wait, staring into your reflection for disconcerting stretches then leaning backward, heaving up your chest and grasping the tree with fingers laced behind your head, opening your body wide and rigidly scanning the northern sky for a pass in the hills across the rose stucco walls of my apartment block. The water runs across your upturned face in a thin caul, it steams. You try to see through it to a distant goal, something still, a skyclad tomb filled with ceaseless empty visions. These afternoons looking cold and steel are vast and hot.

She made out black on black silhouettes. Some forms of tree canopies against the sky, her long shadow, slight eaves, and deep alcoves and hallways behind wrought iron gates crowned with spear points were erroneously placed in the field of night rather than the dew of the windscreen where they were composed of brilliant black pearls of overlooked and surrendered nocturnal fragments. In the distance, although flattened into the panorama, a clutch of apartment blocks descend into thinness, Chez Lax, Velvet Palm, Bride and Groom, Fantasie, Vista Three Sisters, The Pocatelloan, Rexburg Capri, Plaza Plains, The Moon Dial, San Charlus, The Hauser, Willow Flat, Fontana Minnetonka, West 1st de Ville, relieved into the ebony canvas.

You stand in front of a broad plate glass window. The light from the sun, very far to the west, falls obliquely on the glass. Two large panes are bound by corroded and green metal at their corners and crossings. One pane is completely lined with bronze vertical shutters catching the sunlight and drawing reflected gilt lines back across the inside of the glass which sway. The air is still. You are sheltered from the light winds that dance across the waters and into the reeds which sway. The other pane is unobstructed yet befogged with moisture. The green sky reflects Lido Arms, Quadrige Court, Palmus Szasz, The Quarantinian. You approach the unobstructed pane with arms bent upward at the elbows and palms vertical until they touch the glass.

I walked down one street, forever straight, with the same walls coming one after the next taking me nowhere. It might never stop. This street wouldnt end. It would, somewhere beyond where I could go, be washed over with sand and dry rocks. I could get down onto it and brush with my hands and the street would keep going down beneath the sand. The walls would flake away out there. When I look into the whiteness of the sky and fine rain rakes my throat, I see empty glossy walls. I look at things for too long and they become part of me. I think I want to be surrounded by walls. On one street is all of this. My apartment window is black too. I made a day apart from the others. I had wanted this one to be in the middle but it is at the end. I had wanted things to happen. I knew they would.

Artificial twilight settles upon the cavern. The light, gently fingertip touching the shadowless blond drape comes not from the door itself, but from far beyond it. The size or type of illumined mouth is indeterminable. The light possesses a barely saturated hue that is given depth and reach by the promise of its source, a luminous bloom falling open far beyond the membrane of the astragal in the foyer and the antefoyer that mirrors the gray alcove. Beyond, drawn through the fissure to face a gray alcove, shrouded in night, before the beige face of the two doors, a character is erected of the siphoned dew and projected history of the cloud. The stars, falling, glimmering traces on brass, draw yellow patterns against the usual sky, full of light, pale blue.

She is lost in the opaque script of the shadows. Hands wring, shivering into and out of bolts of domestic light, hair sways through dappled apertures and stocking feet stack and unstack with heel on ankle and toe on toes. She sits at the kitchen table. She gives to you a jumble of omens and talismanic body fragments. You know what they compose and where they condemn you. Her hair on the right side hangs long across her face in wet plaits. She feels the apartment on her skin. Its emptiness runs beneath her collar and she adjusts her neck reflexively and widens her eyes to the dark. She is folding cloth napkins slowly into squares. Checked green and white squares divide the smaller folded squares. Her feet alternate one heel atop the opposite foot, filling the night time.

You are barely here until you flail into a pose against the tree, something open to evoke motherhood or fecundity 'though you are rotten and dry. Your face is colorless. The allusions to features are rigid and uninspired and frequently absent. Any encrustation of detail on your skin is unimportant. After the rain smears it, hot stillness dries it somewhere else. The breezes blow away your expressions. That you are there, somewhat physical, is obvious. You have a frail heaviness that rustles the air around you and the breeze diverts in an empty envelope around your body. You could fall over and the upright doldrum would linger. The vision of you lingers. You fill space elementally. You have no charge. I propose my skin, my life could paint over you and equilibrium would be sustained.

She draws back in a slouch from her scrutiny of the windscreen minutiae. Her hands again on her knees, all poses project self-envelopment. Yet, resting back away from the persisting uncertainties of this night, she was ensconced even further in the dark. The light stars, though rare, glimmering in drops of condensation that twinkled in the pupils of her straining eye were distant on the glass. Any real source of light that was not bounced perpetually and falling dead dull on her lap was more distant still. The seat was smothered, the dash reduced to an edge catching a glow, and her posture slithering down before her inky and nebulous. Even alert, attentive, swimming in night left her gasping and fingers wrest the dash to hold fast to something in the dark.

The glass is very cold and damp. The hollow beyond is sealed, excised, solitary. Its refusal is total, it refuses the city, warm sun. It refuses you because it is not there. Rooms do not reappear. They are there to be filled with emptiness and reflections. These are the empty cells where you put apartments, the dust of age and sleep. They have yet to be forgotten. In the green glass a cold gaseous light emerges from a small low point, its source shielded. The light reflects back upward from a sterile counter very close to the source. The edges of the counter are not visible, only the cold white zone directly beneath the lamp, the width of your shoulders, the lamp low to the desk where your bowed head and chest, your arms outstretched beneath them, flatten over your palms.

I wanted them to come on their own out of lifeless things, those things that I have found and tried to fit myself around. I wanted to make a day from the debris field of the days sloshing within me. It would be purely mine, then it would end. It would be of the world. If I could forget what I was made from, what my desires and impulses were pasted from, I could make that force end, the force that makes me crumble into the desk, to disappear for the benefit of places that belonged empty. I made the decision not to go there, on a day with the rest, and because my body, molded from that place, worked into something out of repetition and implication, could not be trusted to allow the day to be, I had gone to the ocean in its fantastic pointlessness. It didnt need to be, but it was.

I am rocked by the wavelets rolling through the curtain, riding the crests of breath having traveled so far that still hang away in this passage falsely tramping through a great night cavern. Each dewy pastel rolls into the next, rolls into cornflower, rolls into taupe, into sand, into the next. I drift with my gaze across the champagne fabric. The incurving edges, where the fabric has lapped back upon itself, rear up to the solidity of opaline dusk, of a slender figure, a chairleg, an ankle seen from behind, a tumbledown tower of folded linens, an outstretched finger beyond these afterimages of an impending resolution to my state, a physicality beyond the trace of my gaze upon the mid night fogbanks. I am evasive the more ensorcelled in the hall of objects I become.

72:

She sits curved in a chair with arms and wings facing the wall. Her still eyes are wandering. She is still. She looks at the white wall. Moisture stands in the texture of paint over painted over moisture. She watches for white to differentiate itself from white. Aged walls tell no stories. Her shadow is still. Long nights have no stories. She looks for things to emerge from the emptiness, patterns, shades of white, glossy profiles, relief, relationships, the wide orange sky, dawn, vast sunset horizon of the sea, glittering golden sunset domes, the emptying of her body into this vessel, the shadow of her empty body rising from the chair or turning to face the covered window. Nothing. The ambiguity of night rests upon you. You bear narrative questions you cannot cast away through forgetfulness.

You dont see an outlet. Things go in order, the wind, the water between your shoulderblades, your acquiescence, your eyes and the light across a dry lawn and a black gate in a stucco wall, then a high wall that plods unbroken for days in either direction, the pale rind of hilltops glancing the sky and housing an end to the rhythm of days in an authoritative dusk where young lives lie down and fold pieces of sky into their disappearance. Lie down on your back, inert, emptied, nothing else, and know what has happened. You look to the east. Increments of measure and distance repeat your walking past without end. A sheer curtain flutters out of an open window with a narcotic nod. Afternoon is slow. It stops. The clouds break revealing more white sky and no sun.

She struggles to feel in her body, even now, with eyes wide enough to swallow her flesh with lids wrapt back all around the soles of her feet, with all the sensitivities which the back of the skin cradles close to the flesh inverted in the night, that she could feel something; the pattern of vinyl against her shoulderblades, the cool moisture on the vinyl ceiling, hot discomfort on the back of her neck warm with tangled sweaty hair, the grain of the dash against her fingertips or some pressure of objects or enclosure to hold her at the threshold of the void. The palms silhouetted against the orange sky bob beyond the fog stricken windows. Their crests rise and fall above the rooflines in a continuous black undulation. All she sees is floating.

The desks are lined with rubber stamps. Painted metal cabinets line the walls. You raise your head. All the desks are empty. Meticulous tasks isolate you, comparing addresses and names to lists of addresses on damp sheets of paper, reflecting the green sky at the end of the day and days before. Straighten each dewy letter when finish'd. The most recent always reflects clearest. Dust settles thicker on finished stacks of post. You are the only one here. You pull your head out 'neath the lamp. Your reflection is strange in the glass. You are too large to fit at the desk where the lamp lit. You are at one of the darken'd desks near the window. The desk is very cold and slick. Rub it with your sleeve. Condensation moistens your palms. Look under the desk in front of you. The tile floor is dark.

When I am at the desk, the destruction of my body comes through routine. It isnt something I appreciate when it happens. The actions are fixed and the setting is inscrutable. When the light falls upon my hand in a particular way I can see through my flesh and know that I couldnt possibly exist. Not in this way. In the pattern of shadows under the empty desks and the cones of light from each lamp I see myself become nothing because those visions have become my existence, and they will not change, and I will not breathe, or cry, or sleep. I wanted to wake up at the beach, and for the desert to have crept to the oceanside so that I would have nothing. I wanted the choice to be made for me but I wanted it to be the other choice.

I skirt close to one side of the corridor, a breath swallows the curtain folds. The fabric comments upon the drama of my movement against the long wall of a theatrical gallery. The entire corridor gasps inward and curls about my gaze so that I can no longer see the icy light in the distance. Upright yet limp, interlocking my movement with the writhing skin around yet distinct from me, I grow still whilst I am ushered onward. My concurrence with the billows, cast out of the insistent exsufflations of an air conditioning register, turns this shivering movement through space into a sheet of frozen wrinkles against which the still clouds race. Bands and wispy weavings of a taupe ground fallen behind the mist step out into the billowing twilight.

Waiting in the armchair there is little to do. Repetitive tasks fill the day and give it cadence. The night is to be waited out and endured. She endures the unchanging light of the apartment. She endures control and its illusions. She controls the past. The odd reflections, the watery stains, the disheveled carpet nap are the traces of old effects. In the unchanging objective light of the milk glass lamps they are mute. They indicate nothing and they change nothing about what she recalls. Only you are distant. It is the muteness of these old effects that causes her eyes to tile them together into an interrogatory rebus. The night has no stories, only the manic effect of those dusk visions that crept toward her in the last gray shades of day played over and again on the pure emptiness of the blank painted wall.

You look at the window, closed, with yellow light hemmed by a flat curtain, a floral print in tiny moments of silhouette radiates a warmth that swims through the heat, a tender warmth that emanates from you, from behind your neck at the sight of it, not from it. It loosens your lungs for a moment. Take a curt gasp and your right eye strays away and returns when you shiver back into suffocation, stillness. In afternoon, when the plaster sky opens slimly through the dry trees, you are alone in its light. The city has space to spare, distant from the morning and distant from the dusk, yawning shadows that dont reach the next body, but prostrate, gaze out across the landscape with its deformities, casualties and obstacles, see nothing beyond the thick light that afternoon spins about you.

Profiles of sheen and gloss whose coolness she can touch but whose substance she flies through, barreling ever inward towards a convergence of dark, damp, her self, and all the bodies whose coatings glow and diminish, snuff out, and swim. A dawn of substantive particles rises each by each through the night. Objects grow from their glimmering edges inward on themselves with creeping luminance. The sky slowly fades, draping down orange across the eaves, the walls, the lawns, the sidewalks, the asphalt, across her knees, her blue floral print skirt turns beige. An equilibrium falls across the city. The homes are in the sky and the clouds float across the grass. Where things fought to disappear they stand to face scrutiny, where she floated on their immaterial lines she now felt mass.

Nothing is here for you. Long headdown days do not wear away your body, they dry it into a bundle of hollow stems. When you crumble and disintegrate you fall in one spot, beneath a counter to clean glimmering tile. You are propped there emptily beneath a lamp for so long that you do not realize you are not there, that you have not been there. In vacuous sunlit hours you weighed the invitation of every open door, every reproducible darkened dim apartment full of texture. You have not found yourself here, in total reflection, it has disappeared around you. Sunlight falls into alcoves, plays across clouds moving by, warm on your shoulders, your oedemic feet lose sensation. You are refrigerated. Repetition makes the city, makes the sea, drifts up dunes and thickets of reeds.

The routine is a temptation because it is a life. The ocean was the other life, a mirage of stability that gives way to a confrontation with the aspects of my body that could never be fixed to my name, my location, or my memories. If I couldnt see now, but only know, that back through all of those empty hours she was just behind the veneer of the things waiting to take me, I could pull shut the curtains and watch the walls take the light from the lamps. I started it. It wouldnt be giving up on the day. It would be stopping it before it had a chance to end on me. There was something from the bright sky that I could take. I went through the metal gate, the courtyard, up the steps and across the walk to my apartment and I pulled the heavy curtains over the afternoon, and began the night on my own.

Proceeding with the presence of a cool breath, and draping color variations through the curtain-lined corridor, the character appears along the gallery wall. The pleats nod invalidly in intersecting wave patterns that send taupe to the recessed pleat bordered then by foregrounded steamy bands of mauve. Then in the same location the mauve pleat recesses to draw the taupe woofs to the fore. The pure yet vapid hue of the dawning light shapes the soft curving edges of the curtain. My view sweeps with the breath across the entire bank of colors. The distant flat rolling of the pleats, where only the dawn illumined edges are visible, diminish into solid color and return, open upon chairlegs and fingers, and bronze glimmers rise out of the cavern in waves of visual peristalsis.

Layers deeper, through all of the apartments that painted away your memories with colors of paint, each more inappropriate than the last, you find flecks beneath your fingernails at night, away from apartments; the colors flake off and dust the night. The past is inevitable. Your past is not. The startling calm blue of sky over dull beige buildings, taupe, lemon, green sea grasses turning black through thick deep water, hot stucco red, and mauve are borne indirectly, transparent and luminous, from the surface of the rippling water. You are not waiting for shadows now; you are waiting for hands. Nothing moves, nothing moves forward. Across your eye the colors tile into different domestic lineages. Red before mauve, yellow over taupe, each ending in still white washing over both cold eyes.

You feel your skin and where it ends and it ends. Your teeth liquefy. Your legs fall through the water. You are alone. If there was a place that was just you would you know you were there. You look down the length of your figure and know it from the clothes draped over its contours. You build yourself up out of cloth and patterns, things you can remember. When you sit in the grass the flowers on your skirt show. The thickness of the layers lets you not need to happen. The world doesnt let things slip away. You make yourself of those things. Things go wrong without cause and you lose yourself in regret. You assemble yourself of parts that do nothing and you wont cause anything. Without them the world forgets you. Things end without hope, without things.

Where she saw edges glimmering with dusk and twilight she finds grainy fields full with detail and space. Windows, drapes, frames, knobs, eaves, shade, moulding, pulls, flecks, globes, hanging formations, fans, drapes, grains all quivering effulgently. She births them into the night with her open eyes. The night is aware of their newness, summoning sodium arc lights to burst across the darkness atop poles with orange grain cast out on high across the landscape and rolling beyond the horizon at the crest of the road, and beyond home. The sky is gone completely into a totality of washed out sepia and orange that nourishes her entourage, expelled from home with her, and chokes the firmament. Drawn open, before her, in the illuminated enclosure, is a fleshly world, again.

There is nothing here for you. Your head down beneath a lamp, your hands move over objects and clutch themselves. Repetition wears away desire and leaves you with absence. The body you began with remains in the spot it began, time has passed, your body has gone. Loss in time is irretrievable. There is not enough of you for time to claim. You watch your hands out before you play across a reflective surface, tracing beads of moisture, where your hand traced a palm print remains spectral, your palm drags across the tile, the light upon a cloud, you etch fine feathery lines into the surface, your impact is negligible, there is nothing for you, the process of disappearing, of turning materials into vapor and dust, you are vapor. The tile surface remains, it stretches out beneath each desk.

The warmth of the absent sun rays in lines across the carpet remains in the brown darkness. I dont recall the day. I settle to my knees and trace the alternating warm and cool strips with the tips of my fingers, lost light and old shadows. I dont know how long the edges of the afternoon remain clear before they cool into all darkness. I havent seen it slip away. I dont see things become other things. I wait for them to be replaced, or I dont notice that they never were the things that I thought they were and their history becomes a useless mystery. The pasts those mistakes perpetuate are messy and difficult. The streets and rooms are littered with the things that couldnt change, or shed their useless shroud of shapes and wear for a new day. Those are the things I see.

The oceanic billows rolling over the fabric cause certain pleats in the sequence to lap up and outside the continuity of the curtain when the wave is transferred on to the next stretch of fabric. When the vertical selvedge of the curtain rises away from the system, a ghosted colonnade of plumb, still pleats is revealed. Splashes of gaseous color slither amongst obscure side passages, slip behind curtains, invaginat'd in a respiratory cycle in which the body is turned inside out. I am lost in the folds left to flutter in breath while the body is righted. The layers of subterranean twilight are laminat'd indefinitely. Drawn into circuitous and ever more slender byways and corridors, my movements twirl in and around peeled away selvedges and dive within the shadowy gray of deep, tight inbetweens.

Her eyes have been open so long. Her glittering old crypts and ruffs wash into all the dark places of the city, into mosaic archways and damp timber passages. Little moonlit pools sparkle at the end of twisted alleys. She could never find them again. The city turns around precious things and intimate places and makes them lost. Dry eyes do not sparkle. They watch. They haunt. Wide dry eyes watch without looking. They see shapes before the shadows and the bodies before their obliterations in mirrors and mirrors. Empty sight stops everything in its view until it piles into the problem of an immemorial life. Your hand on the collar of your smock pinches it shut around your throat, your furtive pained footslides stop in her eyes and are preserved, mothballed.

My curtain parts and I put my face to the window. The glass is morning blue in the dusk, condensed breath and air conditioning. You are slumped against the gate looking down into the thin rain on the sidewalk. Things have to happen. If you wont be the cause I wont be the cause. I notice that the apartment door is ajar. That is all you have. That is the parted cloud. That is the sunset. That is the mirror. Those are my words. You have come through the gate and feel your hand across the metal railing supple with coats of paint and rain. At the top of the stairs you see across the flat roofs reflecting the sky in standing water. White mirrors endlessly diminishing until the last, steaming in the distance, reflects the hills, then the hills again, and the sky again, and my door, and me.

She looks above the silhouetted horizon. The windows of the apartment block are black and flat, painted against orange walls, belying no depth or enclosure beyond, or passage at the very least. High above the lamps sputtering to light, beyond the halos of the lamps, is a deeper orange cloaked in spotty falsehood behind which is a continuous deep and impenetrable purity, misapprehension, and again the world. Shadows of depth, indicating promontories, natural arches, outcroppings, passageways, verandas, are folded flat and applied to a continuous wall against the sky. Her only shelter is beneath the sky with its absent slumbering breath. The empty spaces are her enclosure, a fragile village drawn by wandering, staid only by sleep.

You do not fit at the desks. You fit beneath them on the floors, the sidewalks, the murky canal floors where things pass by above you drawn by tidal action, or by the impulse to work, to repeat, down on these horizontal expanses. You inch forward, you roll over, you recross your path but never retrace it. Your path began at the sea so it must not end there. Nor must it end here, in a dead end, you will continue to trace the horizon. The paths all sink away into a diffused wake, you are left with movement which you cannot stop or you will disappear. The impulses sink away. Impulses are minute, over time they affect solid surfaces and bodies, if the bodies remain long enough, if you can keep from drifting away, or falling to pieces.

The light slicing through the dust in the air is either there when I walk through the apartment or it isnt. If it was, after a still harbored day, I would walk blindly through the apartment without pulling the curtains to lie in the bed and cover my face, otherwise, it was already night and everything is in the same ink that writ me. The bits of dust and breath that turned in the air through the blades of sunlight and were warmed have flown into falling currents, and fallen out of order. I throw my wet raincoat under the kitchen table across the linoleum and crawl to it to spread it across the floor to dry slowly and put on the kettle of water. I pull out the stop and fall back onto the carpet. It is cool and night has dropped into my apartment alone.

There is, in these dawn physics, the calculated possibility of the remoteness of all these phenomena. Character, defined by color and moisture in this venue, is transmitted and recomposed through stations of reflections, breezes, appliques, and misperceived patterns. Colors against the lolling curtain, though recognizable, are so fleeting, diaphanous, that I corroborate the stations against my own repetitive progress, and fix upon the forward fluidity only stable in certain instances of twilight that I chase behind curtain edges. Even when the collusive essences of light, vista, atmosphere, and diligence, disclose a cyclicality of movement, it is not possible to forecast any impending openings at the seams of the curtain, yet they emerge to tow me further into the sequence.

The tide has rolled across the city. It unearthed you, then it buried you in something else. First, the finest dross penetrates the empty textures of fabric, stucco, cracked skin, and oil caked hair. Dry viscous dust, dead skin, bits of pink paper, breath hardened air jostling in a tired cascade wicks deep into the cracks in your feet, the edges of your underclothes floating parched beneath your stockings, flooding across the hair in your nostrils, and lining the wrinkles and folds worn into your still skin. Your breath is a finger fighting against beach sand. The dry chaff settles into chipped paint pits, the slots where sun dried wood has pulled away from plaster, and the uneven terrain of older dust not blown into the air by your fitful napping. The floodwaste is smooth and terribly solved.

You dont ask anything. You dont ask anything of the walls or the black currents, impediments or diversions, and you dont ask anything of me. You are barely here. You look across the panorama of empty furniture to sort out a blank spot, a hard spot. You rub your feet forward in short slow steps drawing the rainwater and sand across the carpet before finding a spot against the wall facing the wing'd armchair with the palm worn cabriole where crawling hands obsessed. Slide down to sit with your knees in front of your face. Eyes feel other eyes before they see them. Eyes hide from themselves. The curtain flutters across the kitchen, outside the same tired and still blue that you saw through the window, the light switches places. Here you are.

The deepening pulse of refrigerant blood filling her fingertips, cooling her palms to blue, the places at the heart of the network sagging into exhaustion, submit to the city lugubrious. She holds her hands before a tree, fanned out, flat with her palm parallel edged to an eave, a fist blocking out the hot point of a streetlamp. All of the surfaces in the auto are shaped around her body. The walls, distant across the lawns hold her from where the sky hits the ground, mountainous undulations rise to hold the sky from resting on the walls. Although it is torment, the whole of a realm caked in orange, in grainy pollen, it is a falsehood that her raised hands might connect with the flat, powdery place, and she is, perpetually, defeated in her forever falling envy of weight and touch.

The window opposite your desk is covered by closed blinds. Griseous dusty light drifts in an unbroken sheet. When the sun falls behind the buildings from whence you came, to the west, the empty room fills with a mute light, the suns rays wander through narrow alleys losing strength, falling away lost and dropping limply at the edge of the sidewalk, only leaning against the glass, barely illuminating the room. Face the window. The light from the sun falls here each afternoon, the same. You rise from the floor and move along a row. At the center you turn to face the window and you move toward it. The intensity of the light does not change when you approach the window. The uniformity of the glow, the boundaries, the emptiness at the edges of the room hold you in place.

Im not wise. Ive lived long enough to take a piece of everything I saw that wasnt mine and build something up out of it. When I see it from a distance, when I wake up to it, Im not able to discern anything about it. It isnt my body or my life. It surrounds me. It grows on me. It is where I put myself, in my apartment, in my visions when I close my eyes. I know that other people are made of those bits that I can remember, not human bits, still bits of immaculate garbage and they are easier to sort through or dismantle. There is nowhere to put all of this that it wont come back to me, or where it wont be replaced while I sleep or stare. It washes downhill or things happen at night that reawaken my vigilance. I dont want the sunlight to fall on any of it. That day is over.

Still drawn in the character of the mercurial pleats, the profiles and edges of potentially familiar settings are described by liquid traces with glimmering accents. The topographic contours drawn visually along the curtain grow more dense the lower I leech into the populace of the cavern: nested furniture, columns of sheer linen, pale blue fingers, slender square edged stalactites, a highbacked chair draped with taffeta, a fanfolded linen, a precarious column of damp bone hued mugs, honed metal tubes, pale blue clothing tied in knots, pillowy pads that sag with moisture, isolated constellations of rivets and screwheads. My gaze races across these phantasms, barely etched in their essence, collecting in the pleats and drenched with shadowy chaff.

You are blank and patched. The tide of objects tumbles into empty hollows. Soft mailboxes, trashbins, pits and cups and storm drains to the sea fill with the collected aggregation of everything you forgot when you closed your eyes. It is scales and carbuncles in sleep. Empty frames and mugs, tins and clocks, dusty candles, keys, jars of sand, dust, shelves pulled over and contents rolling in a grinding wave, islands of tinted glass and crystal, stainless steel objects, formless. Nothing fits you. Empty apartments, closets, empty shops and broad glass windows float across the sea of objects, useless without them, merely heavy. You feel only their weight. With each breath they collapse further and fit your profile more precisely. You and they are perfect when you are crushed by waking.

The things that push you are tired. You cant see the sands shifting in the dark. You feel the vibrating quakes rising up through your skin and the pits behind your ears, an unchanging barchan that has rolled from the day into the night, crumbling in place with the physical song of the dunes. You sing to me in empty voices about your silence. You stroke your chin and your legs grow warm without feeling. The blood pools in your thighs and calves and heels when you stop moving. You feel sparkles and dampness. You wrap a towel around your neck and hold a mug of tea between your palms. Your hands pulse. The centers of pain collect the entirety of your body. The rhythms of heat and throbbing lap through you with the rise and fall of entreaties and naked trusts.

Yet, at the very least, and it is all that she has, it is the end of a tumble through nothing. She flattens her gaze through the north windscreen, cropping out the slender frames and top and bottom edges to search for an entry. Windows with no boundaries are eyes on the breeze, caught up in a swiveling head, showing all but never being admitted to the caresses, the compressions on display. Stop. She stops. The city streets and their contents are arranged around her behind glass. She is drawn and tucked in a narrow frame, a chaste rectangle, undivided and shallow, terminal. She is pressed to it and enveloped in a cloak of glass, engaged, caught by, and cradled in a starched yet diaphanous drape upon which the roads stretching into disappearance are etched.

You carry a shell of twilight myopia. You cannot see the walls, only the windows, and the light. The manner in which you open the blinds is automatically hopeful. You manipulate the wand between your fingers. You can see your fingers, the wand against their blueness. Light does not flood the room. The day is lost. All the colors of the day are provisional. You spend days with projections of what appears beyond the window, which you open alone and too late, wipe sweat from your eyes in a blur of fluorescent light, and repeat each action that defines the edges of your desk and the paces that describe the room. The sun does not rise and set across the edge of your desk. You do not fit. Standing behind the window your reflection is cut off. You see only up from your waist, above the desks.

It was a mistake. I have left things in too many places, too many traces on walls and sidewalks, finger tracks in dust. I havent lived long. I dont know where I come from. I am in and out of the company of things. When I am not it is because I am one of them. I dont even notice. Without the light most of the apartment falls into shade. The sun sets for hours. It is too protracted. I dont want to know when the day is drowning. I dont want it to collapse on my floor. I dont want it to take me with it. I want to dry out and flake away. A corona of brown light rings the curtains. It is hot. I need to be lightless, colorless, trapped. I dont want it to come flooding in here gasping, wet, pulling me down with it. She takes things. She takes their place.

I see figures erect, not moving toward me but I to them. I could see sleep, a grayness beyond this opaline dusk, that in a tessellated reserve, clasps more fragments of a flesh body within the furrows of each successive curtain. The fragments are animated by the pulmonary movement of the curtain. I peer behind the selvedge rising up from a mauve pleat. The seams and puckers of the textillery rind in their soft undulations camouflage the sequential decay of the body into ever-flattened fragments. Once sedate, with the curtain visually stabilized, I stir back the tornadean chaos of the figures into uniform vibrations; I am synchronized with their quivering outlines. They return to discrete packets: fingers, thighs, apples, rendered in the colors of dawn and spongy cold blood.

Everything gets painted over, wet things, almost living things, painted over things. Ancient apartments disguise their owners in the uniformly colored shapes that sink into the walls. At some angles their shoulders and clothes leer in glares. She was painted into the apartment, an all beige night. She spent most of her time in the bathroom and slept there on the floor. When she slept the apartment sparkled in darkness. Domestic lights shimmered through the window and flourished on the imperfect glossy paint. Warmth smothers the place when you turn away, when you close your eyes to sleep. It comes in a fine spotty fire and pricks your skin all at once, all over your body. You awaken breathless, crushed, sweating, suddenly cold and in the bare light of the street.

A word spreads across you, a characterization or clue settles into the gentle stupor of your creation. The years that have lead up to your limp entrance and dissociated gaze were filled with unspoken projections I have forgotten. I casually entered into awkward silences with you in my mind and then interrupted them with cascades of trinkets washing through my apartment. You were the sand and the water, you were lost, now you have me, you have what is mine, you need it, I no longer do. There is no story in the words. They are characters that erase themselves by happening and being recognized. When they become real, shared between us, a little bit of me is let loose, a view, a movement, a lost hope, it could be in you, settling on your skin, it could be lost in the room, amongst the detritus.

In the small sheet of space beyond or before the glass in the frame she is pressed, stretched out, and she impresses her body on a swirling toss of forget-me-nots with tender stems that limply cross and end, snipped during innocence, to weave an open flaccid lattice foolishly bespeaking permeability yet a coquettish promise of entry into the home or room beyond. The blue floral print is sweat stuck to her thighs, slightly parted, letting the night fall gauzy and muted upon the seat in a hall under the sky slaked with cerulean and azure in corners and extents. O, if that diurnal firmament can be warm, this would be warm; for nightblue is only warm with her knowledge of the sun. Yet the sky, and flowers, are stiff when they yawn against one another toward the sun.

In shaded byways, under overhangs for carparks, in the narrow, clotted space between two buildings you linger. The sun passes overhead once and flushes the empty space with light and warmth. Lying on your back you see the sun pass, or facing forward you watch the sky at the end of the alley change colors across your toes. You inch forward, using your fingers grabbing into joints and cracks, headfirst, away from the desk, deeper into the earthy shadow. You belong to the ground. You have not fallen to it. Even in the twilight collapse you had nowhere to fall but back through time in those last seconds, back through tired lagoon awakenings, colliding with funerary islands with your cheek against tile and fluorescent shadows.

There are three lamps in the room. Each against a wall, far from the corners. The corners disappear. They are dark. They arent in shadow; there is nothing there. I hide things in the gone corners, absent from me, in my chair, looking from the chair over my legs, only into the lamplight on the wall. I dont see her face, or folded stacks of paper, or bleak light shining directly into my eyes. I slowly move forward, creeping out of the stillness. There is a texture to the air. I feel my hand stopping in it when I reach out. The light stops my hand. It is velvet liquid. It is vaporous sweat. I feel it against my body. I feel where my body ends. It ends in here, in almost all dark. Back and forth I drift. When my eyes adjust the clutter rises back out of the corners in tumbledown stacks and dullness.

The physicality of a tableau composed of these formations is tethered to my nerves through the layered, looping atmospherics of this tracery hall. I gauge my own reliability through the promises of the voyage, with the thickening concreteness of an environment being coalesced from vapor. The narrowing confines of subsequently deeper layers of the curtain give way to more persistent, yet tepid, luminance at each selvedge. With gathering light, such profiles and characters that accrued against the curtain, now forming a complete dense patternwork across the scalloped pleats, begin to disintegrate. Figures are redefined by infinitesimal increments; a tablecloth develops into a loosely lashed bow. The clarity and pose of the elements refines with each layer of curtain I transcend.

The nights do not pass. Your feet consume you with their feeling of scalding and needles. The street lights are still. The sconces are unflinching. The shadows of dead bugs show. The same dead bugs. Close your eyes. There is no moon to trace your shadow, only the rise and fall of the tepid displaced water trickling into your nose and your abdomen expands with breath after breath. You find yourself awakening in the same state, empty places, rooms and halls that are too large, bits of flat sky visible and the urge to walk quickly to the next incompatible plaster casket to sleep. Something has happened here. You deny. Your feet are alive. Something has happened, under the layers of paint. You sleep outside in the oceanic balm. The city is on the verge of sinking.

You dont hear. I have put my life into my own undoing. It has taken a life to make a life for you to replace. I know that what I leave will remain untouched. The shadows of dried lives rise and set day after day. What I leave isnt what I started. An untouched life, an abstractly written existence, merely has to be noticed, allowed to pass under your breath, it doesnt need to be pieced together. The things you need to hear about the replacement arent spoken. It has just happened that you will be when I am not and that will be seamless. The city doesnt notice those crashed asymptotes. My life wont recognize the replacement. It has no sentiment of this body. Things stay still forever. You cant occupy their places. They cant topple out of the dust; you have to escort them.

Their tones and postures are unrelenting, uninviting, with a folly of false stoicism. Tree branches against the sky, fingers intertwined, low garden walls, hallways cutting through to alleys through metal grating strapped to fence gates lace together in an order of exclusion that hides the city from her. She is hidden within it. She cannot distinguish herself from the fabric. The pattern on her skirt flows onto the asphalt, into the dark over the end of the street, through the glow crystallizing in the swaying high fronds and fans of gypsum crystals. She is nested behind the drapes of urban phantoms, within whose airy stiffness is a guileless proposal that she might enter into the unspoken marriage of geometrical emptiness with already so many years of longing for home.

Your shoes are on the desk, propped upside down in wooden trees. The fluorescent lamp at your desk shines on their upturned soles. The wooden foot shape shows through the worn spots in the sole. It too is worn, unvarnished gray wood hewn from seafaring logs wandering to dry in tidal flats, worn and baked. Your feet have worn through the soles in nightly trips across the floor and through the aisles to open the blinds. The light shows in each bead of sweat upon your face while you look across the shoes, out to the floor from whence they came, outside the door, stacked next to one another on the sidewalk, or the hallway. You walk to change. Your body, left to the devices of the absent tide, prostrate across the tile in the deep shade of a shuttered room, collects dust.

When the apartment is empty the light rises to fill in positions vacated by old things that had cast shadows. The edges of the room disappear in broad scallops where the green carpet and painted wall meet. A roving brown-out with black characters jogging against the dust tingles a cultivated dusk. I look for things in the still emptiness of the lit wall. Vision doesnt arise of its own accord. Accidents of sight belong to a sequence of moments that I cant tap into. It is astride what I convince myself to see. I will see for a moment a face trapped in the shimmer of sunlight on glass, or the veins of a hand on a door jamb laced into the shadow of a breeze frayed palm frond, or skin through parted hair in the flow of storm water through a grate. When I tell myself what they are they are gone.

The bandage before my gaze is undressed, the curtain settles into place behind me. I gaze upon a great dim hall hidden in shade. The stretch of wall to the left of the scene is papered with a repeating mountain landscape. The scallops tracing down the slope of the mountain are washed with mauve, sand, and cornflower. A full night of breath can swell a foreign cave with moisture leeching through all baffles of papers and polycotton pleats hanging sheerly weighted and shifting against yarning breath. Gasps visible in the upcurrents thrown from the empurpled landscape, and red lung tissue aerated to gauzy buoyancy, catch silvery luminance borne through a full basin of clouds toward fair frail palaces. High canals of mauve fog are turned liquid en masse in temperate morning exhalation.

You look for detail and differentiation, a character in the continuous endless mess. When you sleep you leave. When you wake a sharp stria of blond light stretches out and cleaves the rosy stucco wall beyond between to columns of dim windows. It enters you. Would you choose unchanging chaos, endless footsteps, or the pure spear of scrutiny. Change insinuates. Light changes things. Across the stone and shining in the punctuation of wet partial footsteps the light traces across the glowing greensick pool and up the blank wall to the sky and back to her feet with monophobic sweats. The spear of light is empty. Out from her feet stretches old yellowed linoleum tile, swept clean, but worn nonetheless, by sweeping. She stands away from the window. The view outside is poisonous sustenance.

Your eyes unravel. It is late. I sit drying and brown at the kitchen table. The air doesnt pass. I sometimes pull aside the curtain to look out under the desert tree even though you are here with me. Even when I turn to look back at you and then face back hands palm down on the blank surface of the table I wonder what I might concoct to contain you, to lure you into activity, to let you live without the force of the past. You feel the mass of your head pouring in waxy torrents down your shoulders and melting into an upturned spreading puddle across the wall. You are not going to be anything other than the muddy skeleton I first dreamt of. This was not supposed to be about me. You were to come to life. Mine. You are nothing. You are made of nothing swirling about spaces of dead breath.

Surrounding an array of lit windows, stacked two high and two abreast, a reddish wall stands, possibly of a less fiery hue but aroused into rufosity by the orange glow of the streetlamp. The wall stretches out in uniform illumination. Streetsides at night have more purity of light than the day; her feet on the sidewalk are lit from all sides and cast no shadows. She greets the spaces that cannot welcome her. Although the red is punctuated by bursts into homes, those gapes are glazed in a dull passion she cannot share. Out of those eyes the red wall is no more than another barrier, but its shade carries the mirage of invitation and passage. The charitable sky, full of windows and lit portals is alive, is to her a loving statement of unshuttered presence.

Your skin is dry and translucent, a fluorescent light several rooms away, through which nothing can pass without faltering, tinges your ankles milky green where they catch the light, just outside the open door. You do not feel the tightening of the skin because you do not move, you draw shallow humid breaths. You lie through the continuous dusk of the shuttered room. If you were to move after the long day, your skin would stretch in a dry gummy attempt to hold you together, then tear, laying down hairy dust into drifts of powdered blood in the gaps dividing your calve'd body. In the gray heat of late afternoon conditioned air soaks the glossy walls. The fluorescent light catches edges of beads of moisture that mix with your powdery remains and leathery skin turning to soft paste.

The light passes, the water slows, things change. In that tract of actions I fit into only a line or two. It rarely occurs. The rest is nothing more than anticipation. It can be trimmed away with shade, curtains, my palms, black bracketing thoughts that hold more end than beginning, dark on the wall. It is filled with handwritten names, handwritten places and dedications, addressing a world that doesnt really need to exist when I am here where I am, in anything other than name. It is finite. It can be out of order, or it can all happen at once, it may not end, but it is all there, hemmed in from sunlight and warm necks that swell beyond each real name. The names wont change. They will just fade, or get painted over. In each place, each nameless thing is everything I want or remember. Let it stay there.

Lines etched across the view are frosty fingernail crevasses. I visually strode the routes of these calli. I trace out of these edges a chair, a cup, a stack of cups, a stack of linens, a stack of chairs, traced in linework against the linear scallops of the curtain filling the right side of the scene. Along the bottom of the curtain is a broad seam with evidence that a thickness greater than the doubled fabric conceals a series weights to keep the curtain taut. The accompanying greater weight at the loose end of the curtain causes the break in the fabric, when flown open by the air conditioning, to return back to the continuity of the curtain by sealing into the interlocking pleat at the base. In a catenary billow, the joint comes together, the sheet falls, softer, over a discontinuous body.

The sky is flat and empty. It should not be. The courtyard is dry and empty. She looks again. She expects change. Then she can fall apart. The doors are painted shut. She is keeping things for you. Things do not move. These are things that you left. She is putting her hands on things in her apartment to see if they will move. You left things in an apartment. When she pulls the blinds aside with her face the window reflects back into the apartment, across the yellow marbled kitchen table where stacks of folded napkins recede to the wings of a golden armchair over which is draped a beige coat and a towel that has dried in its draped over folds, a pulled wispy bunch of cotton, a hand on the door frame. Between you and her a mug of tea is still. She wants you to take it. She wants an empty apartment.

You have never brought anything to the world. You take from it. You wait for emptiness to become content in your watch. Intense focus, or the posture of it, does not produce a world out of nothing, no matter how many nights you fill. The windows are more opaque surfaces inside this series of apartments. You have shut yourself into them and stopped there. The world made you and keeps making you, youve never let it free from its responsibility, you pretend when you are looking into the clouds or through your eyelashes into the distance that you embrace the finiteness of your self, but you are not there or anywhere in particular. You are a collection. The garbage that you eye curiously for hidden incriminations is roiling with bits of you.

The night, which itself has a palpability across which even the tender, unseen heat from a teakettle, a hand folded on a hand on a bare knee beneath a table, rustling shadows, unforgettable perspectives of the body, or the arrangement of a fork on a folded green check'd napkin could, in their existence in the same luminous powder, wrap a fiery tingle in the base of her neck where acceptance and acquiescence are sensed. She let these windows watch her stride and she felt strong approaching the walls that held them. She gives to each of these windows, each with its own symbolic variant on the tone of its home, ruddy, brick'd, rust, burnt, a memory or a manufactured history; she gives each a potential because she senses a love about the objects and embracing passages therein.

The water level rises to rinse the dirt and dry dust from the walls, you are a slick across its still surface, only rising and falling, and drying again. You walk to hide from the spaces that remain still in the city, dead end rooms only serviced by the tide, which delivers to their confines despondency, dust, and still decay. You move because nothing else can. You wear away your flesh on the pavement so that there is nothing remaining to ride the tides into the backs of shops, flotsam of skin and dust beneath a desk, rising to open the blinds each dusk. You can be replaced. There are enough reflective surfaces in this city to leave her here at this desk, and deep within that apartment, to watch until she gets up to put her shoes back on, clean out her tea cup, and get into bed, or return to working.

I didnt write any of it. I didnt name any of them. There are things coming from outside of me, swirling into my day and night, and propping me up, and coaxing me forward. Without me, what would the need be for the apartment or the ocean. Those things make me happen. Against their eternal stillness I know that I am not still or endless. They set things up in a chain that leads back to me. Those bigger bodies that make this day of mine dont comment or shape; they are silent. The silence is incomparable, but it isnt new. Her name is not among the displayed. I have looked for it. I think she is too new. Or she just isnt. Something that cant find a place, jostled between where I am and where the ocean always will be isnt named. It doesnt leave prints in the dust. She is where I end.

The casting off of a dew covered silk coat previously bound tightly around the neck, the fog on a translucent section of pleated curtain recedes, I see them there, huddled beneath two columns of stacking chairs, awake beyond the nightfall. The aggregative capacity and purpose of this mess of bodily components is foreign and silly in its gestures and poses. I wished I were ice. The untouchability of a frozen condition would be welcome if only to be of a matter that had the potential to be touched, pulled open. I watched my own gesturing arm pass through my presence unhindered when I clenched my gaze in an attempt to harden the misty curtain I floated through. Freezing then, if only all inert forever, would lock me into the vision of my body.

When you find your way back, when, of an afternoon, the sky is swollen and opaque with clouds, stand on the sidewalk with your arms crossed and watch her window. See how her face must look. You craned upward to expose your throat to the fog. When she held the warm mug out to you you refused to take it. Each thing she has collected, each the sole purpose of her existence for just a moment, is another thing she has to lose. They are strewn throughout the city, each icon of guilt, slowly replacing her with the worthless seconds of her intentions to construct a trail of life. She wants you to relieve her of them. When you touch the doorknob and feel it in your hand she feels her hand annihilate the doorknob. The guilt of an historical life is no longer hers.

The tired and submissive apartments where days end stuporously are bedecked with you, with your useless desires. You didnt march into any of this, you just move and it remains inert around you. If you could stop the forward movement you could stop it all from coming, you could stop with me, a fixed distance away from the end. Although the grid of possibilities is finite, it must complete itself. With a single cell empty the whole is useless. By merely existing you believe that you are proof of something. You believe that you are proving it to yourself because to not exist is the most tremendous departure from the physics of dependence. You are a drain. How could you not be. There was nothing left for you to offer back, but you couldnt end until it ended you.

With each window, a lost trace of the sky from the fallen away day. She constructs vague memories from colored glares on the inside of the glass, shadows on far back walls, love in a place setting, shod feet astride a table leg, toes pointed together, a door ajar with a light showing out from the jamb, or turned down bedclothes on a pallet. Behind a gingham curtain, a rose-covered drape, red on cream pastoral toile, and a rubescent translucent veil, lit from within, are scenes for plays of potential escape, descent. The street reaches out behind her, perpendicular to her movement, curving in her peripheral vision, racing beyond the horizon, stretching out before her again in the next line of the grid. Her eyes squint, her nostrils dilate and draw in night air.

These places were not for her body. She saw reflections of them and herself outside of them in unshuttered windows and wavelets on the sea. When she walks she is standing there at the door or prostrate there on the bathroom floor. Her vision beyond this room depends on the imperfections and subtleties of everything she passes, windows hung crooked or drawn inward in shrinking refrigerated rooms, mirrored doors ajar or swollen slightly out of their jambs, water vapor against a sun warmed puddle. She cannot see herself awakening late afternoon, only each stage of the arcing sun, each detail in which she saw her self captured. The history of the day continuously multiplying in reflections depends on these minutiae that move her further away while everything behind her continues.

The apartment grows cold in the dim. The afternoon rays would have warmed it. I skipped them. The cycle of the day is a nuisance. It stops things from happening. I work through the sunset and sleep through the sunrise at my table. The apartment is scorched by the sun and abandoned by the day. I hide in closets. If I lived in the day it would drag me with it, sweating, heaving, looking askance, and finally shrugging into the foamy edges of the sea. So much is lost, but remains. So many things forgotten, but only by me. Waiting to come out into the world through me, the thoughts to be sorted and grouped under fluorescent light are left to disintegrate in cubbies and slots, gone by morning, gone during the stopped night.

Full close. Full splay. Full close. The crystalline mirage is still parted but has recently not been or soon will be thus. The mountain, textured and upright over a reservoir in a single peak is marked by scalloped chutes. These four hard brown lines converge upwards and curve slightly towards one another before truncating. An inverted crown of refrigerant ice is tied by capillary threads leeching mineral rich water down through a stony fibrous network to the shy reflected formations of the cavern. The formations of this oft night platform are drawn with a sheen of age secreted in a process of reproduction controlled by the reflected thicknesses and topography of its outer shell. Each shimmering formation hanging therein, seems to be a recognizable fragment of an whole self.

The things you left behind were not talismans or cabinets filled with stories. You left scraps in tall reeds, reflections and glances on hands; other bits floated away in canals and storm sewers. The more you cast off the weaker you became. Emptied of cargo and clue to fill in your body you were bared to a vacuum and bits of you began to wander into place out of the evaporated lights of dusk. Where those parts of you had been left shameful dirt on the skin and inexplicable stains on the clothes, finding you in total a filthy collage of caked and cracked black silt in thin skins, starchy dried wet clothes, scratch marks of inhuman black blood, dry foamy crusts of ashen mucus and saliva, patterns pressed in skin, whites are red, pinks are gray, the night is bright, and every thing is on display.

The opportunities that might have given your fate shape earlier were taken by hidden, more complete people and then they were gone and there was nothing left but the refuse that was a product of their deeds, cities, sun scarred earth, paved mountain passes, waking and sleeping visions. The labor was done. But you kept on. Only the skies in a day were yours. They made the skull around your eyes shrink because their promise of openness and liberation was always framed or injected with the rooftops and the disfigured tree canopies scraping the departing clouds. You circled the block without stopping, for days, you were uncoiling the time, using the energy, and occupying the stageset that had been meted out and was left in the world that had no use for what you might do with it.

She breathes in the moistened lateritious sediment of the lighted night floating between her self and the wall. Her body is afire, awakened in the streetlight that throws itself out in all directions. The sky is hers with the walls, with the lawns, the dark hollows beyond the horizon at last were hers because she could project herself out to them in an endlessly roaming breath of luminance. Out from the windows cascade the recalcitrant nights of awakened apartments, the glimmering seeds of containment, pink, rose, the brick dust of crushed histories, the tangible nights turned to ephemeral stucco cocoons, bodiless, wrapped about untouched utensils, and stacks of unsorted things. Each particle contains the spark of a situation, the beck of the emptied home covered with inviting openings.

The walls spanning out on her sides, mirrored by seas balmy flat and those that rise to be mirrors splitting the sky reflect articulately straight into a point. Walls close down upon the horizon placing you in their disorienting circuitous maze. The streets and the paths may be straight or convoluted, chambered, but they do not encumber her movement, distinctions about geometry are the musings of the lost. She merely continues. The walls, assuming the ambiguity of dusk, are liquid and featureless. They form a second horizon, a shade brighter, beneath the sky. Her reflections carry the streets, narrow high-walled slits opened into the spaces between buildings, where buildings fear to press shivering close but breathing against one another.

I dont need it all to move past me. I sleep through those moments that might grab me and hoist me back into the tide. Those are moments when one thing becomes another. I dont want to lose anything for what it might become. In the off afternoons I sleep in the north room and the sun banks off of the brick wall across my bed, hot and limp. I fill the bed with sweat and I cant sleep. I cover myself with sheets and pillows. Nothing matches. When they soak through, the sun yawns brown through them. I hung heavy blackout curtains in the front room so that I could make tea while the sun suspected the horizon from the noon, and I forgot the day. Steam puffed out of the spout. The air was cold and moist and loathed the lingering day, then forgot it while your tea grew cold.

All of these glimmers, enumerated individually, are discrepant with the orientations, postures, and locations of their apparent counterparts. The shadows from the chair legs bleed out in immediately broad zones across the landscape rising up in their midst. The shadowy pleats undulate softly although the chairs and the light source are still. The heap throbs out from me in viscous eddies, frozen drapery steps out hanging from arms with an oscillating bland palette of pastels and wallpaper field tones. The unisonous movement of identifiable pairs of characters, based on the color and level of wear of the clothing, could be briefly mistaken for an integration of body and character, given location and posture beyond dreams, were they not describable from without.

These are the tired facts. Facts resist causality. They are borne each after each out of the grainy night suns. Each fact is an ominous fragment of a day, long and compartmentalized in which each stands motionless before you, tempting you to lurch back toward it, deeper down to where light cannot penetrate the sediment to be alone with each part of you and falsify the precursors to the state of you. Mysteries are useless. The things that have happened are obvious. You have long sacrificed interrogation in favor of motion. You beat your feet into the pavement to stay ahead of the things that have just happened, until, in the spring moments after the streetlamps are tricked into darkness and the air is a lightless silver vault sealed and timeless, you lie oblivious in the seconds before dawn.

You hardly looked human. You were made up of pieces that didnt seem to fit. There were ledges and crevices and shadows cast back on yourself instead of smoothness and skin. Light from the lamps direct down from the opening in the shade above you shown straight through joints where you should have connected to yourself, through your shoulder and knuckle and cast discontinuous shadows on the ground. You couldnt have moved this way unless you were dragged draping in the slipface of sand upright at 32° in a perpetual swoon on your feet. When you collapsed here I thought I would have the recollections to fill in your silhouette. There was a time when I saw hordes of people and their names and when I began the day they were full in my head.

The light from the windows falls on a pale wall bathed in aureate benevolence. She outstretches her arms horizontally from the shoulders and kisses the glass. In an apartment home, blond wood floors are sealed with ancient shellac. The floors creep throughout each room and out of sight. The grain of the wood is indistinct and hazy, blurred and refracted through the thick carapace of yellowing resin. The finish is damaged by prolonged exposure to sunlight. Idleness and neglect have left her skin lying out in the day drying, gathering a fine coat of sweat that when grazed or rubbed scuffs the fine outer layers until they are worn down to tanned, leathery flakes. The dampness standing here, refrigerated, carries the skin away from her body, evaporated into the interior cycle.

The narrow streets trail her heels after the unfurling canvas threads and frayed rubber strips, reflecting one after another blinking together into the mightily still wash of silt on which you stand with boundless freedom, yet sinking. All points from which walls turn away, eventually, flow on in the moments at your desk, at the moments just at bleak predusk, your eyes and feet fill the continuous outdoors. You are walking at the edge of the wide boulevard at dusk. For you the clouds are still. There are no clouds, more reflections of beige streaked across the sky and to the horizon where it meets the floor, dissolved in dim. The undifferentiated street environment slows around you. You seek to move through it and further from the desk, toward open doors or ajar doors.

I dont expect the steam or the empty air to reveal anything to me. There is no augury in giving my eyes over to things that are on their way out of being or slipping forward from contemporaneity. They wont take me with them. If they did, and I saw her on the sidewalk under the tree, in the real purple flood of night, I still couldnt get back to put things in order. Staring at the empty teacup doesnt tell me that it will have mint tea in it, steam swirling around it, a hand and hand cupping it, it is kissed and tipped, that it will sink out of the lamplight, it will stay whole forever but cease to be what it is in this moment, empty and expectant. I can pretend that it is influencing me. But it is still and what pantomime I put it through is no evasion of what I will do with myself. Only I have the choice.

I am passenger of the dewy night, a floating transport of my gaze. The heaviness when I fill the clouds with the cold beads carrying my reflected vision, draws downward the night with its moisture towards the groundcover. Moving in low across the waxen verdant landscape with a wavering presence, I draw the familiar background of hundreds of small strias of light upon beads of dew. Gazing out from each orb I follow the breath of its light ascribing minimal liquid traces to formations reaching out from the ground. Tendrils of moisture that have diverged come together with the fullness of my presence to form a limp sheet of dew. In a catenary billow, soft, a sheet falling over a discontinuous body, I drape the expanse of carpet.

The way is marked by persistent absence. With the sea at your back there is always a looming presence. You focus on the bare and lightless whiteness. The uncertain fog moves toward you and you into it swirling around you, parted by you and runs out cleft into diminishing tendrils. You do not turn. You are immobile. You avoid the mesmerism of the emptiness, the dangers of passing time. Time passes. The milky light yields, still distant, the afterimage of a dim bedroom. When you travel long, the things you have left return in front of you. You are facing a window with lipid horizontal blinds receiving and obscuring little bald light. The walls have a resplendent sheen that softens the corners of the room around the bed against the wall under the window. Otherwise the room is empty.

Your head falls forward. Responsibility, commitment, and support are human. Things dont fit you. You try. You keep trying. Your shape is flawed. You dont cause anything. Those attributes have destinations that you cant engage. You cant make something happen. You are the effect of majestic arithmetic, the tail of shame, the waste, the spume, the wretch, the broken dry soil, the terminal end of any action, after the goal, the lumbering ennui in which the spent old woman, a shape, nods her head at the futility of putting away another day but watches the sun rise, folds her hands and feet at a table and sees right through it to the same glossy blank wall, and waits through another day, and you have been lodged in that moment since you rolled out of nothing.

The skin, in a jaundiced uncinus runs back up the walls. The sky seeps through a deep orange around the walls of the box. The stage flats are pried open slightly. The walls, floor, and roof invert and refocus continually so that once she is within and contained she is at once spread out beneath the continuous night sky dome, draping down all about her and in the distance, across four fields of dew stippled lawn on her four sides, stand four walls. The treasonous home, without interrupting her cagey suffering beneath glass in a rolling vitrine, has enveloped her in the topology of the window, the wall, and the city of walls and windows has cradled her without touching her, and has spat her out in a phlegmatic glob against the sky.

A pale fabric unfurling breaks the endless continuity of the street where glass covered in fog and damp stucco whose color is deeper in the damp than in the shade it casts upon itself where the cross chop of the breeze upon the lagoon has risen up with imperfections, hand marks and the wakes that fingernails leave in sweaty dust. The movement of the slight billowing pale brocade, distant and oblique, twists the street upon itself with the eruption of softened reflections. The street billows in the breeze that arises. The breeze arises. It is perceptible on the hairs that trace down from your knuckles. Your eyelashes fan and your eyes vibrate with the movement. It is all more pale than damp stucco, softer than the reflections this tableau contains.

I make all of these things happen to me. If I never touched the cup, it would never move, she would never arrive, and I would never choose. In the very long accident that I keep falling back into, nightly, and in those moments when the rush of things looses me, it is easier to try to fill the emptiness with the bits that I remember, from the things I didnt choose but which struck me hard enough to change my shape but only damaged me, I didnt really keep them, and when I try to reach out to them, in the midst of a wide blank wall of an icy green light I only find their names written on paper. I bring them back over and again because there isnt anything else that can stop the time from just disappearing and me finding myself let go, back into it all.

I sense the watery presence of me aloft across this flattened basin. In the space of my travels the cloud of me has been drawn apart in a trace across the entire route, leaving fragments and spreading thin its occupation. I am an airborne condensate, I am not cohesive, not liquid enough to settle, yet fine enough to stand in individual beads on fiber tips. To be touched, a cloud must thicken, and thickness is uncloudlike. Exhale. Gaseous extremities leech out through glistened walls or spread across the ground cover in a dewy cloak. I see an awakedness beyond the nightfall, the hortulan array of the carpet, the long periods of scrutiny in which all is inert, the movements of night folded into the stillness of my gaze. Layers of the heap are separated only by damp sheets of night air.

The more you sleep through the less you repeat. The soft flash of distant silver impossibly outside the bedroom, outside the tangled city, rises to fill the room with imperceptible light. It washes over your pale eyelids. Routines begin in partial light. You are impatient for the beginning to end. The bland rising rays fall high through the blinds drawing few lines high across the opposite wall. Slowly the shadow of the brick wall outside the window sinks. Each line increasing in brightness expands and consumes the next growing imperceptibly into a single inescapable day. When late sleep is foiled by hot anxiety and you have blinked with avoidance into the day the day goes on in blinking still moments. It is the same day. It moves too quickly because it never began. Days fall apart.

This day wasnt a chance. It was the whole of time. If nothing filled it, you are to blame. You are the bottom of a shoe, the black guts of the ocean, the rotten plaster of the desert, the things that I, falling asleep at the outset of evening, shut out of my thoughts. Without the banal and wretched doubts that you are, I would have nothing but several gasps and a hole in the night. You dont have enough to lose. I will never see you and you dont exist. People have been gone so long now that they arent more than the words that recall their faint presence in the dust of my apartment. You are too much nothing for the something that I barely am. I need you. For so long I have been so little, in the end nothing, I want to leave nothing, but forever, you are endless nothing, the sea floor.

Awake, in a vestibule or alcove, stopped, bug repelling light fixtures are clotted with webs and wings. Yellow swags of light hang in stillness. It is very late. Slumped against stucco, in a vessel to bear witness for the apostasy of her hiding, her shelter from the nightsky, her figure beneath the dome light in the auto. She lurches forward, the reflection of her upper body on the windscreen rolls out of the alcove. Her shoulders skirt low windows on each wall. The reflection of her face is obliterated in optical plays which she sees straight through. Across lawns and framed by twin palm trunks and running across the night a long low apartment block, covered in gray stucco, stands dimly, to the left and on a corner, or fallen off terminal at the darkened end of the route.

Atop the street stretching out is dappled with shallow inky puddles where the asphalt is crowned by a tiny wavering segment of horizon, black forms rise into a continuous butte in the shadow of the earth. At its crest a veil cloudlet trails in the breeze, stationary but horizontal and slumped. The connections are weak. Your steps are faltering dives. The tip of the cloudlet curls upon itself into a roll and coils back across the horizon and the black emergence of dusk, all beginning to reflect and replace the beige straightness with hollows and elusive night shades. The night butte flows upward. It flows slowly and the skin on your fingers begins to turn a chapped red where the red sea washes conversely over the sky behind your shoulders.

The days end. They end early, before the sun goes down, shortly after it rises, either by rotational force or habit. There are a few seconds when I am waking up that the whole sky lifts with my consciousness, filled with energy, the absence of material is whole with the exploding emptiness of the sky. The crowd of forgotten objects rushes into it and my eardrums are drawn outward with the absence of pressure. It feels right. It pulls me to pieces in a short breath, and then there is nothing where I was, the shadow of a labored vacuum at a metal table, a lump beneath the sheet, but not me. In that instant every part of me is the furthest away from itself that it can be. It can only begin moving closer, and the days wandering toward each other, becoming one unending.

The points where furniture contacted the ground were coordinated, seemingly borne simultaneously with major geographic profiles of the body. The right hand rests atop right calf and curls limply about the back right leg of the left chair column. Drops of dew reflecting brass traces collect in creases of skin on the palms. Two feet face one direction, the right heel touching the right front leg of the left chair column. Two knees, pale blue floral fabric tugg'd tight over the lower, are stacked between the back legs of the left chair column slightly askew. The back right leg of the right chair column stands in a triangle of clothed limbs: right tricep, thighs, chest. The chest is facing away from me. The spine sags, a posture of night breathing dissolved with each coat of dew to reflect anew.

You fight sleep early, wide awake in the dark. You have seen it all. The day before laid out in square steps, interlocking with places, straight through into the night, before you have even gained consciousness, you fall into the day after, into those places you have already left. You try to sleep through the long sunrise to evade its traps. In the first rays of the sun, creeping into your lashes, are luminous reflected images of askew medicine cabinets, of your eyes opening, your hands absently moving, your back hunched over, turning slowly against the sun, before, again, a claim on the day from the decisions made long before the day before, from a forgotten coerced commitment, locked into the rigid ebb back toward a rote day at a table. You keep your eyes closed. The sun sweats you out.

I need these things from you. These things are real and there is a real loss, a real bequeathal in the sense of the intangible character, the schedules and habits, but the bodies remain, matter continues, things remain. Put me in salt and sour water. Stop me from aging and let it fill the room. Let it wash over me and let it run through your nose and burn away your mind. Breathe it in and choke it out. Watch me stop. Watch me until I know that Im gone. You are always the end, end me, seal me, pickle me, fall into my eyes and see, take me to the end, finish the task, take my breath and suffer my cycles, use my body, pickle me and come back when you are done and you will sink into the brine next to me, but keep it living, barely, in the manner that I barely lived.

The night sags, a heavy lid falls upon the horizon. Somewhere else the roads continue, maybe beneath her, maybe over a high plain, maybe in the violet shadows she toes into. When the road ends in the city it is with sorrow. Lawns and buildings prolong the ambling stasis of forgetting, they are immovable weights. They sit on the horizon to halt the endless motion and division that allows her to not remember and to not record. Here stands the terminal ash to be shaken off into the night. The edges of lukewarm things, when half in shadow, half inviting, although so continuous and impermeable, are crisp and glistening in twilight. The end of the road dissipates into gray. Where the asphalt meets the sky and yields, the sky turns gray in deference.

How many evenings does that redness on your shoulders carry? You slept in them all when their waters, which have washed through and down from the first floor apartments, which have been in gray shade for hours already, loop around your ankles in smooth caressing shackles. The dusk brings the liquid bonds of freedom that tether you always across the horizon to the next sunrise, back behind glass. If it is dark and all of the flakes, turned down edges, steeped pages, drifts in corners behind things that do not move, things that do not move, the frayed plastic tips of shoelaces touching gingerly and unwavering against a tile floor, but the shoes were taken off and washed too by the creeping dusk not to exist, or swept along with you.

I feel spaces in me. I feel a distance between my heels and ankles and my feet flail when I shuffle. There is a breeze that blows through my diaphragm where my chest is independent from my abdomen, and whole areas of me are gone, and where they are there is again space between them in which nothing happens. I feel the day pass between the omissions in my self and the day ends when I feel myself all coalescing back together. When the darkness, or the confrontation of some incursive process, changing atmospheric effects on my body, makes my body recognize them and pushes me into one place, into something with edges that ends, whose influence ends, when other stars appear out of the clearing sky above the ocean that light me unreservedly, the day ends.

It was with vaporish slenderness, spawned upstream from this magic aerated reservoir, that the distant terminals of my presence cut slowly through cloth and hair, dew and sweat to condense across skin. I rode an illusion whose conjurer had long since lost, in its own sleep, some secret method for terminating somnambulance. Stretched into thin flowing scapes of moisture drifting out upon distant promontories of my self I commingled with a sheen of shimmering refrigerant dew, my surface pulled apart by probing digits of festooned vapor swaying from the cavern roof across dimness stretched. My gaze swings low across the carpet pattern and module, built up fragments of diaphanous tissues, slithered and pinned to the hewn floor.

You are ahead of the day. The action that becomes living is the repeated recognition of your old traces and the resurfacing of the objects that catch you, tie you to rooms, and flood you, awake, with the subtle horror of routine. You have been here before. Your forearms on a table. Your hands track around an apparatus. Every moment is an interchangeable plat of stained irrelevant objects, and exits into guilt, emptiness, or the next plat. The end is useless. It is the beginning with more guilt, more left in the world awake. The locations of all of your mistakes mar the moments in which they fell, inconsequential to you until they later ruin the lope forward when you are caught on things, the shoes and your hands, the sunlight high on the wall, the mug of tea, your reflection, her eyes.

A long stillness becomes apparent to you. It is a space for you to enter. You notice your feet on the carpet and the light falling on them and the empty chair. When you go to her, step silently across the carpet, bring your shoulders and eyes, cross your hands below your waist. When you go to her, her feet hang out from the ajar door. Her knees block the door from fully opening and a long vertical slit with your cheek against the damp doorjamb has her calves, the hollow behind her knee and pale veins, desert dry stiffening tendons, a heavy skirt over a sharp hip, with other shades of skirts worn for slips falling in scallops on tile, into a dress over her shoulderblade and hair spread across the floor before the bathtub. The stillness of a body is the most shoreless stillness.

At the end of its route, her gaze falls upon a shear gray face. It looms. She faces it directly and its solid edges slip away behind the night into the violet space upon which nocturnal things lean. The profile of the block, a single lit face presiding over a dim lawn, inverts and recedes to become a vessel penetrating the sky. With shadowless and flat faces it is possible to see, in the benign lack of depth which the gaseous streetlight has rushed to fill, a hollow, a shelter half mourning its incompleteness. Textures, mauve undertones, and minutiae of value allude that this shape is not the enclosure of a space but a distention of the night, behind which lies a vast griseous demesne of endless identical passageways, curtainlined corridors, disintegrated halls erased by currents of moisture.

Windows, fogged by the slender breath of night, diffuse all. Her disintegrated features are there opposite your eyes, that face with the kisses of mint tea, grout impressions on the cheek, with stale eyes looking toward some horizon, the curb of a bathtub, meeting the night. That face, this face, a glass slide slivered into a cloud, is forever turning away into the direction where night arises. Your eyes and hers timidly want to look back toward the red sea sky where more daylit footfalls trail out in a sunlight waterfall over stone steps and other horizons, and her face, that face, when you step backward to the door, is washed over in the shadow of her own dark cell, red darkness floods the windshield, cloud, and street. Night inside is no different than dusty day without a memory of the sun.

The pressure of walls at night or in darkness turns wet air into ice. I feel myself at the center of a hardened tomb. There is nothing outside of my skin. I am getting smaller and the apartment is drifting on shifting sands or opening into a mountain pass accepting the orange sky. I pull back the curtain. Purple light shades my fingers and washes across the wall. I know the sun has set and no tricks will prolong the day. I need to get a hold of something. Events grow so imminent in the dark. Things feel closer. The sense in my skin and my short hairs that something is moving toward me. When the sun goes down I begin to know all the things I havent seen. Their complicity with the darkness makes me want to throw up the window and reach my arms into the slim steamy rain.

I promote the insistence that these phenomena of light and the manifestation of the cavernous formations are reflections. Through the atmospheric theatrics of vapor an emptied environment allows the surface characters of sheen and glimmer to prevail. These are subtle performances, the edges of characters. Little light reaches into the shallow dips of fingertips where I pool. My presence is far too sparse and oblique. In a downcast vista I receive distant and detached twinkles traveling through liquid gauze. Each drift of my milky cloud, growing more distant from the touch of the lipid light, has resulted in a softer rendering of the heaped body. I settle to await the transubstantiative dawn. I submit to the pliability of dew.

The innocuous table settings and furnishings you conjure out of the shadows and array through the slow timeless dimness hang plaintively alone, harboring a whole that is beyond use, beyond investment. They are warmed by lamps on tables and fabrics that you can see through windows. You sleep in the dust. If you walked all night you would only see more yawning apartment windows yellowing the night with other bleak stage sets. The burden of a populous life would drown you. You start when you wake up in the dark. It has all ended. The day is sinking back into the stable tomb of that morning, below the paralytic sea, obscure. The bare peak of a choppy dark wave flickers out of the shadow, salty foam crusts the corners of you mouth, finite on the broad lagoon.

The water is high and undulating with the force of the running faucet hidden by the door. When you go to her the water in the bathtub is risen to just about the profile of the rim where it rolls outward to form a lip. It doesnt raise or lower while the faucet runs but it changes when water pours in to displace the water you had seen, moving imperceptibly from the visible sliver of the tub. Her face has ocean eyes, the steam of water dreams in a sand sea. Your cheek against the wall is cool. You force your face further into the narrow opening of the door. You want to put your face on the tile, to complete her curled form with your body. When you go to her, through a cascade of reflections, her eyes are shallow allusions. Their stillness is eyes on a sand horizon watching for the sunrise.

That slickness lines her downy arm. Her arm is parallel to the window horizon, slightly above it because her hand grasps the top of the seat. Her lips rest against her forearm, dampened. Her eyes are fixed low, where the building meets the lawn. There is a border of dirt around the base but no plants, no coverage. The void or corridor disappearing into the center of the ground level of the building, a continuation of the sidewalk that is cut diagonally across the lawn, is gated. The black wrought iron or painted metal tubes are capped by flattened black spearheads with very slightly rounded points. The gate, covered with flaky grime, is the only portion of the home that does not glow. The wall stands immaculately illuminated in the absence of moonlight, a surface cleared of all texture and grain.

You back into spaces. With eyes closed, the compound reflections that you face on the windscreens, windows, and water follow you backing toward the ajar door. You back into a brick wall. The bricks are warm in the napping dormancy of your inert world. To sleep in the sun is surrender. The grout is damp and leaves a familiar residue on your fingers when you rake across the wall with your heels and shoulderblades. You are narrow. You feel against the wall your slenderness in the world with which you flow between things or become them, assuming their texture and skin. Against the wall you do not cast a shadow. With your fingertips hooked over the vertical joints in the brick, which align vertically up the walls, you pull yourself slowly to the east dusk.

I only pull the curtain back slightly, holding the base against the wall and pulling back the midsection with my pointer finger until it just breaches the jamb. I look out with one eye into the swirling night. The streetlamps light slowly from across the horizon in the earlier dark and pace slowly toward the ocean in segments. These are still dark but the moisture in the air is already orange and has a living glow to it, and gives it to all surfaces and soft shades of brown shape her out of the dim beneath the tree. This time I will let that day happen. So many bits back, when was that day, did it start and finish. What she wants is what I make her want. Where she is is where I have put her. She cant see me. Maybe she can see my shadow on the curtain.

The top surface of an arm with accompanying damp beaded hairs rises gently from the tessellated rind of the heap. Tracing moist fingers upon that body, lying across the hall in a continuous contortion beneath two columns of stacked chairs, a full night of breath can swell a foreign cave with moisture leeching through all baffles of papers and polycotton pleats.

I trace shadowy contours along the path that defines the body in folds and flexures, to develop submerged properties, to invent my distance in this dusk. I am close and the breath that rustles past me is cool and moist. I produce my tableau from beyond the body to compose its dark side with pastes of light running through slit'd runnels between limbs. Breath barely tosses my cape up from the floor aflutter.

Beneath you and all scattered around the dark are those junked inventories from the sunken city, threatening with the complicity of the tide to disrupt your sleep and corrupt your innocence. But you will not see them. The moments when the city darkens before the dawn, all the streetlamps snuff out, the hallway sconces, the shimmering light from the courtyard, the muted shadows and glimmers from the windows, the cold sea lights, concede. Beneath the skirts of the earth, where you can rest, for a lingering moment, your eyes race across the fullness of the dark for some fragment, a touch of pain to reconcile your presumed fears against the offer of peace. You will never have control. The things do not have stories. The things are gone.

You push high on the strike stile of the door. It gives inward in a dry elastic strain and then returns. Her feet topple. They are bare. You lean your shoulder against the door jamb and will your vision to see the carpet bleached around the feet and the white feet mummified and undiscovered and nameless and the name and history irrelevant. Salt water and vinegar burn your lungs. Behind the door, when you go to her, nothing. You wont force the door open but let all of the mysteries of closed doors bloom and choke your projections. Her feet below you, and then, exquisite endless sand, the deepest emptiness, her face, blank and foamed over, a straight lipless line for a mouth, a high window and a dark line of hills and a purple sky.

With the same wan posture, the shape drifts toward her, framed by smooth trunks in variegated silver and gray that grow slender while they ascend, and identical formations inverted from the sky beneath a gathering cloud ceiling. At the threshold of descent, where the sky settles to meet the earth beneath the horizon stand the purgatorial intrusions that the night spueth out. The shapes are borne atop the stretch of her arm, a shimmering horizon crenelated by dull jewels. She reclines, pulls her chin out from the night, draws her arms from the door, buries her feet into the darkness beneath the console, and looks out into the vessel of night. In the street, her last resort pacts are imbued with repentance, they lack seriousness, verging on untwinkling sleep.

You tap the back of your head against the wall rhythmically and lean back in order to force open a door should you come upon it. Your hand instead discovers it sliding palm flat against the surface no longer brick and pushes out a wake of paint flakes adrift on the smooth forgiving wood of the door. The flakes, breaking off in acute fragments, lodge their points beneath your fingernails. You continue to slide and push. Your hand and elbow press beyond a faint axis whereby the door falls inward and around your left shoulder on the brick jamb you fall with it, backward still, shuffling your feet heel first into a stale room steeped of afternoon disuse. Sightless, you feel the dry stillness creep over your neck and shoulders with heaviness.

I step backward into the room. Maybe she saw the sheer curtain folds waver or whisper out of the window when I let them go. Maybe she knows I am alive and that she is alive and that is the remarkable depth of understanding that is our limit. She knows that our pulses are not any more delicate than the eternity of inanimate objects. We can come closer together, but we wont feel anything in the air, only pressure. Because I know that this day is finite, I know that she is the way it will end. When things change they end. I am not ready to start over. I wont. Things have been slowing. The days end. In the night I am finite, but the darkness is filled with unknowable multitudes of other finite bits, and I havent time left. It will be she and I.

Fine spun hairs sprout forth between the skin and fabric running with sweat caught from the air. A pelt which was matted down, yet rigid and bristling, would catch slight friction at the reversal of its nap. A fragment of the body is in slight motion. I watch the bicep drawn back across the skin, pressing the fabric down and raking the hairs through a coat of sweat. The immediate sheen on the skin plays against the position of the body by rendering a wholesale reflection of the hall across its landscape. Refrigerated strings of crystalline night air woven together draw out moist hairs and brassy screwheads in a pointilized tableau on the contours of skin. Shivers with an hesitant range of motion becoming vibration, press deep into the piled carpet with a pale digit.

These were all gray. You saw them in the long darkness, each with a prick to your independence. You left them behind to comment on you, but, you were and you are absent. You saw a pair of canvas shoes, slightly worn, one next to the other in careful opposition with their toes against the threshold of a door but not entering the room. The door is ajar and darkness amidst light infused steam sways over them. You pick them up, they are filled with cotton. The air is wet. Walking all night in damp shoes your feet grow soft mashing into a trail of gray paste and pulpy paper. You drop card after card until your entire stack of scraps and their borrowed insinuations disintegrate behind your head. Your shoes, your papers, your feet, float into pulpy back waters.

You look across the counter into the kitchen. Rain light in streaks faintly glistens on a place setting, and several rings of keys. A long chino skirt and tunic drape over the back of a chair. Coupon circulars, alms requests, clearing-house booklets, and real estate takeaways are stacked and gathered in a paper band. Something is written into the condensation on the window, across the crown of the street tree shaking in the rain. The apartment is too empty and prepared. The things that are in it make it feel emptier, more abandoned, already. It looms ahead of you. Another sure sunrise, awake somewhere strange, or stay awake and make your way there through the night and sleep through the dawn. Walk into sleep. Walk away.

The street does not gesture, cringe, or shrug under the received tribulations of an entire city night. It seems always to remain in pale balance, with almost rosy undertones, when she glazes upon it the sorrows of and the blame for its barren perimeter. At high curbs she creeps to fold, shoulder to shoulder spanning from roadbed to curbtop, her face into a cavernous stormdrain, the rosy throat of the road. Where streets end in the city they do so without curbs but with walls. The walls hit the asphalt in a perfect intersection of vertical and horizontal. She can squeeze her presence to the width of a crease and disappear into the intersections of things, allow her self to slink into the storm drain, to sprawl in the grass with joyful delirium, face down, eyes dewy.

When dusk light, falling with powerless crispness through deep metal blinds, washes in decayed lines on wood panel, whose grain and joints show no signs of sea damaged silver but reflect the yellowing that accompanies aged plastic on outdoor signs, the entire space, circuitous and dead behind closed doors full of mystery and color, is only that spot of false wood, limp in light, that your eyes first open upon. When was this? You see nothing else unless filtered through that stale moment. The skin on the back of your hand in this shade is tobacco yellowed. Caked runnels of fine silt run from the cuff of your sleeve, dried quickly but with a well worn matte surface that diffuses light without any crystalline properties. The hairs on your wrist stand proud through the silt.

Some time has passed. I feel the moment where I left in my skin with a cooling wetness the very same that I feel when I return. All of the days are over. The one where I spent down the sun doubled over a desk, the day in the sun and the rain, the day hiding in my own shadow, softened by the sheets, and the blinds, and the brick, and the crown of the palm, has fallen useless and unconnected into the blocks behind me. Which day wasnt filled with hiding. Which one was me with all the events in clean a line that told a story. How long do I remain when the darkness lets me not be seen or see myself. When night falls on each body and each thing in each of them it tears away only their one shadow across the horizon. It stretches but it doesnt break. It disappears.

In the wisps of moisture I saw the body waver. Ribbons of pulmonary slumber wrap and isolate each limb with brassy resolve. I draw closer, riding the pleats of moonlight in waves that spill drifting dew over the body to halt the approaching sun. In the wan phosphorescence of a stuck squint, laced with the soft edges of a cloud, I see the quivering machinations of sleep shuffle out of the grayness. The movement of the continuous surface of pale floral fabric, knees pressing toward neck, throat pulsing, wraps around the catalogue of the body, no more a finale of an internal convulsion, a sleepy twitch gathering more limbs into its writhe, than it is a current initiated by atmospheric conditions working over the throng with its moist reflectivity.

Your feet are caked in plaster. It penetrates the cracks and fissures when it is viscous. When it dries it hardens into chips that break your feet into pieces. You dip your feet into the black sea water and the plaster trails out in sinewy clouds of silky dust and briny blood and is gone into the unknowable fullness. The water is taken up on the hot nights when the night sweat cools the sky that is disappearing. Your punished feet dry, giving over the foamy destruction of your flesh to the cycle that lays clouds across the city, over the bodies of land and shut away empty bodies that lie just above the high night tide. You fold the collar up high when you walk beneath trees so the water cannot run down your neck, beneath your hair and untouchable betwixt your shoulderblades.

The high lit window over your shoulder sloughs away with the things you know she had forgotten and you need to forget them too. A forgotten day was balled in her throat when the breath tapered into nothing, when the wind blew her clothes through with clean sunlight long after she awoke and she arched her back with her arms above her head and felt her entire body at once to be complete and continuing, she slept full of the sun and her head emptied into her body the dark contents of its rich blood and dream, her bare skin felt nothing but the pressure from within and the sea washed over her through the night. She awoke surrounded and confused. Everything you encounter stands alone with ponderously silent significance, but you cant place any of it.

In a city of chambers, quadrants, halls, and depths, she is drawn through inbetween spaces in a constant train of the changing skies. Her exhibition, a floating-eyed scrutiny that forms a globe about her, is necessitated by her movement. The glass wraps around her body on all sides plastered with the faces of the low hanging sky. The clouds do not trail through apartments, caves, or kitchens. Darkness does not fall on promontories or rolling continuous plains. Where shall the lights not cast out onto the lawns? Where shall she lie at the frays of the violet unknowns? The dew from the nightsbreath runs in currents toward the curbs gathering into still pools and gently flowing streams that meet the horizon, and slip beneath it.

The flesh that holds your fingernails is thick and deep yellow riven with cracks that run up to your first knuckles. You set your palm on your knee. Feeling discomfort before opening your eyes, you felt the dust on the sweat beneath your collar, creeping beneath your shoulderblades and the dust drying your lips and slowing your breath while it turned to silt in your moist lungs. You fall to be seated in a dry, lit tomb. You kept your eyes closed a moment longer. This city is filled with single rooms, none of which open onto one another. Another room, perhaps the same one from before, with the trickles of fat discoloring portions of the wall, now thoroughly clotted with fine hairs and dust where it had been still running yet slightly gummy liquid in the early afternoon sunlight warmed room.

She has been waiting with each day, in this one form, mostly absent, but waiting. I dont know why I kept her there, and so easily now, I gesture from the window. She puts her palms atop her hips and arches her back with squinting eyes and her dresses fight across her chest in tension. She puts her hands backwards around the tree trunk. Her skirts shift and she looks at the ground. She looks long because nothing happens slow enough. The grasp of her toes against the sidewalk is a whole night of streetlight passing and another when her heel leaves the ground, and night after night she has walked slowly into this cold mess and what do I expect now that I unlock the steel door and leave it ajar and pull the curtains tight over the windows. I expect to stay here. I am all that I expect still.

There is the appearance of constant motion in the presence of liquid; it is numbing yet attractive. With each pass my cloud deposits skins of dew. The body is covered with all tiny spherical reflections that describe the contours of a landscape, low, sprawling, and quivering, that has not the bounds of a body on a carpet. Their trajectories wander off across

the cavern, under the doors, and roll into the city to loop down into false built up hills, recondense in a stand of tepid vapor on pavement, and leech down, dripping into a distant refrigerated cavern. The landscape shrugs off dew to run beneath the pale floral collar into disappearing contours of blue skin, lightless, the beads grow cool, dark, relinquish the conveyance of image and sense to leave only irritating trickles between shoulderblades.

Transparent gelatinous pills are laid out in offset columns and rows on a low glass table framed with deep gilt carving. Each pill catches varied colors from the stained carpet across the daylit spectrum of turbid Adriatic seawater lit in the afternoon dim by table lamps moved to the floor. The colors shimmer through the grid of pills when you approach them, wavering to and fro, idly bound between the dull gold walls. You sit in front of them in a golden wing chair. You look long and deep within the frame and the bilious greens and endless virid blues loll and transpose in waves across the mosaic. You check your head is still and the apartment sways. The cooling tea you set on your knees drifts within the walls of the mug. Your feet wander through the mosaic, toward the bathroom door.

She had asked you to wait for the right time, if waiting was forgetting, to wait outside the apartment so she could watch you. The path you take to run away from the last charges will not fan out behind you into an incrimination. She isnt looking for you. She had already decided it would be you to watch her, if watching is seeing, if seeing was the creation of immediately obsolete impressions, never filed, sometimes they slip down the back of your scalp and run between your shoulderblades. You cant be counted on. You knew that. Her failure couldnt be helped by yours, but you wanted to hold her head while it ended. Merely passing by someone in blinding white, both remaining obscure, commits you to more travels than are possible on these straight roads.

In slender reflective threads, the stored radiance of day sputters together into cohesive bits, entries back into awakedness. Meticulously patterned fabrics hang in a sequence from frame to frame that stand around her, capsules of the city reaching out to her in elongated streaks, the fresh sap of the lively inner world prick'd and drawn across the night whilst she races away from their false hospitality. She looks to the reflections in streetside puddles that remain still 'neath the streams which bear them rolling on. It is through reflection and projection that she inhabits and carries the spaces of her memories. Only in these memories can she inhabit the cobbled together reflection of her body. The wall becomes more broad in proportion, panoramic, she moves ever away from it.

You are reflected into found situations. Through optical sleight, portions of your body, recognizable with their imperfections or the edge of a piece of clothing trailing into the tableau, become familiar with their surroundings. Your foot curves in its shoe over the narrow steel ring around the base of the stool which stands behind a counter. The counter has two sides which meet at a corner. The stool is behind the portion of the counter which is opposite a wall with two windows and a door. You face the window, the register tape fed out of the top of the cash register which sits unadorned atop the counter. Each action your body finds itself performing, when you awaken to its movement from long dazes, is one of these reflections, borne of an initial faraway movement.

When I wheeled around to look back into the apartment everything was closer in to me. The ceiling was enormous and small in a way that made the walls need to taper inward to hold it in place but its surface was so upon my face that I couldnt see its edges. The room had more corners and each corner had things spilling out of it, pieces of furniture backed into each other and stacked, beige foam, bits of glass beads, crevices jammed with mail circulars and unpostmarked envelopes, trinkets and fetishes from dried out gutters and medians, each appearing in mirrored groups with other corners and vertices of shadow. The room encircled me and if I found a bit of wall to focus on while the time passed a jumble of old papers would slide into the space. It was one space facing inward.

Were the body rind to split, the satiny lubricant hanging from the cardboard undersides of the stacked chairs and draping across the undulating limbs in mackerel folds would calve and waver off into pleats of lavender night. The surface of the body is riven with long folds and crevasses of blank gray. In shadowy ripples, I fill the puckers and crevasses with a regenerative spray of reflective mess that spreads across the body in a sheet. Puddles form on the outer crusts and leech slowly through layers of trickling subterranean formations. Damp tendrils constantly traced with the moisture that carries my code, the reflections and refractions of my route and my character, move toward the peaks and crevasses of this familiar outcropping.

You bend forward letting your hair fall wet across your face and shoulders heavily, parting about your neck. The towel is soaked through with black water. Other towels are rolled against the threshold of the door discolored and stiff from drying in place, distressed. The long hair strands waver in an unpredictable undulating carpet when the water passes over them slick in the water with old slime, the erupting foam and saliva from your hard mouth, the dirty oils and compounds from your hands, the gray water that you pat out of your hair and catch at the hairline of your neck. The towels are infused with the liquefaction of your body that cannot be rinsed out. It lingers in stains and you recognize that it catalogues moments and causes, but no reasons. Nothing speaks for them.

This is not the time to recollect or sort your faults into cause and effect binaries. She asked you to allow for your own predestination of guilt, so that counting out the pills, holding her absently while she foamed and turned cold, watching dust in the rain spin outside the bathroom window, putting her in the running briny bath, and locking the bathroom door from the inside before shutting it would only be another place in a life that was now yours. If it were so linear you wouldnt have six chances to speak the words, for the wind to blow your eyes the other direction. But it is simple. Something must come at the end, in the sequence of parallel pacts, one lies at the bottom of the stack, this is the route you take away, let it be the one to close the circuit, to fill the morning with clear light.

The windows, streaming forth verdant waves to enfold the car, hold her in the waking night, where things come into contact with other things, actions take place, things touch places for days, years, and reactions are applied to situations that occur between her self and the objects that she encounters. The light from these windows casts long expansive capes of diffused patterns across the lawn reaching just to the edge of the curb. These are the memories and sensations she holds at a distance, the regeneration that the day finds in the night. Her constant movement toward that freshly born dawn, although lost, is an act of hope. She slips away across the curb and down the eastern slope of an incessant hill, ever toward night.

Your feet in the waves, bland morning sun on steel water retreats back across sand littered with bits of paper and cigarettes where each fold in the surface of the water, each crystalline grain of sand propels the reflection of that moment of you forward, onto another surface and another, you stand near a table by a window which extends to just above the floor where steam rises from a teacup, the water vapor carries you out again where you meet a woman from the beach who stepped out of the water in sock feet and laid onto the hard low tide sands with her cheek on the sand looking out across the sand longways up the shoreline, behind the counter you tap listlessly on the keys of a metal cash register and the tape unfurls, a white pennant in the breeze of all those breaths that pace the sunset.

I looked away from the edges of orange light detaching the curtains from the room. I turned off the lights that were wedged into the bedecked shell of the room leaving on the tall gooseneck lamp that illuminated the chair that faced into the room with a low table before it. Both sat alone. The far reaches of the room were gone again, not into the shadow, but into nothing. The beige light leaned in from the open door and I sat down in the chair. She shut the door behind her. She was transparent in the shade. She was wet. She watched the warm rain fall from her fingertips to the carpet, the damp blotting out the color of her hair and skin and falling long and still blotted out the sun and inversely riled the orange sky. No one really needs anyone.

I condense myself across the skin, within the heap, to give it ease of motion. The settling of this dampness allows the contorted topology of skin, draped about the slender formations of the hall, to be seen in one skin, reflecting the night about it. I lie across the reaches, veins, and knotted hollows in the dew. My reflections in the liquid shiver in miniature increments on pale blue skin below the outcroppings of awakedness. I see sleep on the skin of the palm, laid bare by tracks across which I trace imperceptibly to apprehend myself, still lying there, stationary, pulsing in the glistening dew on that shoulder. A pale blue fold, a cuff, billowing away from the slick skin, wraps over me. I am fixed with my reflection. I and a breath tracing down the neck sway.

When the shadows take over the night your tomb becomes airless. The shadows of all of these things you cannot resolve replace a solid world where light swells perpetually outward, holding the walls and the sky aloft and visible. You can see them but they are blank. Not even the occupation of honest avoidance can bloom just before dawn. You cannot continue to face the blank wall or the blank patio, to find an object that buoys your descent or adopts the causes of your decay. Upon the ocean floor there is nothing to transfer your body into. You begin to panic. You have no mass and no extent and not context. You feel your hand reaching out before your eyes but it is not there, only the ambiguous white abyss of dawn. You cannot confront anything or flee. If it all went away, could you breathe.

In the wordless gestures of habit she described her life to you by sleeping though opportunities, sleeping through awake wanderings, and living for years in silence. She asked you to sleep in this bed struck into the crook where it is backed against the wall, sweating at night for the morning and soaked by the sweat soaked sheets when you wake up too late sweating and racing in your head about a sequence of events that you have slept too long into to affect, and sitting squinting at the kitchen table when the bedroom was too dry, when the light of fires played gray palpations across the blank walls of the bedroom, or when the open window nights were too full of the desert and you woke up afraid that the powdery dust in the folds and wrinkles of the sheets was you.

Capes and puddles of light hesitate, peek out, billow and lap at the street edges running with water, await her footprints, lick the tire treads, shiver it all forward. Solid orange luminance swells in the streets, fighting the sleep seeking, seeking the dark edges and overhangs. Transitional hours are filled with reclamation, yet counter to the character toward which they ought to tend. This night is swollen with light and agitated grain, a night that tolerates not the darkness which is its gift. The daily movements of the sun seek to obliterate lightness by allowing all corners to find shadow each in their own time. The city night expands in all directions at once until it has met the hills. There too, after long swelling, near to midnight, it yearns for final repose.

Your breath rustles the blank tape. You crouch over the register. Shelves line the walls beginning behind you and running to the windows, six abreast, on brown metal standards. The slots in the standards are trained with dust and hair, white earthenware fragments in fine drifts down the vertical line and the shelves are mostly empty. They bow upward between supports even where there is an item or object, unidentifiable. A handwritten list of items to be requested is on the counter beside the register. You fold it twice and slide it into your empty chest pocket. The list is meaningless under any banner and the cans and bottles speckling the walls are covered over with a gelatinous fatty brown ooze that drapes the labels or is clotted with powdered rust.

She looks at me tentatively, into a shop window or down a long street that converges on itself, concealing things, and beyond me from the shadows through the light and back into the shadows. What do she and I become in all of this, together in a series of relatively small bound chambers, we have the night to play out. I could draw things out from her, origin stories, tableaux, schedules, habits. How do you survive without anything but your body. How do you survive without that, still amidst all of the rushing forces of junk and debris. I didnt need to know. I knew. If you were all of those other things, and they were forgotten, washed away in the high water, would you blame them for not swimming to the surface, or not sinking to the bottom in the right order.

I draw close. I ride within the pleats of a dreamt dawn in waves, each spilling me over the body in dew. A pale blue fold ever expanding wraps across the hall drawing with it a new horizon that revolves about me at its center. The cornflower and beige pallor, the similar clothing on each limb with corresponding colors and level of wear indicate a unity. Bodies bloom under my breath, pearlescent azure vapor. Under my coat, they shiver without communicating. The extremities and the palliations of the cloth, though they pursued my shadowy gestures when I in turn trailed them, in the dusk and the setting wakedness, were foreign and pointless to me. That skin, beneath my watery skin, was too continuous, too bound. These clouds we inhabit race with our thoughts. We came to rest here.

With each breath rushes all of the night shivers and imprecations from your still sleep into a torrent of pasty foam and beige bile slaking your lips and face, out across the sea floor and into your hair. It happens gently, with the unseen loosing your numbness into the wet and tenuous essences of spume and tears. When you cough more your body gives nothing up but crunches smaller and smaller, folding in on itself. You cough when there is nothing left, in you or around you, a barely living reflex that keeps you made of body. Fluids slow in you. The egesta should float away into tendrils of invisible powder. Without your breath it should dry up. Without sun or lamplight it should not be. You lie with your cheek in it, your eye looking across it, something finally terminal.

She asked you to dress in heavy smocks all at once, to wipe away your face and the messes around you with layers of clothes, to build up a thickness that was a body on its own so that you wouldnt need yours, the stiff fabrics that she preferred stood up on their own or held her up when she faltered in a day. She asked you to walk that route, the convex in the morning and the concave in the evening, to sag toward the sea that might some day want you, to want it secretly so that life didnt stop, but ended in the way you looked at the still objects around you, to forget the sun, to live outside the body when you spend the rest of your days at a desk, to search for shadows across the things you see every day, to see if they move, if time passes.

It is in the city, when the day remains, a limp sheet cast from the distant dusk portcullis, becoming night from its distant edge, the face to the east she toes into, beyond the violet veil, that the luminous arms, reaching across the globe and up into the plains recede, drawing back a blanket of darkness and with it her vision in which the trailing edge snuffs out each sprig of the grass, each kitchen sill, each concrete pathway, low wall, each glimmering puddle, her folded hands, fingers ceasing to rub the opposite knuckles, and where her fingers trace its passage, even the stored breath of day, in each chamber, loses ground to night, slinks into roadside burrows, is washed back toward the ocean, leaving the plants, the grasses, darkened in degradation.

Every room is empty or stopped. You stop in each, the curse of your footfall and of your eyes, stopped each morning on the sand when you walk east all through the daylight and twilight. You make movement and you make trails that bind the pointless disparate cells of the day into action, continuous and seamless. The misregistrations lie in the failures of the city and its failed languishing bodies, neither of which can move forward, or rise to seal their pact with the day that they will await its return. You are continuous. The sunlight dross wavers through the shoreline tall grasses across a speckled lagoon riven by avenues over sand, infertile and inhuman, scalloped by her footsteps whose heel crests cast shadows over the smooth water and bears a golden crown with red corona in its sun.

Her bare feet dry on the carpet. I get out of my chair to get a towel for her hair. The bathroom door is closed. The towels are in a hall cupboard with half of the doors painted shut. She pats her scalp with a mauve towel, wraps it 'round the train of dim hair. She sits between a chest of drawers and boxes full of photographs against a bare spot where the wall and floor meet. I put a mug of tea on the glass table and sit back in my chair. Things have order, they are ever fortuitous. I feel things stop inside me when they reach a point in time that their action fits. She and I breathe. The steam between us responds. Ill fall apart. I cant see the moment. I think of the conception of our parallel course. She would be a figure beneath the paint. But she and I breathe, exchange damp air, and convey silent secrets.

Deep toward dawn the filmy cell of my visualized territory contracts to the fluid empty shapes that trickle through the apertures and ajar portals profiled by wrists, elbows, buttocks, and heels, into soupy, tangible dark. I settle across the sere fabrics of clothing. The surface of the fabric is pulled tight and captured between the limbs appearing to be two distinct pieces of cloth whose fragmented repeat patterns do not align. Sleep wraps and isolates each limb in a mat of gray void. Still lax, languid, limp, breaking apart, I apprehend that body is a series of self same pieces from which the disintegrated form scrutinizes itself from a distance. Still, the distant facets of the body sought the compacted grayness of sedimentary sleep. Still lying there stationary, it continues to softly sway.

Night is too accusatory. Have you done something. A streetlamp fell on a patch of concrete in front of the apartment building; yellow reeds aflame parry forecasts of your ill history. A tree trunk stands at the opposite side in shadow. The focus of the lamp is empty. Something belonged or was forgotten there. She leans against the tree with her hands above her head looped behind the thin trunk. Her eyes are closed. She faces the apartment window facing the street. The streetlamp blazed empty, continuously. The light vibrated. You stood there. Night is trouble. You made a mistake. You disappeared. You are slowly disappearing. You dilute into the stage sets you have fled and the gentle disruptions your hollow body had sifted into still afternoon air where you trespassed. Night is needles.

She asked you to take her pain and forget it. She had forgotten the feeling of it but she knew it was there, it was visible in the shape of her spine and the way the white pillows that she stacked across the bathroom floor turned gray in the parade of nights where she hid. She didnt want this train to continue dragging, but she knew that it couldnt break apart, the world is built on the complex arrangement of things, every thing relies on the perfection of stillness, and because she brought nothing to it, she could take nothing away, and so much was piled atop her birth. She asked you to fit so perfectly, no matter what the shape, into a life that was never lived, to end it properly, if things end in darkness, to let it end being only a result, if anything were to ever cause it.

Atop an Idahoan precipice she straddles the night and the dusk. The dewy streams slip down into darkness to a point where the glimmers on sinewy currents taper into blackest descending oil. The last crystal streaks of the haunting limbo, the final exhalation of those moments in which all the surfaces gasped to hold in the final long rays of the sun, are slowly wrapping away behind me. She is upright against the sky faced away. The near sides of her shoulders are bathed in old rose light, the choked out long red rays from the depths of yearning homes and hollows. The flowers wheeling blue and patterned across her shoulderblades are dipped in violet growing deeper into the inexorable repeats beneath her arms. Her face and chest, her knees and toes tip into midnight.

The tip of the register tape has reached the floor while you drift and on the other side of the counter you trace its edge with your hand until it reaches your toe. A purple imprint in soft foliate type with the paleness of still air which has preserved it from before you may have possessed any involvement with or affinity for its subject: Venice Boulevard. Through the blinds, or inland from them, she is left again in twilight and all detail escapes into the rinse of seawater and dusty air, neither of which is visible now yet both clog her dry nose. Twilight clings to twilight in each cell of each late day cell in a bleaching wash to an evening that is pure gray. Should those old moments of focus come in her life let them fall in the sea whence she has marched around the globe.

Sitting in the light cone of the lamp I can see her feet reaching out of the dim, stacked heel on ankle through the glass of the table. Her shins taper into the shade of a dress and a body, tapering into nothing visible. The territories that crush my mind lie strewn across every day but are absent. Undiscoverable territories hang in the questions stamping in my thoughts. I will never occupy the chambers of my heart, the crevasses of black cold ocean, countries filled with people, alive perhaps, and the paradise of thoughts behind the eyes I see glimmering. They feel impossible. This apartment tomb is a persistent memory. Every unknowable shadowy supposition invokes the world that is mostly empty. My questions disrupt me with more and more empty space.

Fields slick in this satiny dew refract against the skin a floral pattern of small stems, milky stamens, pale petals, and buds cast in the unifying cyanosis between a pressed together palm and calf. Somber floral profiles stride in reflections before the stria of light at the door. Each new character entering the hall fills the body with dreams of other histories, and although I drape the body, dress its contours, its processes and promises are encased beneath the flesh. In the dusk interior to the folds of the body, I gaze upon fingers slipping between a calf and hamstring. The digits, back to the wrist, to the arm, to the trunk, all encased in my sheen, are not in my possession, do not reciprocate my inquiry. I become skin; still I ride the night, immediately distant even to that which gives me form.

Foam clots and smears diminish out from your cheek across the glossy tile. You cough out wet breath from your throat throwing bits of foam toward the wall of the bathtub. The water runs from the faucet into the tub throwing sheets of steam up across the tile. The window above the tub is dark. The foam has dried around your face situating you particularly on the floor, away from the faucet and bathtub and water. Parts of you are strewn around the floor. Your stocking feet slip out the ajar door stacked atop each other. Your dress is let out around you in an irregular cloth pool. Your hands are curled atop the fabric. You are paralyzed. Your eyes are fixed on the rim of the bathtub. Do not look away. It curves toward you in the periphery, encircling you, drawing you in.

Pleas and aspirations are grains of the sweeping dune mess just next to the junk, stockings, clamjamphry, vespers and squalls, sandhills, caverns, maremma and melancholy wastes, moonstone, hemlock, gingham napkins, salt cellars, dust bunnies, phials, slips and the things that trail the darkness behind you forgotten. A hope is a chance quickly dimmed by the flood of living. You cant see them through the mess. All the things she wanted for you cascade down the leeward slope of the night where the apartment door hangs open. When you began she was reborn. But nothing happens. Things are still and you lose rudder. A commitment is a moment, a look that you wear on your skin, where your blood is reborn in darkness.

She sinks, high within the hemispherical cenotaph of full night where the clothed windows of that final outpost, that terminal Idaho avenue, show distant among magnified points of starlight. The feelings beneath her fingers, pressed out from a void under her skin where erroneous ascriptions of docility, and tactility, and vacillation mistakenly characterize those objects which she grasped to anchor her sleep into the day, are the touch of wasted gifts she is leaving behind in those rooms. The sensations fade across her skin with the light fading into the ether softly falling beneath her eyelids and over her skin, beneath her clothes, through her hair and down the back of her neck, window panes mockingly kiss her shoulders and are consumed.

The trailing away of the sun across the vast skin of the ocean where she floats on her back leaves no stars. The slow tug of airless lungs and salt turns the eyes white, some night seen through grayed out pupils. She coils the register tape around her palm. In the rose gray nights the city evaporates or drowns. Can she be something with eyes open floating through corridors of her choosing. Nothing else but a faint desire to stay awake can arise from the high tides of dusk. The murk of sleep coats all. The body melts. Gathering up of her skirts and stockings and squinted eyes she can tread through the rising gray tides, with faint consciousness and rote steps she folds the paper from her hand into her breast pocket and steps backward from the window.

Statements form in my head, questions, accusations, statements bond into fragments in which settings are appointed, passed time prior to the setting provides arguments and causes, potential can be intuited, the marks of narrative punctuate the place but withhold it from annunciation, hold it still and silent from her narrow tight mouth. They just appear in me, but they are hers. I see the curves of her face in each setting. The abject dark inside is far away. It approaches me, when I am looking at her mouth or eyes in the shadows, and I watch the bits of a situation form around her, or after her, playing through the shadows, until it envelopes her, or makes sense of her, and then she and it are beyond my reach, beyond my apprehension, hidden within me.

I reflect pale blue from the fabric I slink beneath. I refract pale blue through each dewy bead of me. Pale striated reflections on the joints of the fingers encircled an ankle and were pressed beneath a calf. Fair and pale fingers, tinged livid nail moons, hook through the dew, press out against the fabric, and dissolve the continuity of the floral pattern. The fabric, swaying, traces a brocade of fray edged pale blue fingers, an abridged vista, across which I can see my own character, centerless, a single repeat cluster of stylized flowers multiplied into patterns of cuffs, sleeves, hems, wave. The risings and fallings of the flowery cloak drawn full of breath, respond to my isolation, the coolness of the moisture she withdraws, by spreading me, all at once, over the curves and folds of this body.

On the tile wall opposite the rim of the bathtub fluorescent reflections of lapping water flow. You are watching the reflection of the water lace across the chrome faucet. Milk green silty clouds sweep a wake around two paste white feet; they rise and fall breaking the surface and sinking into the cloudy water. She is floating in the water. You see her feet in the reflection. What floats is in pieces. They collect in waves and are thrown apart on currents. Nothing adrift coheres. You let your gaze stream out across your body, seeing bits at once, your dresses draped over a collection of marooned curiosities. Beneath the fabric are hands, legs, knees, pits, napes, hollows, splits, thighs, clefts, furrows. How do you put them together. Let them drift apart. Let them sink.

You wont see her. You have old remembrances that wash out from her feet into the spot she lies. They have faces and requests, distant eyes behind windows, distant bodies over the horizon living different lives. Thoughts, from moments ago perhaps, when she stood on the carpet with her skirt over your feet, with face in the dim, weathered away, hard from regretting you, are hidden in plaster envelopes and dropped into the inhumating path of wind driven sand. You wont see her because you dont want her. Seeing yourself in her eyes stopped and dry makes her yours, indelibly. What could you do with that thread of a life. You are looking at her feet. Her toes are purple, downturned, born, worked, and retired. You are not the mirror at the end of it. You are the stage set.

Cloaked in an actual blackness, her body trails her in movement, she sees it plodding behind her, acting, posturing itself to the city, pressing itself in exhaustion to surfaces and enclosures, aimless and half aware, foreign and silly. The vague line of the horizon there between her and her body, separating solid from void with no distinction of color or weight. Her pupils, her eyelids align and her hands stretch out to find her, waving with a blind uncertainty that comes from a life backed against walls. Those arms reach out, beyond empurpled straining skin growing darker with the depth, through diminishing twilight, through airy, cool darkness, through soil and rocky veins leeching smooth dark air and streams of sweat, to a true night departing.

She wheels backward, falling away from the streets, away from the roads that without definition dip beneath dark continuous overhangs, the shadows of sea blanched timbers silver in the borrowed moonlight, and emerge, possibly, into winding valleys between windowless walls, or where walls would be is dark that she dares not reach into to break her fall. She, ever deeper in the distant light, still lapping at the blinds in the front room, is lost in the curving mess of her descent, back to the earth, where it slumbers beneath the vaporous and dingy sea in an open space created by her breaths falling slower above her. The open air cells, through an enfilade of doorless portals are separated by more featureless gestures. Apartments are the dark space between two doors.

Then she is again there in the crook of the wall, resting on the carpet in the same place but deeper into the night, surrounded by different circumstances, and with more familiarity. I forget. She describes the edges of the shadows with the profiles of faces, still splayed black fronds, long stretches of sharp fence pickets, succulent spines, swaying fabric seams, and hands reached in from the darkness poised to grab at her while she sits there. Her presence populates me. I grow crowded. None of the situations that contain her apply to me. Nothing associates and I sit illuminated, on display, waiting for her to just take it all away at last. Each fitful start forward has days fallen in between and each starts with something lost and something useless gained.

By folding sheet upon sheet of dew, my gaze folding back upon my self, I can see pale cloth with a hinted floral pattern hung loosely about a hip. I continue to be pressed more finely in subsequent turns and configurations between limbs blooming all at once across the fabric firmament. The dawn, a vision, wakes with waves of dew soon to catch the pale sun. Skin, almost sloughed away yet taut and blue is beneath me. I am a fleshless dewpoint, I raise the fabric away from the skin with steamy breath. Dampness laces me when I kiss the collar of my shirt. Sleep, or at least a condition counter to endless tramping, comes fragmentary, sparse, vaporish. The stars, foliate blue and pale pores in my flesh gather in a show of corporeality. I alight on the ever inward sky of myself.

On your knees on cold wet tile, your eyes drag upward slowly through the steam. They tingle benevolently and your shoulders melt into your neck growing soft and languid. Your dresses are warm and wet, each blanketing you in viscous grog. The dress against your skin gathers around your joints with thick wet folds. The next approximates and smooths over the disruptions of the last. The outer dress is a smooth rind over a heap of useless limbs, the whole mess growing heavier, warmed by steam. Across your thighs the dress spreads out across the floor blending into it. Next to the door, you pick up two white canvas shoes. Each ponderous move pulls you deeper into the sagging landscape of your dresses. You slump your face out the door, into cold dry air and liquid light.

You didnt organize the city so that you could come upon this image, but you would. The scenario is old, but you didnt feel the burden until it actually arrived. The moments that you knew to be prefigured, the set aside images that clog the plats that your story left empty, where bare floors run with fluid from beneath doors, leaden clouds ride dawn breezes, her half curved smile and pleading hands are the conspicuous evidence that you have caused something. You lost your life in a short old thought that a day and a night would fill the empty space that no past and no future leave, all the empty plats that one day and one night could fill over the many days and nights it would take to accumulate them. But it was only a thought and you never acted.

She is disintegrating. The linked rifts of midnight that have sorted her stand alone in humility; the space between them is at once intangible, useless, and expansively impenetrable. Her hand grasps for purchase on handles, edges, loops, rings, pulls, brass stanchions, runners, seams, brocades, matted and diaphanous when they fade behind fine curtains, misses altogether and coasts deeper through the darkness, casting over the windows waves of earth and shade, following her further from the inevitably wide sky. Hollows of the void fan out through systems of descent, into drain pipes, storm sewers, grates, trenches, culverts, throats, natural entrances, vents, and clotted caverns. Through them, ahead of that sinking reactionary sky, she falls.

She falls to the ground, through a door, in a brick wall, lit green, at the mouth of an alley that lets onto a broad asphalt parking lot. Back west into the alley is that gray twilight filled with temptation and the surrender of the day. In grayness you awaken on a beach, back on a beach westward. She lies on her back in the alley, pointing north her left cheek on the asphalt sticking to fine sand with the night above her bespread, it claims the firmament. She turns her head against the sand to look directly up to the sky with no inclination or focus. The city is sinking. You can feel it with your back and with your equilibrium. Around the perimeter of your field of vision are the cornices of low apartment buildings flanking the alley to your feet and to your head.

She has fallen asleep against the wall in the midst of some papers. They were covered with names in unfamiliar handwriting. She had the gentle touch of a corpse. The air fell to her, reserving vacant packets found beneath an afternoon bedsheet, when peace is found drifting away from the stacked masonry of accusations that build awakedness. Where I saw her leaning is completely dark. I watch the empty space with dried ink eyes. Nothing poured into them. If she was gone then I was done with what was long ago born of a single body cleft into a population. If she was gone, the desert breeze that dried her skin could whisk my blood and bile into the atmosphere. I want to rain far out from the coast and sink through the brine into the rocky sheets of space that house the blind.

I am situated beneath a formation of chairs and folded linens. These are stacked in a dim hall. A field of brass chair legs, arching forward over my back and neck, rests on the carpet before me. My neck is midway between two legs that lie several tiers from the clearing and the stretch of rug that runs out into the gray. A surface of worn cardboard spotted with reflective yellowed and deep brown labels spreads out at the top of the chair legs until the perimeter of the formation where the space floats away vertically out of the vista. I was built up of fragments and diaphanous tissues. My right leg lolls and kicks back slightly against the base of the front right leg of the lowest chair of the leftmost column of chairs. Liquid traces of bronze, brass, and condensation reflect the pale blue of my skin.

When you are adrift, you drift apart and you drift toward. Hope is pointless. Things happen. You see your shoes peeking out beyond the skirts of flowery cloth. You gaze into her secure plainness, hoping to reach a togetherness, clasped from one day to the next, waiting for a final whole, a body with sense enough, whose origins you place at that very moment, with time enough before you drag the whole thing sleeping beneath the surface. The white edges of your gray face are still. She does not return the gaze. The city is asleep, she is gone, the courtyard is dark, the streetlamps, the timed floods, the nightlights of the damned have cried pax after an anguished night. The corners of your mouth glimmer where bubbles of saliva burst. The clouds light only the sky and the water.

If you are now seeing something, her stretched into nothing behind the door, if you leave her dried out next to the bath, where you found her, you pick up her shoes, if you put them on, pull the curtain, look out the window into the night and walk out the door, you will see what you have seen then, already thrown across the midnight from the bathroom mirror and noted casually in the clouds that the white day cool into rain, and it has happened and is over, before you even realized that what you had been waiting for was that lost moment, when you swung your arms out of the darkness and took a step forward. Now there is nothing left, you have a new pair of shoes, your first conception of a nebulous conclusion with little impact passes, and time is left now to fold only out of itself.

Descent, or prostration, is defensive. The deepest tongues of night sink into self conservatory slots, behind shutters, underneath feet, eyelids, between apartment blocks, shifted veins of rock. She is defensive. Wholeness, reflection in the dew of long nights, and looking down arms to hands from eyes are the forms of self accusation that drive her down and apart. She is only being pulled along, propelled by the sequential sorting and division of her self, each fanned sheaf moving faster away from the light. The waves of motion fold the matter swollen and skimmed from her into the profile of those great palmy trees that crenelate the horizon. Deep and gone into the sleep that forgets the body, she divides into each feathery, scalloped, eroded pocket of the purple nights matter.

In the starless mauve sky the arc lighting of the parking lot has eradicated the momentary hint of moon off of sea. Perhaps it still streams through that window, or others abandoned, you will not find them again. You look into solid colors and into blank surfaces, so rare in the day, where you find only dim, slow rolling over or finished lives, still beneath slowly settling, not anymore real. With each night sky dropping down again yet not quite to the same depth, the ground, silty ground is falling away from the sky. Where you are flat on your back you watch the emptiness above for it to change and awaken with imperfections that you might hold fast to lift you where you might see the rooftops, and the grid of streets, to where they end at another sea.

My eyes burn wide open. I drag them closed bound with my dark vision and the traces of her profile begin to alight in negative on my mind. Her eyes are closed. I looked at her on the street and saw just a person. She and I are barely people. We are a series of moments when we come into each others view, and then there are moments of absence. It is debilitating to sustain the constancy of the relationship, or at least the coexistence, of both she and I together in time. When I see her from my window, one of us is not there. She slides right through the moment, eyes on the sidewalk, weeks or days before my gaze existed. I cant describe my appearance in bits of her life. I wasnt there. My reluctance to enter this plat that would house us both was a product of the conditions which made us apart.

The foot of each chair leg meets the rug and slightly compacts it with noticeable discoloration where moisture was forced outward. Each chair leg anchors a discrete terminal of my body by either falling in a void between my limbs or by forming a retainer against which a surface of my skin is forced. The sprawl of my body has the appearance of being borne of the landscape, or being left behind by it. The physicality of the vista containing both my legs and the chair legs is tethered to my nerves by some looping and wavering corridor of moisture that seems to stretch parallel to my gaze and translates visual characteristics to dreams, memories. These wither in the growing light; dreams become sweat in dawn. I acquire the uncomfortable sensation of dampness accreting behind my neck.

The corporeal landscape of pain and cause, made of captured silt and dry dust, retires to a haunted and transparent, shadowless and detached distance, and you are loosed from it into the obscure airless stratum between the clouds and the reflective sea glimmering. In all of the days bound together, a monstrous plot, dawn is the interruption that drops you somewhere new. You must watch for the instant of absolution in the cresting sun to recalibrate the machine. You are ruined. The bloodless choke of the city lights, the shivers of tall reeds, the paces of her feet beat knotty patterns through the night, into death heavy involution. You waste the peaceful awakening by sleeping a moment. Shortly before the sun falls over the city the long shape of a lit window slices across the pool deck.

You turn around and see the funereal apartment blocks packed down the slow slope and the windows are all darkened. Did you turn off the lamps. You wont find it again, those rooms, yours. Places are never the same twice. It has been too long to remember where you fit into a particular denouement, lost in the middle of an unbroken day, a grid of locations and sun angles or hypnotic street light clouds, that you played some key role in perhaps, the significance of it, now that you see the horizon high above the alley ahead, would surely be better at the convergence of someone else and a long faint story. You walk briskly, steam fired and frenzied, each step a spasm that runs through your body, shake yourself apart, into the thick night.

Inky and fine, a paste of her self, smeared upon the flattened silhouette of the natural world that grows up to stand in the city creating a stage set in day, but is needed elsewhere for nights beneath the sky and beneath the high plains, a primeval crown of black fronds engaging the firmament, draped with crossed wires, hanging conical stones, and cradled by shear black faces. It was all draining into the pores and openings of the earth to populate her slumber with different things, transformed shadows of their sunny countenances and dusky pools of essences to anoint her sleeping eyes. She reaches out from beneath the earthen cloak and drags it down into the crook of her arm with all of her fingers, a mortuary shroud for a slumbering cloud.

In the absence of imperfections, colors from your eyes bloom in the sky, soft edged taupe and gilt floating rings and clusters. Your eyes are dry and cold tears collect and run into your ears. The discolorations of the sky, frozen vast pinholes, begin to drift open from them, exposing foreign imperfections, clouds wheeling out from orange streetlights, edges of moonlight, full fissures to brown black beyond. The sky is expanding while the city sinks and the crumbling silt your hands claw slips away. In years of days these streets and alleys will run with the tides to inter the desiccated corpses of dry eyed afternoons, to float us out face down and deeper into the full ocean on a sinking current. This evening we are afloat in a sky great beyond the wheels of her eyes. Brown with orange stars.

I thought perhaps she was forgetting me. I dont know that she was aware of me at all. If time was meted out by increments of envelopes and letters and circulars I sorted them until they were gone. I didnt lose time. It fell away. It first became familiar, then was easily forgotten. But there kept being other things, and the reflection of a woman that traced desperate tension around these increments remained mediated in the cold things that reflect light, so distant that they became unnoticeable. The reluctance of chance, to put her here, became familiar. Every night in the apartment I knew that I would be alone. I had surroundings. Why did I need vision. Why did I need to see behind what I see. Why would anything beyond the surface that I am and that I plod across have anything for me.

The formations of this waystation, an oft night platform, dress'd in the dullness of the approaching dawn, lie awake to absorb all light. Each whole component I catalogue becomes an increment in a greater patterned landscape, not a continuity. I inhabit the spaces between the repeats of the pattern with my fingertip. Outward vistas down the length of my body are framed by fragments of my body. I raise four splayed fingers out beyond the forest of legs. My fingertips carry the dampness from whence they pressed into the pile of the carpet. An highbacked chair draped with pale taffeta, a fanfolded linen napkin, and a precarious column of glossy, damp, bone-hued mugs glisten in the reflections at the webbed base of the slim portals between each of my fingers.

Stop. You teeter on the window light between days. You can sort the next events while they unfold. Each has its light, its toll. Behind your back, out against the dark street, the lingering night washes the stuck doorknobs, the place settings, the sunless horizons and the blocks and blocks of blocks, the sand running through your fingers, the trees against the white sky, the curtains pulled aside to watch the rain, the chair pulled under the table and room after empty room in gray water, eroding the connections and the causes into a dusty soup. When you look back, across the beach and road, it is unrecognizable. You hold your breath and it scatters back there. Things stay in places forever. You blow away the dust that reminds you. She is up early, or the light never turned off.

The night is at your back, darkness before you, and thoughts and bits of terrain or light are lost throughout, and lost within them are effects untethered and cascading. They sing out in wordless and silent accusations of friction and movement, not knowing where you are to them or where they are to the causes that make them seek you, they rumble noiselessly in place, never moving, lingering implications. Walking through the dark parting the pure black sand smoothly around you, you leave nothing behind. The night closes behind you. You pass through stages of experience, lined up for you curtain to curtain in a seal'd corridor of imagery. You leave nothing because you take nothing, vision is useless, your interests lie in erasing it all, not taking on more.

Her breath, the extreme unction of black bile coating each memory of day into night, of the walls her hands supported her against, of the arms of the alcoves that held her, the garb of the exorcist, violet, the barred fences dissecting her with shadow, of the final laminated gasps of the sun drawn across the horizon. She lay there in an unreal night evacuated of endings, horizons, scale, evacuating her experience of dusk up to this moment where, on her side, knees slightly drawn up, feet stacked at the ankles, arms outstretched yet crossed at the elbows, head turned and eyes buried beneath her and burrowed into the pile of fabric, she is draped in a fair blue sheen glimmering on her pale skin, through glass, in sleep, streetlights.

In their palpable light she settles again against the earth. She is on her back across the smooth striping of an asphalt parking lot. In these higher grounds bodies touch places for years leaving no other trace but a lack of dust. They leave the hundred shadows of ceaseless illumination. Things will touch places forever that she will never apprehend, things that are not hers in an empty world hardly belong at all, or things that she has relinquished do not exist to her any longer. Such things she carted along with her, once no longer with her, were something other, on their own on barren shelves, afternoon lit kitchens, in the folds of weakly thrown bed covers, without her ceaseless mobility, and there forever starts for them, at rest.

It isnt a puzzle. The pieces go where they are and they dont need to come together into anything other than a length. Why should I see other than what I see. I see her in my closed eyes, unmoving, but real. She is not a sign, but I know things are hidden in her. I can only see her in the dark by closing my eyes. She is not a harbinger because things have already begun to end. She has been imminent for so long that I know the remaining bits will be filled with her, and here she is, and she is asleep, so I know that they must be few, and although she is here and she will fill the frame, these last bits are only my own. There are too many people. Too many names that must be people. Am I one. A pasty, pale lump, fragile. I wont last. But I am not alone.

Festoons of pale fabric hang parted before the opening to my hutch. I splay my fingers and peer at the grayness bisecting the web at their base. I press the fingers toward the fabric and part the two cloaks further toward awaking from the dim that draws gray moisture across my skin. All of my body, seen refracted and already broken in convex droplets, is segmented further by the chair leg staccato. In the refracted images and droplet vistae, I am a hand, a floral pattern, an ankle. In this specious wholeness is the risk, where things appear for other things, of an entire twilight comprised of objects and characters; noplace is there only dark. The population of this near-dark field by my own real body is possible only with the projection into the night of the opposing lack of body.

How long would you stay in there at night, with the light on, visible from the street and the courtyard. Inside the apartment, with the lamps lit, the rooms are complete shells, the curtains are opaque, and the messy presence of the outdoors withdraws. You feel alternately secure and aware that although you have the shelter of the walls, the carpets and closets, control over the temperature, illumination and the tone of the apartment, that you sit, above the street, surrounded. You are in a shell full of things. Things do not move. You float from spot to spot, touching the painted drips on the corner of a wall, kneeling with your head between your knees on the carpet, sitting upright in a spacious cold chair, the light illuminates discolorations in the wall, where old paint coats muddle through.

These things you shelter in your body, you know them to be yours, and when you are torn to pieces, when you dry out in the arid end and your fine blood, the secret of your vessel, yours, blows into the dunes, the things that were yours the least, the shoes, stamps, and rooms, are all that are left to make you exist. Those traces are barely aloud, nameless things. You havent been observant enough to populate the passings and surfacings of those things with their own particularities. You dont recognize their physical shapes enough to let them inside of you with other things, to change and no longer rely on the signal of shape. Ambiguity becomes yours, you can erase from it what you need to, a benign presence, emptied of itself into you. Things are your enemies. They are silent.

Night, the space qualified by darkness, is bound to her while she burrows into sleep. The high walls at the edge of the flat landscape sweep up and the night pools there, and the earth rotates, and the night follows; she lies still within it. Caverns puncture the plains of sleep, twist and contort back on themselves, some open back to the sky, some end abruptly in small concave stone cradles. Regardless of how deep the cavern, there is always a point from which she could go no further. She was unaware of these boundaries. Her momentum continued and grew into less defined spaces where the earth has dissolved. She seeks shelter in sleep, the loosened cavern that trudges through the darkness with far walls and flat, open expanses.

You awaken on your back. Pebbles, refuse, and small drifts of sand outline your body where it touches the asphalt and sticks to the dew on your skin where your dress has ridden up. You cannot fall asleep on your back. You fell asleep elsewhere. How many chambers in this platted land shelter empty and unmade beds this dusk. You awake with the full sky, which so many havens obscure in this city, spread in intimate proximity to your cheeks. Hesitating, the night is a pliable mask for you to wear. With its streaks, furrows, blotches, and sparks, it radiates the imprint of your face out beyond the space of your gaze, around which a strung chain of luminous and burning night lights throw and coalesce spumes of orange gas into trembling bodies that cluster in the air.

Nothing makes sense in the mess of surroundings. Things are real when they are alone, with their essence bound, when they are falling or forgotten. Context is a burden. A description of the most recognizable element of my life could drag on without end because wherever it slips to in space it is never without the magnetic collection of my surroundings. It hasnt ever mattered to me why or how things end up together, on a shelf, drifting in the gutter, but what they are, where they have been before, what they might have been witness to, not how they move, but how they pose when they are still. This vision makes time useless. I dont want to see new things, but with juxtapositions that I cannot avoid, new moments will ceaselessly appear.

I withdraw my arm and wrist into the den. My fingers trace the moisture across the metal chair legs. Long rivulets of condensation, beginning their downward peregrinations, skirting the light, came to drops hanging from beneath the chairs and fell through the dim to fall through my clothing and soak the hairs reaching out from my skin. I feel an outcropping of legs pressing damp strips across my shoulderblades that I cannot reach to wipe dry with my cuff without rolling over. I cannot roll over. The furniture, the stalactites cradle me, all turning inward around my limbs to stay my clanging. If I could ascertain the preoccupation of my body with its own machinations, I would give its reports of my position little credence and await the sun.

You sit at the kitchen table folding napkins and at a low glass table lining up spherical transparent pills. Why should any occupation of time be any less than grave. Objects and effects are ordered, in sequence, one after the next in time. Dust is laid down in soft carpets that you never fall between. Where are you in time. If you turn on enough lamps in the apartment the day will never come. How long is a night. What would fit in one that would not fit in all of them, over and again, slowed until it is no longer moving, with arms on the arms of a chair, you sit timelessly, counting back through the layers of paint, a night, a glance, another night, until you have unmade yourself. You stand up to pull the curtain slightly. It is still dark.

The blocks of buildings continue to come. You are stricken by every thing. In the apartments lining the road loom significant collections of old junk and useful placeholders. Your experience is impermeable. The scraps of parallel lives, and worse yet, abandoned lives, jeer passively. Each hurls unintelligible secrets about you, each is unidentifiable horror. The world exists outside of you. It is terrible and relentless. You are not observant enough to recognize the same things again and again and each new glimpse down the road is filled with those old apartment hauntings, covered with your fingerprints, swimming in your spit, and bound with your old hair. What do you expect it to do when you leave it behind. Things are still. Secrets need destinations.

Light sinks to a certain point before it must be shepherded away from the night to which it belongs. The grains disincorporated, continue to fall captured in leeching water, in fanning trails and considerations, leaving the color it bore on craggy rocks upturned toward the moon and the matte ridges of her fingernails turning pale blue. The vein along which she gropes, damply, lead through the darkness by senses tuned to vestigial light, reaches to that innermost or distantmost concavity to which all the longing domestic phantasms and all the fragments chewed by night, fall reconstituted into tableaux of scrambled relationships, a transported diving hall of wallpaper glazed into a flat sheet of space, stretched to the cusp of dawn.

:139

The sky stretched outward from the center of her vision. She was afloat in it. Your feet touch places forever. They never leave the pavement. Do the spots where your sock feet smoothed aside the dust on a hardwood floor remain. For how many dusks have they been there. In how many will you float directionless with them, submerged. You lie now with your toes against the sky, each moment it changes in your eyes. Each time you blink the dusty light of night suns flies out from your lashes in radiant haloes around your eyes. The night swirling with orange clouds is dry. On the shores of a great sea is a desert and your eyes are dry. They ratchet through your head tracing clouds of vaporous dust that pulse outward and then driven hard down to cast your body for evacuation.

The apartment and its contents are inert. I line things up in my vision. I kneel so that the empty mug of tea floats above her head. I close an eye so that the slope of her shins under the dress follows the strike of light across the far wall. The flower pattern on her dress from beneath the window, where powdery light leaks, is luminous. It flattens her. I give these things to her or leave them with her, or leave her and them together, after me. From the hallway, with one eye free into the room, I can see only her bare feet on the carpet. I am behind the wall that leads back to the bedroom and bathroom and then she is gone and the apartment is gone. I think they exist, but, now that they have been, there is no reason for them to be again, not tonight, not in this order reversed. I slip into the bathroom.

I loupe my fingers before me to frame my knee and the point at which it presses into the carpet. A soft light falls upon my thumb and its web. My pointer finger is in shade. The morning sun, in absentia, grows vibrant beyond my fingers and I am orphaned by the night. My circled fingers draw a throat upon the dawn through which facets of moisture exhale their smooth light. They exhale accidental color; pale blue and the glow of moist fabric ensconce my gaze, overflow my fingers and wash toward my chest. The dew draws a roseate pallor from the hall where uniform wan light grows across a coffered ceiling, across the outward surfaces of the chairlegs, my knuckles stand out from the pale and gold with the dry cast of morning sun.

The darkness of the night compounds its length. She began waiting for the faint race of dawn by turning at sunset back to the east and setting up before the east facing window with a chair, a low table, and an occupation. The window treatments are bound tight to block out the orange scrutiny of the streetlamps and to bind in the incriminating heave of her table lamps and her reflective skin. There is nothing left to do in the halted timelessness of the apartment. She has stopped for interminable gasps, prone on the floor and lit uniformly, shadowless for a long night. She throws open the curtain and turns the blinds to watch for dawn to augur the sunrise. The lit apartment windows over the street stand alone, still with her folded into the light, seated, absently occupying the room.

You page through images and names looking for an exit. The buildings keep coming. You stay on your feet and walking. If you close your eyes you fall. You want to see emptiness and distance rising in between all of the things, through the mold in the stucco where wind should blow and the streaked glass in the windows full where rain washes the sky. You walk until it is over. Things stack up in time. A teakettle is covered with cooking grime on a clean stove. There are trains of thin grease chasing stilled droplets on the glossy wall stilled over years by paint droplets. The walls are thick. Seeing the teakettle through the high window, just barely the crown of its shape, you know the rest. It is half empty with cold dark water. It is cold against your hand. It sits untouched for days.

She is laid out beneath the city, her recomposed body stands or huddles intermittently, laid bare to the grid of lit streets and sky partitioned aglow over the crust of asphalt. The logic of the city decays immediately, it does not repeat; the veils of stone, soaked with greasy runoff, conform to her body rather than containing it. Out across the distant plains rolling beneath her, each circling vision she has glimpsed of her body is present, and her body, seen, is different from the ground, standing out against the continuity of the inanimate earthen chamber. Long, lanky projections lie fragmented by clothing; tapers, bulges, and divisions cobble together in a discontinuous heap. In its hollow poses, her body appears too human, too gaseous, too propped up by the earth.

When you awoke you were cut from the tangibly orange night, now it mummifies you in its growing dust storms. All around the parking lot glimmers of orange bloom in drifts against your flanks and across the pale white flowers of your dress arise the lilies of night sun and also buried in the night. Your body touches this parking lot forever because you have left it here. Your body is an imprint in the night, embossed in its material. When you awaken, you become part of its scheme. Night freezes parked autos in lots, it freezes sleepers, you, and the sky wheels on around you, spinning on axis with your eyes but not revolving about the earth to bring you the wet sun of morning whose sweat washes the body from the dust that buries you. In a spinning sky where will you find the morning.

This was the first time I had lived this way, or at all, but it was my whole life, years fell into it, everything is deferred to a gap in this experience where I can turn around to survey it all. I have just let it all wash over me, it hasnt been stored. I know it is behind me. Sometimes faces and shapes arise that turn my spine to ice, then they sink, steam wavers from my skin. I have known about it all. It was clear from the start what would happen and where and when it would happen. But in the midst of obstacles, familiar things becoming foreign that couldnt be avoided while the city swelling with lives each night grew around me, what I thought would be early white noons, or long mornings, or slow dusk, became a perpetual night of curtains and windowless rooms.

At dusk, in vapors, I was forced unquestioning from the day. The ever escaping territories of my body that turn to mist in the suns warmth ceased their truancy when the temperature dropped. The cloud, the moon, and sleep exert subtle controls. No history of me, drawn through the night within a spectre, could have compressed the distances within my body to a singularity. The motion with which the atmospherics held me and my character enrapt to night was one of a parallelism to such emotionless despondency that even the cave walls appear frazzled to me if I am seen to open my eyes. Liquid sensations again trace my skin, I am felt to run into the night to all points equidistant from where I lie, nothing is gained from the return of the crushing weight of these lifeless limbs lifts.

Hanging clipped from the dark, the narrow figure in the window is lit from behind by two lamps, her face is in shade but painfully visible, wrapped in the domed pupil of night. All of the luminance of the city is alone on her skin. She is at the center of a tremendous emptiness. With repeated nods of her head her hair swings longer into the shade of her face. To concede to inspection she puts her hands on the table and begins to occupy herself. You are there. Her hands trace lines out of the dust on the table. When the coming of the day counts on her eyes, her presence, she can only let it. It requires of her her shadow. She can cast one, lifelessly; dust casts shadows. Her collars stand tall. The room behind her is sallowed and still, bare shadowless walls frame her dim face.

What you are sometimes doesnt register. You slip out of alignment with what you have been made into. Sometimes you are a shadow. You see what you are doing and wonder about it. Where was the decision made that you dont care for tea. It gets cold too fast. It is for after a day that has passed without you in it, where parts of you are lost in scraps of paper or in the cycling of a fluorescent light. You make tea to be a lure for yourself and hold cups between your palms burning at the start, then warm and numb through swollen blood in your hands and then cold. It is a registration process. It is a physical passage of time after an abstract one, barely bridging into the darkness where you sleep in your body at the end and awake, beginning already gone, a cold kettle, a dry mug.

It is her charge to turn and prop up the earth and the mirage of the city with that new body. If she can not hold it back, stand pressing this terminal concavity in the sleep of the rock, it may flood with bland light, become unfathomable and organized, recoil upon itself, draw itself back under the sky, right itself with a final predawn glimpse of clarity and intention. It will eject her. A night awake is very long, because it is improper. If she is not able to hold the ends of this cavernous night, how then shall she remain in service to the earth, how can it make a home of her. It is of her own charge, were she to see the sun rise on Idaho again, that she exhales across the stone, warming its moist metallic veins, and gives herself to the night and its discrete shelters.

You leave yourself to be one of the objects of the city amidst receipts with diaphanous blue print, cigarette filters, fine dried twigs, stiff slender straws, soft undulating tooth prints, tabs and strings from tea bags, newsprint, teeth, mail in dark maildrops, footprints, parked autos, cups that leave moist rings that have dried, weeds, all the skin given over to dust, dried and hollow corpses, thresholds, storage units, driftwood, fingernails soft with undulating tooth marks, short hand-written notes, a house dress, reflections and horizons. Into the night tide of objects you recede, into the sensory state where you can possess the forceful stillness, into canals with no horizon, all rises and falls in place across the swells that gather to pass through to the wide open night of roads.

The things that I knew would happen still did happen. They happened in the apartment, in the dark, or apart from me while I labored upon time and geography. I thought that I was catching myself and falling back into a sequence where the impending moments were caused to follow, if not by my actions, at least by something old that I couldnt know. But each of those last moments, where I folded myself into sleep, where I saw the days in sequence, was a chain of waste, with no cause, because there was no me in those moments, only what I had surrounded myself with. Only this moment and the ones that it causes are where I am and will be. I can work backward from the end and find myself here, but not back to each other night.

At the edges of the silvery slick upon bronze, a gilt corona rises in the dewy vapor. Skeins of moonborne false golden hues roil against the incursion of tones carrying the warmth of all the bodies of all the cavernous breath. The warmth of awakening is tinged at its outer crests with silver. I awake before the dawn before the colors have engaged the hall. The anticipation of light stretches a blinking moment in which I sense the presence of the sun, a sea bearing light, around the twist of the rio, in a long gray yawn. Each shimmering formation catches light, striking each silver dawn instant on one contiguous contour, seemed a recognizably fragmentary delineation of an whole self, a night of increments: the leg of a chair, matte raised mountain peaks of the drab wallpaper.

The street is silver. In between the lamps in the room there is a darkness that is not shadow, it is nothing. In the doorway to the bathroom and bedroom there is no light. The night, while it moves forward to its apex of stillness, its end, flows into those spaces between the lamps. They are not corners, or dead ends, or crooks. They are flat expanses of endless depth. The room does not tend toward evenness when the sun rises. You do not turn off the lamps. The lamplight eases back toward the two lamps, day falls. The city is made of finite quantities, and beyond them is nothing. The streets end, the apartments grow scattered and interspersed with low cypress shrubs, dry dusty patches, and further out, traveling on high blue breezes, reedy estuaries swirl out to where nothing can happen.

When you see that every whole is a transitional element between some unseen sources and aspirations, points in a day that have edges, that are discrete and will never happen again, you become increasingly isolated from the selections of the narrative. Things happen to you, they drift over you windblown and, although compartmentalized and granular, leave nowhere to grasp, nowhere to reach out to. You stand in the stretch of sidewalk near dawn. You feel it in the muscles of your neck. The road curves around dry silver trees and disappears. Moments pass and leave nothing but their increment in your flesh, less a breath, less a breathless sigh, you shake your head at the walls and lights go out in the apartments lining the street in no sequence.

Reassembled and too large, the complete innermost darkness of the cavern is not enough to keep from betraying the openness of her hiding place. She has crawled long and down to reach stone landscapes, kiss their benighted surfaces lost from daylit scenes. The sun knows that these rocks, these porous cavities and catacombs, lie in the dark holding an imagined understanding of warmth. They are among the continuity of the earth; a stony breath drawn into the rock and back out, is of the day and of the morning and that flash before the morning. She knows that the sun is there, racing toward and away from the plains, and although beyond the creep of its rays, she sleeps filled with its light, dreams hand over hand in observant gropings. :145

With closed eyes she feels movement, a tender rise and slower fall in her throat and her stomach. Her movement is irrelevant because it is without consequence, it is within the domain of darkened eyes, of dark apartments. She had not seen the mug of tea move against the marbleized pattern on the table. Do things move. The sky with imperceptible breathing breezes moves across the skin, the sun draws across the days, night swells beneath her in the spaces where her body is freed from the asphalt, until she feels the full movement of space flowing beneath her dress and her body, until she flies in the swimming of her eyes across the sun, where flares and stippled bursts arise from her eyelids and move slowly across the wrinkled surface of burning seas.

I had never slept in my life. Each night was a waking disappearance, a purposeful relinquishing of will in order to remain surrounded, and not to become something. I am afraid to face these moments that I am causing. My fear is heaviness that grows from inside, it doesnt crush, it is expansive. It is inside me, but the fear is not mine, it is of the desert, of emptiness. Its sands fill my chest. Each breath draws in more sand. I am being crushed from the inside; I fall to the floor. My fear is living in each moment. I am alive in the bathroom, in the dark in the back of the apartment. I dont fear the cascade of shadows that my body will loose in the dark. In the string of events, the reluctance to let the end begin was not out of fear, it just didnt have the cause. I had to let it happen.

Scaling marks I have struck on the leg of a chair to insinuate myself in the crown of a distant mountain, flattened into a wallpaper repeat, drip and gather in the crook of my arm inside the elbow. In a type of darkness whose lightened edges could be seen in dawn carried on vaporized dew, my gaze adopted a cadence. I rose with that portion of my breath that was a dream. I chased myself into the antechamber. I pulled apart a lashy coverlet to reveal the vermilion band and undulating plane of vegetal textile woven out into a gray planar bed. The columns of chairs, linens, and cups rose up accurately represented. I isolated them in steam. I pulled apart the pleats of indoor night. The sense of the void beyond was tangibly pale, when exposed.

You feel lost things, not because you have seen them, or because you want them to be there, but because of the emptiness where your body stops. You and they are not here, only a bit of light in the city. The spaces around you are dim, walls, tree bark, thin fabric over thin worn fabric, lightless alcoves to splintering dry doors, dry empty air. They barely are at all. They are diurnal approximations. Where will you be when the light leaves you. What will you find you have sunken into or floated away from. What have you caused. What have you added up. What have you counted and indicated. What have you discovered and unburdened yourself of. Does it survive you. How many days will a footprint in dust be legible. Does a handprint in condensation outlast the dawn, at least to sunrise.

You lose your cadence. You lose the sequence of colors that allows one setting to connect with the next. You are released. You know that one thing never connected to the next, but you see the tether that is strung through and around the city merely by your passage. You didnt try. When you sat and waited in the dark it didnt mean anything. When you end it will be an opening in the air for a moment and the moment that preceded it will find the moment after you are gone. In the windowless room, with no vantage point, the colors pass before your eyes, yellow, gray, black, white, green, rose, rose, white, black, black, orange, blue, red, yellow, gray, green, black, violet, violet. After they line up they happen again, walking in a loop from street to street or staring into the blank wall of the apartment.

Sleep, in a fashion after the waking, is the state of awareness in which she registers senses with her physical body, although with the detached diffusion received through a new, or recombined body. Cold bands of damp metal impress on her clothes, decaying stone enclosures leave pale slicks of grime across her skin, the hardest surfaces grow tuft'd, forgiving, absorbent, her sweat against the carpet eases her movement. She has provisional control over her movements when the forces of coincident systems of movement do not intersect her own. Her body is of the dampness that soaks the night city, moving with the drifting mechanics of the cooling asphalt respiring, the swirls of flecks and dust clouding streetlamps, the cascades of dew and dark through slightly parted doors.

Pebbles of tar broken loose from the asphalt, rounded broken glass with the milky film of the aged sea, drag across her back and lodge in the folds of her belted smock. Small stones fit beneath her fingernails against the brittle tip of her finger and pry fissures open with deepening distress. Each nail latches over rows and groups of stones for any excrescence of stability to draw her along, sliding footward downward down toward the north, keeping her head up. The open city skies never cease their battle with night. In shutting her eyes she is no more recognizable than the reeds that ceaselessly rustle in the sea and current or the refuse that shuttles past them with automatic motion, never demanding dusk, never commanding dark harbor, but receiving only how the tides allow: she sleeps afloat.

I counted while I sat stopped on the floor. I counted backwards through the things I was letting go of. They were changing. The apartment was still, the tables and the roads sank and the lights weighed them down. I wasnt letting go. Nothing is gone, things just happen at different times. There couldnt be a sound. Some thoughts put life into a trajectory. I felt partly mechanical and the rest air. Night is not a medium. From underneath, the passing waves effortlessly emit silent thunder. Throats dont need voices and there isnt anything to say. If I had anything to share it was that everything was exactly the same for me and for her. Some situations put us to those slender graces of power apart from each other, when we pretended to make settings for our bodies that the other might find.

In the alcove, distant beyond the doors, there is a presence, a waxy light drifts within breaths sifting through the doors. I await the caress of these rays equidistant from the doors and from the sun. Pores alight on my skin, casting away blue tones for a wash of rose. The drops of moisture poised at my fingertips refract more gray character of the roseate dawn; this light does not emanate from the drops themselves. I construe the space beyond to be equal and opposite to this dim hall in its physiognomy and its physics. My body sprawls in dreams of an opposing catalogue of atmospherics; the alternate dawn body, diaphanous, lies awake and washing over constructions that mimic the stacked ephemera and filmy shelters herein. My gaze is punctuated by brass storms arising.

Does the swell of light rising over peeling walls and cracked sidewalks take the light from your skin when there is none left. When you are the emptiness, does the lack of scrutiny decompose your body. You lose your edges. You become gauzy. When all that you had left behind becomes visible it takes your shape and adds to it and you find yourself over a hill, in a sewer to the sea, holed up, lost in a mirror, already at a desk, gone. There is only a bit of light in the city. When the sun crests the rooftops the walls and the windows turn black. The light rises across you and grows up walls and spreads over the city and pours into the ocean. The light and the constructs within it are silver at first and then the colors of things fade into themselves. They are familiar. Their wordless secrets return.

You find yourself staying up into the night, partially awake, but upright, staring into the historical smoothness of the blank wall. It is only to stay awake, to let the sequence of colors keep playing out. It is not out of love for life, for the saturation of time, but a rot that lingers from the day that has degraded your capacity to change into a sleeper, or a walker, it stills you without aim or identity and over the greater sequence of nights it has encrusted your apartment with sifted out throngs of unidentifiable filler. You have forgotten all of the origin stories. They dont have origins that connect with your life. When you look across them you feel your life beginning. They just accumulated and whether they were gone or multiplied you wouldnt sleep or want.

At this depth there is only stillness until all things ascend with the dawn. Stopped in one depression for long stretches, her perception grows riddled with tiny chinks broken through the uniformity of sleep. Light shows through them, or they are pocks in a distant cave wall, catching some character of light saved in the atmosphere from an instant, a sequence of jewelled reflections speckled across the earth that transmit frayed grains of the antipodal sun with coincidental continuity. When she saw it reflected or admitted from those distant situations, a scene out of the night arose, stitched together by glimmers: a sleeping woman, an alcove in shadow, a drift of dust. It was more atmosphere than memory, more current than those places faraway passing through afternoon haze.

With quiet exhale she settles against the worn asphalt. The pebbles relieve landscapes into her damp calves and silt in sweat gathers behind her knees straining. She inhales and her body rises on her clawing fingernails that scuttle lightly through empty space where light now trickles out from alleys, corners, winding gutters, and ajar gates. The night tastes domestic. She exhales, settling swaying back down, her skirts riding higher upstream uncovering the backs of her knees and thighs while her stockings unfurl at a slower pace but reach almost to her knee before ceasing, rolling out over the silty sweat. The street lights fall, on her bare legs and brown veins and brown bleeding fingertips, and fall heavier and fill her gasps with steam and orange, molten frenzied grog.

I thought, early on, that what I left for her would hold, merely because I had taken the opportunity that surplus provides, to forget. From that point everything was moving away from every other thing, alone. She and I moved at the same rate. If I could stop she could fall into me, replace me, she could surpass me. I thought that things would stop and stay, that marks in the sand would coexist with place settings at a table or a turned down bed, or a note folded in her pocket with the rest, I thought it would stop shy of the need for comment, without breeze or other hands, until the absence of any other context beyond those that I had littered let them untethered in oblivion. There would be something where I am. I gave myself the crown of the final force and I left her where I was.

Auroral lights ride upon dead orbs and land in a scattering about the hall. Dawn taps a bit here or there. The movement of the dawn, with my fingers stippling the dew in the sorting arms feathery sway, glazes my hutch into day; chairs are decrepit, peeling, tumbledown towers of linen kicked through a night of filthy white sneakers, untied laces, bunched clothing about my waist, collar astray, sweat dripped. These are outlines of night that look foreign in day and I cling to them. These moments in between sleep and dawn hover continuously in their simplicity. I gray things out in the full sunlight fighting the complexity of day. Remembrance of these moments gently falls balanced with the call of sleep, the loss of night, the jab of day, and the promise again of night.

A thermos warms in the light, a mug, folded plastic bags, a plate with crumbs pushed to its side, and a towel hanging over the back of a chair, tartan, bone, white, pale foam, wet fabric, all colored by the sun. You reach out and feel your skirts rising. When it cascades back from the sea the light pushes you outward. You claw at the concrete, into dust and weeds to hold yourself down. The ceiling is pink dressed with dry gray mold. The sky is white. Your fingertips pull away from your nails, you pull away. The things are arriving east, arising into themselves with what recollections they can hold, a fingerprint, traces of saliva, a hair floating in tea. The light slides beneath you on the pavement, under your gray skin. Things touch places forever. The light slides beneath them. They float on it.

You find out very late that there is nothing about you of consequence. You stand up infrequently and round the apartment checking the tableau for some kind of change, some layer of age peeled away to reveal the real thing inside it. You see if anything has moved, someone else has been there to rotate one of the candle votives, perfume bottles, mugs or table lamps in the dust. You are concerned about circular things. You feel the night in the roof of your mouth. Another windowless room. It could be night or day. The follicles of hair on your scalp ache from being flattened against a highbacked arm chair; your neck tingles. All that happens to you comes from within. Where else could it originate. There is nothing beyond these dark walls, more dark walls and an endless dusty floor.

When the sun passes, it halts for an instant, deep beneath the ground opposite her, or behind the roof of an apartment block, a burnt corona profiles the shivering silhouette of the earth entirely. In the plain city the trace of backlighting rides across the silhouettes of the trees, the rooflines, the stark streetlamps, the street reaching a hill crest and diving to day after day, etched in the unraveled circumference of the sun at night. The contour, appearing for that instant, changes color from object to object to surface taking the hue of smoldering leaves, fronds, shingles, copings, outstretched finger flesh. The bodies of streetlamps, nightsuns, afire beneath the horizon behind her with dusty orange vapor. In another instant the sun begins its creep back toward the city.

Impregnated with the night light, with the empty night, a relinquishing of the body extents, the closing of eyes and all begins to race away with shorter steamier breaths. Little nightly suicides dissolve the body. The senses, burdened with the day that they cannot rest from, with mysteries and with confrontations of themselves and their reports of infinitely reflected glimmers of the world at the surface, obliterated in windswept ripples that trace across the water for miles, sink deeper each night. The location of vision and touch in the body vehicle grows more uncertain and the pressure of distance increases while the column of night that rides your chest stretches further through the sky, further while the light of the city reaches deeper into space.

Without the sound of warning, or the wretch of movement and friction, the rebus of my days slipped out of place, was buffed away, turned slightly, or withered in the light, where I had been tossed by the dunes that collapsed under my weight or bled inside when I exchanged tissue for air. It was slight. I kicked lightly across the tile and set my feet ankle on ankle proud of the ajar door. Because I passed things by, so was I. I couldnt expect that the consequences of my actions meeting the entropy of the rest of the days would precisely accept her in my place. But I would know if they didnt. Ciphers, you and I only mail rent checks, we dont find ourselves in letters, with names, proliferating. We disappeared before we realized we had the choice. We leave vague stains.

The moment of stasis recedes into misapprehension. It is the decay of the tableau, caused by a night of my own movements, that has ushered forth the inevitability of the day. Lying awake at dawn is damaging. I watch while those things whose sleep I stole awake. A distended cloudband, unwrapped and unraveled, with the density of a filter clotted with refrigerant, catches at my furthest radius of recognition, stipples of oiled cerulean gunblue with a texture of beige that sparkles and draws up toward the horizon, distant mauve morning. The warmth is too quick. My lashes, pulling slightly with them a crown of dewy tears, refracts the haze of colors in twisted interlocking arabesques, into a final solid-colored cyclorama of dew.

How do you find the morning. It starts in you the fear again that it is going to fall away. The morning ruins you. You lie in it, opening and closing your eyes in long desperate intervals. The palms scratch at the dusty window screens. Day sends your body into bits and each bit carries the fear. Do you scramble upward into it, slide into the stream, the tangible light pressing against your dress, fitting it to your skin and you fight to walk. The flaked away dirt clusters around you. Every bit of you is bound by hundreds of cast off scraps and tokens. In the light you are undifferentiated. The things being themselves in the light ignites shivers of guilt when you consider them. Where had they been yesterday. The feeling is crushed beneath the weight of the things.

Your toes throb and your calves tighten; your spine atrophies. The last color is a long empty white, without the black figures and characters, and it sticks. The grit in the air sticks to your skin and in damp hairs. Your skin and flesh are inert packed sand in a particulate atmosphere of lamplight. Your breath is everywhere. It is caught up around you and your face sweats, your clothes bind over clothes against your skin in increasingly damp layers and you struggle, but grow numb. It isnt a process, it is merely a state. If you could control it this would be the instant of your corporeal birth. It is every morning that distraction hides the auroral instant, and again the weight of day and where it keeps you. Each day your body goes. Where do you go. Where are you.

The night seen in a rearview mirror is irritating and feels that it is running down her neck beneath her collar. The night, pocked with retained bits of the last tangent of the sun gasping is something registrable. She closes her eyes and the particulate intangibility of the void sinks about her, levitates behind her back but does not touch her. She senses it is there, she does not need to see or feel it but only needs it to haunt her into sleep. The city jockeys with the night between streetlamps. Her eyes flicker open involuntarily. What she looks out on, directly forward, above the black horizon, a surface upon emptiness, framed through a pergola of dark streetlamps, and frayed by the shearing fronds of ducal palms, is not night.

:153

The night looms and retreats beneath her hands and beyond her feet in alcoves of apartment homes and shimmering courtyards. All around open spaces and snaking through dark corridors are meek inlets to quiet rooms. The currents, the torpid waters of impulse that exist outside of you, drop you in these domestic nooks beneath overhangs for a moonlit night or a damp fog covered moonlit morning. You lie with street empty stomach. Expel the bilious essence into the seas that take you from your body, from the plague ridden convolutions of Venice, horizonless and dizzying, until your bare thoughts, your tired eyes, gaze upon the glimmers of insect repelling lamps upon breeze licked waters from beneath to conjure a submerged home alone.

I ended the moment she passed out of my vision, and the apartment fell away with her in it. Walls belong between people. There isnt a need for both of us. Things spread out their emptiness this way. The choice to allow her anything was no longer even mine. It was barely hers to make. She towed my wake of secrets. I no longer know what they were. I made a decision at the very beginning to let myself float upon all of this. I left nothing to be the shadows of sand onto sand. I left her the space around my body. The sun doesnt touch the earth at dawn. It passes by it. It doesnt ever throw its rays into this bathroom. It doesnt even move forward now. It is filled with dry sand while the water rises. All of the water and all of the sand cloud together but havent moved. Nothing moves.

In the upcurrents thrown from the enmauvened landscape, the red lung tissue of morning gondoliers, aerated to gauzy buoyancy, is borne fluttering in a full basin of clouds toward fair frail seascapes swept in stucco. High fogs of my breath are turned to scalloped liquid en masse in temperate morning exhalation. The warm bronzes of sleep, swept pale by the silver of morning, are remembered by day with its gold etchings. Each token of my nightlong somnambulance within an orb of pulmonary moisture gathers the golden slow apparitions of the sun. The warmth is intangible, irritating. Together they collude to draw me out, dragging this corporeality in tow. Toward the sheltered area where my body takes leave, a refracted erasure flowed in to define my character with vapors.

You feel the weight of your limbs and all of the things tethered to them. You swing them away but they cannot move. You are lost. The moment when the light left you has passed. The alcove is in shade and filled with garbage. You lift yourself out of it and beyond it, sliding against the stucco. Continuity is a sickness. You force yourself to stumble. You press yourself to single out one changed memory. There is never a moment when there is not dark and there is not light. There is never a moment where there is not stucco, or smoothness, or dust. If you could choose to forget, would you let all of this happen again. Would you hold yourself down. Would you gulp and suck air from the slender spaces between your limbs, filling your lungs to become buoyant to the day.

Too much of not you surrounds you. You crane your neck and your hair slides down your shoulders. The trees drop away and you see your eyelashes. The higher you walk the further out into the distance you see, it is too big, too still to fit you, into the morning sky, green for an instant, then softly tapers and you see it changing from the right side of the sky to the left in a flash across the top of the ridge of hills and then it is white, an empty unchanging morning fills half of the world and stops. It is filled or empty, but completely one or the other; it is unambiguous. You are involuntary. You forget yourself or you recognize yourself now in the brown bright breath of the earth sweeping you into its cycle. and another day claims you.

How can it be night when she is not exposed in it, when it frames not her. She was standing below a streetlamp, lit, just at the edge of the corona looking up and the haze of gnats aglow each falling further from the bulb to alight on her skin, each knowing it was night. Here, through the windscreen, is a darkness absent of her. She is looking away from herself from in front of her and she sees that streetlamp, yet it is still darkened, and she sees the curb bathed in light and it runs past the rearview mirror and out behind her though she is no longer there. It appears again, from racing about the earth, running over the crest of hill which the sun had sunk behind, slightly further up the street, shortly before sleep, in the rearview mirror.

Water logged eyelashes fan slowly. Breath retreats. Darkness slides beneath you, moving beneath your skirts and rises through you. You descend with nothing below. Slowly, with breathless buoyancy, a sheet settling through pale light, wavering, you are rocked gently approaching the lower banks, in gentle shallows. Rolling over in spaces over to your face down descent in the absence to face the distance between the surface and the horizon, your ground down stubs of feet useless sink and surrender. All of the surfaces in the narrow space where you can fit soak your clothes; your hands swim across porcelain or glass and brilliant reflections of your eyes at last immediately before your eyes swimming, then stopping and sinking sweating stopping and closing to feel yourself hit the bottom.

It is dry and clear. It leaves only former states of its character, descending arid breaths. Its movements are habitual, in predictable stations. It is a cloud that would be silt, but the water has gone. It doesnt last. Things disappear within the midst of greater things, threads from wide sheets, buttonholes on dresses, digits in geographic locations, a banister from a stair, the peak of a mountain, tongues, dust clots in the real things that are growing old quickly. It is not approaching dawn. It wont be. It is covered with the driest sweats. The tile floor is dust, the tile walls and the towels are dust. It is overcome with air where it had been held together. The air is not a breath. It is a hot wind, and the dust is blown and it swirls in bunnies through the sky and a dry foamy rain falls, and goes on falling.

Leeching from the roof of the hall, my fingertips, and lungs, the transubstantiative dawn casts brassy coins of material light into the place of each wavering drop of water. I curl my body about my hand which dips into the shimmering carpet. The last of the moisture catches smooth light while it is exhaled, wanders off across the city, to loop down into false built-up hills before recondensing in a new stand of tepid vapor. My lungs awakening have cut rifts through the dawn, each limply flooding with dull spangles and pulling apart to consume the space in a single sallowed axis of widening sunlight. Sunrise, the throwing open of a drape, double doors are agape in taupe shadow; my submerged palm closes, the mechanisms cast me off, and the carnival bursts into the street.

You are upright and defervesced, rushing forward in the dim, wavering water lights the ceiling in shimmering golden nets. Rush forward with the tide away from the alcove and opening doors cracked ajar with their still blackness, the brown light waiting for afternoon. Evade the leaps forward in time that apartments capture. They sit in perpetual afternoon. The flood of light, solid but you wade into it, beyond the walls and edges and lines, breaks into droplets and disintegrates. You are white against the sky, bound into the light. The black sea is draped with a lifetime of sequins, and your face, gray amidst it, erodes into the glare. The sun warms your soaked dresses. Shuffle out of the tide and up the dusty sand on the dry and empty beach.

Too much exists, all too spread out to be lost all at once. What is lost is what remains. You forget in increments, each without duration, and time doesnt pass in the empty air of morning sleep. All of the city is still laid out beneath this section of sky, still happening, or left alone, sealed and covered, partitioned off into divergent possibilities, or forgotten, untethered to now. You are about to cast aside the whole lot of them, the years and the nights for a thoughtless dawn where the sun is the sun and the dust is the dust. On your back in gravel, or dew damp sand, or dry grass it becomes all one recollection, ongoing, you lie at the crest of the northmost hill sweeping away to nothing and the luminous white sky reaches around your body, full of vacuums uselessly beautiful.

Decatur, Georgia 2001-2008

IF I CHOOSE TO STARE THE WORLD HAPPENS TO MY EYES

A Conversation with John Trefry and Joe Milazzo

First appeared on Entropy Magazine, October 21, 2014, entropymag.org

I owe what I know—and that appeals to me as only a little, still—of John Trefry's novel *Plats* courtesy of Michel Butor. Not that either John or I have ever met or chatted with the man. And not that Butor, to the best of my knowledge, has read anything either John or I have written. But we know each other to the extent that we do because of a shared interest in Butor's work, itself an investigation into notions of textuality and, more precisely, of language as filament, story as (to rely upon *Plats*' own vocabulary) integument, and setting as mindfulness. Can friendship, being itself enveloping, also be textual? In origin as well as scope? I wondered as much as I read *Plats* and discovered the surprising ways in which my reading allowed itself to approach John's troublingly beautiful and remarkably self-possessed writing.

Yes, but what is this writing about? A description of *Plats* risks much, and I wish to recommend the book without describing it. However, I appreciate the perversity at work in such a wish. Therefore, synopsis. The book's publisher calls *Plats* "a masonry text built of modular narrative elements and settings, a textual city to be explored by the reader" whose plot revolves around "inhabitants struggl[ing] to observe the passage of their lives… [t]hey steal each other's shoes, mail, apartments, and identities with the hope of getting one step closer to distinguishing themselves from the refuse of the unchanging city." True, but *Plats* is also a visual object which reminds us in multiple ways that surfaces are interfaces and that syntax is phenomenology. Perhaps the best context for another reader I can provide is the review of *Plats* I wrote for Goodreads, reproduced here in its full rawness: "Still processing the complexities of this text. Shades of Butor, Philippe Sollers and even Baudelaire in Trefry's careful, even sometimes carefully grotesque, prosody—so, French—but this is a book that is deeply American in its concern with the self. *Plats* is also one of the most original meditations on sensory experience I can recall reading. And, yes, there is a narrative here, and it possesses dimensions (modern as well as ancient), but this is a book the requires you to perceive it first and only to read it 'later,' that is, through the medium of your own deliberation."

In my experience, slow is better than fast when it comes to friendship. Ultimately, I think the answer is yes, friendship can be textually construed, and I trust the following exchange of Qs and As provides some support for this supposition.

...

JM: As both a textual object and a narrative (or system of intersecting narratives), *Plats* seems to require a different kind of absorption from the reader. In fact, the book seems not only to permit but invite a certain drifting of readerly attention. Who is the reader of this book; that is, who is the reader while they occupy the spaces opened up within this novel?

JT: I like that word, absorption. I look at it in relation to duration, as in how long the reader lingers on a particular territory, whether that is a word, or a paragraph, or a spread. I write to the type of durational reader that I am. I am more of a skatey reader, a looker more than a reader, maybe. Sometimes looking at a page in its entirety can give me what I want from a book. At the very least, I find it difficult not to be aware of a relatively broad surface around a word or line while I am reading. Reading line-by-line, and this probably is more common with readers of conventional prose, there is an oscillating immersion in the creation of meaning from the words in sequence, kind of like building a critical mass that gets processed as a chunk. I don't think readers of prose, except maybe an editor, or other people, I don't really know, but not me, reads every word in order and determines its meaning and function in a text one word at a time. It is really impossible not to see the words around the focal point, for them to not impact the connotation or coloring of that focal point. So, I guess this durational quality encompasses both the absorption and the attention. Absorption is the processing, or the depth of processing, how much the text gets your brain wet, and attention is the collecting... the sample size! Structurally, the book forces what I think of as a tidal attentiveness. The rhythm the book sets up makes it difficult to read without allowing that drifting attention to take over. So, yes, fostering that broader type of attention was important.

Despite the more inviting pronoun choices, it is difficult to define exactly who the reader is. I would say simply, the reader is the reader. Like you said about Butor's *Mobile* when we first talked, it is a "book." But to me it is eminently immersive, almost inescapable. But there is no human foothold or vessel to enter, to occupy like a little submarine in the text, the reader enters the book as the reader. Similarly here, I don't think the reader is anyone but the reader, but perhaps because of the intimacy of the situations, they are the reader inside the book.

Plats is a rather short book, the right length, I think. I think *Plats* is a book first read as quickly as possible. The dot product of the book is only possible with the experiential facet of disorientation and cyclicality, and then the closer allusive reading. Maybe I should have printed it twice inside the same cover. I will never have the benefit of reading the book for the first time, so I am not able to say how many qualities of reading one person can synthesize in one occupation of the book. Because *Plats* is not episodic, there is no "Last week in *Plats*..." type of recentering; the reader can not expect that kind of registration. The increasing familiarity of the reader with their variety of contexts takes the place of those kinds of causal signposts, so does the constellation of objects. It is an iconography, almost like landmarks that themselves have a transitional quality in relation to the narrative, the location of human figures, in relation to each other. These things primarily constitute the reader's progress. I think there is a time zone in *Plats*, but that time zone is far more meshed with the reader's than it is meant to be discretely representational. As with most experiences, we push away the just-passed moment. I equate reading a book such as this more to real experience than I do to the traditionally displaced temporality and causality of the novel.

I do think that a tidal attention allows the reader to define their role more. There are all sorts of other wrenches in the assignation of the reader's identity. But that shaky platform of drifting commitment to the self as a reader allows you to often take on a more integral role in the book than would typically be the case. I can see three potential relationships, reader-as-reader, in which you are aware that you are reading a book, and you are focused on translating or manifesting its representation in your mind, reader-as-person-in-the-world, that is, not really reading at all, but looking around, distracted, a distracted reader, which you might have with any text, but which some texts are damaged by, and reader-as-text, in which the reader's consciousness is displaced into the text, is more integral to it. Of course this last one requires a sort of distraction, an inattentiveness to the practice of reading, of actively translating, or the mechanics of reading. It is like involuntary reading. It is the drifting attention you described. To me, this is the optimum kind of reading, but can be sustained only for short periods of time, and would be useless without the other two.

JM: As I read, I marked passages in *Plats* that I either wanted to refer to later, for the purposes of this questionnaire, or that I considered "favorites." But about midway through I experienced the peculiar despair of my highlighter not leaving the page for pages and pages of text. Every sentence throbbed with significance; every turn of phrase argued for its singling out. And yet the text is quite compressed, if only because the structural paradigm of the book requires a certain economization of language. How did you reconcile the flourishes of this subtly virtuosic polyvocal text with the rigorous uniformity of the book's surfaces? Were there any darlings in previous iterations of *Plats* which you had to strangle?

JT: I am afraid I didn't do much reconciliation! In fact, the constraints, as is often the case, pushed the prose to the place we are discussing.

In terms of quantity, I wouldn't say I produced more than any other writer might for a 150-page book. And I wouldn't say that in editing and formatting I lost things I was overly-enamored with, although the structure of the book necessarily forced a pretty merciless cull, the things I lost were the duds. Often they were just clauses, or bridging devices in sentences. I just wanted to string together the jewels. It was more of a process of distillation. And that distillation was really only possible, or was guided by the compartmentalized structure of the book.

As I was saying about reading speed, or the level of focus, the opposite was true about the composition. It was tremendously slow. Perhaps that made it more possible for it to be read in that involuntary way. You said that every phrase argues for its singling out, of course the opposite is also the case, depending on what kind of reader you are. If there are no valleys or passes, there are no peaks. With such an encrusted prose there is nowhere to go so you look for other rhythms and other hierarchical devices to guide your reading.

What really does sadden me, although it is crucial to the psychological foundation of overstimulation, is that the things I do care about, particular words or phrases, are subsumed in the wash of it. It is Rococo. But again, I am just projecting my reading practices. If you are only writing a sentence a day, you want that sentence to be as satisfying as possible; or I did; I find joy in the visual beauty of language. So there is more than enough embroidery and lividity in the particularity of the prose that a reader very different than myself, more meticulous, could profit.

JM: To spend paragraphs in a novel describing phosphenes is to make an argument of sorts. Much in the same way that John Coltrane's famous "cellular solo" on *Impressions* (recorded live at the Village Vanguard in 1961) constructs a kind of argument. Viewed from informational perspective, what is the smallest or more irreducible bit of signification within *Plats*?

JT: As far as it being an argument, yes, I guess when you consider it against the norm it must come across that way—I have had seemingly thoughtful people accuse the book of being a put-on or an elaborate joke—but for me it is a perfectly natural expression. I see something like a 2000-word sentence by Claude Simon as being natural, or Roland Kirk inhaling into the mic as natural, if you want the jazz angle, because it is part of a functioning body, it is the labor of the thing, so I feel a little weird calling it an argument. I don't want it to sound like a "put-on" or an exercise. But I do know what you mean.

In elementary school my teacher started a class by saying "Today we are going to get inside a 3×5 card." It thrilled me. I started thinking about this little terrain on the surface of the card, of being small enough to occupy it, to dig in it and carve out a space, to swim in its material. It turned out that we just cut it in a way that allowed it to expand large enough that we could stretch it around our waists. I think something like spending a few hundred words representing the visions we have when we press on our eyeballs is a way to reclaim that initial fascination with a level of inconspicuous detail that swells to take over the entirety of our reality.

As the person who wrote it, I would say the smallest bit is the book itself, especially in a book like this. It sounds cheap, but I have tried to excerpt it and it doesn't work. I think, like you pointed out, there are lines or chunks that are slightly more shimmery or shiny, but they just keep piling up, they don't do anything on their own but bewitch, and that is dangerous, or suspect to see in isolation. I think those bits say something, yes, but not what they say as a whole. I don't think a word itself, without the rest of the book, is able to present the proper connotative meaning or possess the quantity of information without the rest of the book, or a pretty significant portion of it. But there are object words in the book that do tend to stand on their own in the book.

If you are looking for a signal and noise distinction, I am not sure, I probably don't fully understand the concept, which is normal for me. I wrote the whole book, so I see it all as a production, as contributory. If you subscribe to Barthelme's position on noise and verisimilitude, which I do in a representational sense, in the sense that something might appear to be noise to the reader, but in the compositional sense, the writer is writing, it is words on paper, black on white usually, and that is all, and that allows an excessive amount of control, of fidelity, of willfulness.

I am an architect, and the idea of non-authorial, true noise, true compositional noise, is something you learn to work with, to embrace, because often, not always, the raw materials bring something of themselves to the picture. I wonder if an artist like Jeff Koons, who does none of his own work, is ever surprised by the outcome. The jazz analogy is interesting too. I love listening to different takes of the same piece by the same line-up, especially when I am very familiar with the most popular version. It is unnerving to see that we could have received any of these possibilities and integrated them into our lives, whichever one the people who get to make the decisions, for whatever reasons, chose to freeze the process on. That is what we know. It isn't errant. But even in this narrowing down, the raw materials of that kind of playing have so much chance, so much real chance, so much real noise to them. I feel like the ability to control in literature is more gripping and paralytic, or at least has more potential to be, and in my case, is, because the raw materials themselves contain no flaws, once they are assembled they are, or should be, exactly what the writer wanted.

I describe *Plats* as being a place, but I don't think this is truly possible, or at least not in the way I am thinking about it from the author's perspective. For the reader perhaps, who has not heard the other takes, and isn't privy to the mechanics of iterative creative pursuits, then I think *Plats* is quite effective, both in structure and in the argument of its prose, in being noisy enough to be real, to be a place.

JM: There are figures who move through *Plats*, but I am only sort-of tempted to describe them as "characters." I attribute this ambivalence, in part, to a distinction that the narrative seems to draw between active memory and passive recollection. Are the human actors in *Plats* being recollected by their environment as much as they are remembering their own histories?

JT: That is difficult to answer specifically. I don't believe there is a particular conceit about the characters in that way. Human experience, once it has transcended the immediate moment of our sensory processing, becomes a memory, is the same material as the chair we sat in, no different from qualities or forms we would associate with human beings. It is lovely to think that we can distinguish a human face from wood grain or asphalt or a tiger, but I don't, I think it is all a soup. The problem with books is that they are a displacement of the representations of our consciousness, they are always in the past, but deceptively always in the present of the reader, they are outsideness and insideness, their humanity is always inseparable from their deadness, their uniform materiality. So in my mind the character in a book never had a chance to be more than the chair. Sadly, most people just don't write about the chair with the same level of empathy, so we tend to think humans are crucial to literature.

I would say the memory aspect is interesting, insofar as the book is a feature of your present and of the constellation of the things that make the present, each present, and that the words exist only as objects of meaning connected to your memory.

I don't want to say who is doing what or what is present or physically causal and what isn't, if that is a worthwhile distinction, I don't know, but the entirety of *Plats* is real in the context of itself. How could it not be? What I would say has more to do with the language, which is modeled on a characteristic of schizophrenic thought and language called concrete thinking, in which everything is real, everything is imminent, immediate. There is no analogy in the book for instance. This has a certain effect on the presence of things and people, their roundness, their edges in the book get defined in a way that is a bit disconcerting, by not coming through the typical filter of literary representation, it seems too real, it seems inappropriate. But as distinct as these things become it also makes them more inseparable, rendered in identical materials, because again it is words, it isn't real, it isn't a chair or a person. There is no recollection but yours, everything is in the moment the words are incanted.   :167

JM: Roughly speaking, there are three narrations running in parallel throughout *Plats*, one in the third-person, one in the second, and one in the first. How would that first-person narrator, that figure who is often seated at that metal desk housed somewhere (everywhere?) on Sepulveda Boulevard answer the following question: "When is a body a body, an anatomy, and when is a body an object, a thing solid in its thinginess?"

JT: I think the question of 'when' rather than 'whether' is key. The body becomes a thing, a solid, in the material of the text, most clearly, when it is stripped of any capacity to be controlled by human consciousness, in the night Idaho plats (top verso) primarily. I want to stop and think about the conditions that make me visualize myself as meat. It is hard to do. I assume everyone does it a various points. It is a fleeting sensation I have frequently, but I can't really say when it takes over.

I like that the body, even when possessed of an implied consciousness, when fabricated in literature is almost indistinguishable from the material around it. I think of a painting by Seurat in which the representation is fabricated by identical marks of paint, of different colors, yes, but equivalent in value. We see the edges of things because their colors change, because we recognize the approximation of their forms, but the project of verisimilitude ends there. What the painting does, in fact, is bring a quality of buoyancy, of airiness to everything, to water, to human flesh, to the wind and the sunlight, even to the opaque and massive trunk of a tree. Its values are in its texture, its wrighting.

If we want to say this woman is a woman, then she would be aware of herself as an anatomy, because even when we think of ourselves as meat it is a reflection of mortality, on the kismet of our being, which a thing doesn't have, the potential of meat implies a phase change, or an energy transfer. But if she is aware that she is made of ink and the alphabet, she must be a thing, not a thing that lacks consciousness or will necessarily, but one that has no more or less than a shopping cart or a pillow.

JM: How would you define nausea?

JT: It's been a dozen or more years since I read the book. Is that what you are referring to?

JM: I was thinking about Sartre's *Nausea*, how the narrator of that book interacts with objects. Nausea, to me, well, the whole of Sartre's novelistic oeuvre showing the way, in some sense, for the authors associated with the nouveau roman.

JT: Refreshing myself a little bit, I think my ability to situate the actual sensation of nausea in the same context as Sartre is minimal. My equitable, contemporary response is paralysis, or panic. What if I am distinct from these things around me? That is more terrifying than not being distinct. I get panicked in antique stores, especially cluttered ones. I think that the disappearance, likely the annihilation of the owner of the things around me, is proof that those things had no meaning, that those things didn't disappear with them, that they were in fact separate from them. I am not talking about possessions in particular, which I don't really care about. Just the things around us. Whatever they are. I don't think the preponderance of 'things' in *Plats* necessarily functions in the same way as it might in *Nausea* because I find them to be a relief, a savior, a surrogate, rather than a struggle. Perhaps this is a perception only possible eighty years down the road from Sartre. I think it could be seen as nihilistic, but I see it as optimistic, because I want to subsume what is around me, make it valuable to me.

Nausea as an actual state has a special place for me, in my physical world. I don't use drugs, so my consciousness altering is primarily limited to my experiences with nausea, which affects me pretty harshly when it comes around. It completely rewires my perceptions. Visiting a friend in San Francisco a few years ago I got really ill after a dinner consisting of multiple course of potatoes at a vegan diner in Berkeley. During the whole drive back across the bay I stayed in a pink and white tunnel of light and fog. I was there. I could hear his voice telling me not to get sick in his car, but I was also not there. I was inside myself. Many hours I have spent in a pool of sweat on a cold tile floor. Nausea has more of a displacing quality to it than a sense of immediacy, or reaction to stimuli. It isn't a lens or a barometer of judgment. It sounds silly, but it is more of a threshold into my body's pure physicality, the pure physicality of the perceptions without the stain of judgment or consciousness. It is quite wonderful... after the fact at least.

JM: Place, as a concept, is overwhelmingly real in *Plats*. But time, as a concept, feels increasingly impossible as the novel works towards its resolution and denouement. What makes time in *Plats* possible?

JT: Time passes with the reader, regardless of the representations of appearance or temporal keys on the text. That is my reading practice at least. And that is more of the practice *Plats* encourages. However, the composition of the narrative is very time-dependent, not because of some kind of Rube Goldberg plot mechanism, but because of the effect of qualities of time, and when I say time I don't mean passing time, but time as a location.

The visual depiction of time does have a function, perhaps more of a function in relation to the characters than in relation to the narrative. Recently something stood out to me, in *The Fassbinder Diaries*, which I read in one sitting on a city bench listening to a restaurant's Huey Lewis Pandora station, Pate's use of a time stamp, 3AM or thereabouts, seemed less to do with placing a moment ahead of or behind another moment so that it could cause or be caused by something else, but for the environmental and connotative qualities of that time. Its repeated appearance recentered, not the narrative content, but the radiating tone of dread captured by that time.

If you think about it more cinematically, which I like to do, rather than something being contingent on clock time or duration, the time of day presented visually can be used to situate events, not necessarily temporally, but in terms of their appropriateness. Something that has always stuck with me, and I rewatched it a few months ago, it still affects me, is Michael Keaton home during the day in *Mr. Mom*. The quality of light in that closed-up house during the day, the ennui of afternoon, made the whole scenario seem inappropriate and difficult to watch.

JM: Perhaps because Plats reinterprets the topography (not to mention topology) of Los Angeles so unusually, I found myself at times superimposing Maya Deren's *Meshes of the Afternoon* over the novel, or at least projecting that film, split-screen style, alongside the imaginings prompted by the novel. If you could liken *Plats* to any cinematic expression (that would include films never actually filmed), to which would you liken it?

JT: I hadn't seen that. I had to look it up and watched it on Vimeo at 6AM in the dark… in Kansas no less. I don't know whether it should be embarrassing or relieving to have just seen it for the first time, because there do seem to be a lot of familiarities. The multiples of the woman, the iconography of objects, there was even a very brief montage of a foot stepping in sand, grass, and concrete that could seem structurally and content-informative, but nope, hadn't seen it! Maybe that is a positive – in a bad way – thing about Los Angeles? That is has the ability to manufacture similar reactions, at a detailed level, over a sixty year gap?

As far as my own cinematic reference points, I would point out a couple, and they are not complete films, just fragments, for instance, all of the scenes that take place in Diane's apartment in *Mulholland Drive*, all during the day, all tremendously suffocating and dreadful. There is a scene in *The Beyond* by Lucio Fulci that I watched for the first time on VHS one afternoon when I lived in LA, where a corpse rises out of a bathtub and attacks a woman. It takes place in the middle of the day, in a well-lit room, no shadow, just fully on display, very yellow, very grainy, or perhaps that is just my VHS resolution memory. One doesn't know if Fulci filmed it like that because he was just trying to stay on schedule, independent of any plot mechanics, of which there really aren't any anyway, but it struck me because of its inappropriateness.

I perk up at anything filmed day-for-night. Most cities have that night glow to them, but Los Angeles had it bad. I think most of *The Tombs of the Blind Dead* movies have pretty great day-for-night scenes. I tend toward the visual qualities of movies more than their storytelling, at least in the recollections I draw on for work.

I don't know that literature owes too tremendous a debt to film. It has affected us culturally, but the things that we like to think are cinematic, literature had already been doing, especially poetry, things like juxtaposition or parataxis, montage. So I guess my values are a little bit skewed. I have pictured how a film could be made from Plats. I always grimace when someone refers to a book as unfilmable. It just sounds so lazy. I picture a movie that looks nothing like the book. How could it? I don't think it should. Because of the values that *Plats* has in relation to the reader's experience it would need to find a cinematic way to accomplish that, not just taking the words and assigning images to them, or using the structure as a storyboard.

Also, a movie came out a few years ago called *Beyond the Black Rainbow* that was supposedly based on all of the science fiction and horror movie VHS box covers the director saw in the 80s and attempted to visually tell a story from those box covers, not their context, just their imagery. I think that is the type of relationship my writing practice has with movies.

JM: When I first entered this text, I was a little puzzled by the title *Plats*, but the more I entertained the implications and dimensions of actual plats, the more I understand how that image served as a governing conceit. Plats are surveyors' tools; they are also both records and reifications of otherwise immaterial and invisible divisions (property boundaries). Plats are guarantors of access and right-of-way. Plats are also an invention without which urban development would more than likely not have redefined this continent, especially in the American West, as it has. Perhaps most importantly, I think about the size and heft of very old plat books, they way they themselves parcel out information via these beautifully standardized, boundlessly repeatable templates. That being said, if you were required to come up with an alternate title for your book, what title would you choose, and why?

JT: I can't pinpoint the arrival of that particular title onto the scene. It was originally called *Lost Again*. The folder on my computer is still called that. *Plats* would have come after the structural decisions that characterize the final form of the book, which came maybe a third of the way through the work. Genette's *Paratexts*, and his discussion of paper sizes and margins was formative in this shift, and probably in the title too. I was very interested in these paratextual factors and giving them a more active role. I think the title is never not in that role for a writer, so I would like to think it is subservient to those other functionaries that it connects to. I am sure if I called the book something else you would have just as skillfully picked the lock and left the door wide open, but the things you point out are valid and were on my mind.

I think Baudrillard described Los Angeles from the air as a relentless gridded surface. When you fly over Harlem from La Guardia and you look downtown along all of the avenues, that to me is actually a reasonable facsimile of being on the street there, geometrically at least, but the flight over LA is not an acceptable presage to me at all. Its geometry is far more inscrutable, and on the street you never really have much of a clue what its extents are, what will be coming next in terms of physical contents. That is one reason why I like your plat book analogy. Each property has its own page, discrete, it cannot be looked at in relation to its neighbor. I like the implications of that on the city, and on the book.

As far as other titles, I don't think the original title worked, obviously. Maybe one of the dingbat apartment names in the book? *Vista Three Sisters?* That seems a little on-the-nose. It doesn't ask enough questions. Maybe just *Dingbat?* That would give you a pretty different book.

JM: If *Plats* were a retelling of an ancient myth, of which myth would it be a retelling?

JT: Honestly, I would have to look something up and lie to you to give you an answer. There wasn't anything structuring the story outside my own schema. I would rather hear what you think!

JM: The action in *Plats*, the way in which the sunrise and sunset operate throughout the book, the sense of bodies atomized and reassembled in memory, over and over again, with ritual care... I couldn't help but locate an Osiris-ian narrative at work here.

JT: I see what you mean. That narrative and its imagery are definitely part of my cultural consciousness. I had not structured the work on it, or even semi-intentionally meditating on it. However, I know it is big for me. The book I am working on now, *Apparitions of the Living*, contains a significant reconsideration of the Osiris, Set, Isis triangle. Sometimes we just don't know where these things come from. That is beautiful.

Inside the Castle
735 Missouri Street
Lawrence, KS 66044

www.insidethecastle.org

John Trefry lives and works in Lawrence, Kansas.

80653678R00112

Made in the USA
Columbia, SC
12 November 2017